I0583431

The Dandelion & The Thistle

Makers Market Book One

Pip Dolyn

For anyone who's been hurt
and scared to take a chance on love
and letting people in.

You are wanted and worthy of effort.

A note from the author

This book deals with some sensitive topics that may be triggering for some readers. Please take care while you are reading and take as many breaks as you need. Your health and safety is more important than finishing this book. Seriously, you have my blessing to DNF this book if you need to.

This book contains:

- MC with Anxiety
- MC with PTSD
- panic attacks (on-page)
- abusive relationship (recounted)
- religious trauma (recounted)
- transphobia (recounted)
- death of a parental figure (off-page)
- sexual trauma (recounted)
- social alcohol use (on-page)
- anger issues (recounted and on-page)
- abusive family (physical, emotional, verbal, neglect) (recounted)
- homophobia (recounted)
- racism (implied) (recounted)
- child abandonment (recounted)
- wind/storm (on-page)
- bullying (on-page)
- abandonment (felt) (on-page)
- verbal abuse (recounted)
- cut/bleeding (not intentional) (on-page)
- explicit and consensual sex (on-page)

Table of Contents

MAY

CHAPTER ONE
Addison (he/they)

A few things happen at the same time. Micah hands me my lavender vanilla iced latte with oat milk, and a large crash sounds behind us. We flinch, and I most certainly would have dropped one of the other beverages I'm holding if he didn't have the forethought to give them to me in a drink carrier. I hastily stuff a tip in the jar Micah has set up on the front ledge of the My Chemical Brewmance coffee cart and rush off to investigate the source of the noise, drinks in hand.

"Good luck, Mr. Mayor," Micah calls after me. I roll my eyes playfully at the nickname my fellow craft show vendors bestowed on me.

Before I can make it into the row of tents across the way from where the food trucks are parked, I'm met by Cordie, one of the vendors here at Makers Market.

"Addison, thank God. Lane's booth—it's a disaster," she tells me, slightly out of breath from sprinting to find me.

I nod, and my pace quickens as we both head towards where I know our resident woodworker's tent is supposed to be set up. She briefs me along the way.

"The base for their wall display snapped, and the whole thing just toppled over. There's glass and splintered wood everywhere. It's a mess."

"Okay, thanks, Cordie. Is Lane okay? Did they get hurt at all?"

"I don't think so. Someone told me to run and grab you, so I did."

I run through some ideas in my head of different approaches to take, and we approach to find a crowd of vendors and early patrons have encircled Lane's booth. The crowd parts to let us through, and I get my first view of the damage. Lane's once tall wooden display is splintered over a broken table. There are shards of glass and mirror fragments in the pavement, and some of the wooden frames are cracked, probably scuffed beyond a quick fix. I notice that Lane is sitting on a chair in Ola's booth being comforted by the macrame artist. I make a beeline for them, ignoring the calls by people in the crowd asking what the plan is.

I approach cautiously, giving them a brief once-over to see if there are any signs of Lane being hurt. When I don't see blood or obvious broken bones, I address the two friends huddled together.

"Hey, Lane, Ola. Are you okay? Did you get hurt at all?"

"Just a bit shocked," Ola responds.

"And frustrated," Lane adds.

Shocked and frustrated I can work with. "Lane, I'm so sorry this happened, but we're going to get it cleaned up for you. Before we start, though, I have to ask: do you still want to try vending today, or do you want to go home and rest? No pressure to do either, but I want to help out as best I can and get you all set and ready to go with whatever you decide before the market opens."

"I still have more I can sell. I'd like to stay if I can figure out how."

"Leave that to me. I'll handle it," I assure them.

Now that I know Lane wants to stay, it's time to get to work. I turn to the other vendors lingering around and start putting them to work, getting a couple people to clear out the broken pieces and having a few more go in search of extra tables and supplies so we can put something together. It doesn't take long to convince people to work on things.

While it started out as a bit of a joke, I do take my unofficial position as 'Mayor of the Market' seriously because people tend to rely on me for pretty much anything and everything that comes up at the Makers Market. Even Seth and Lilly, the event's organizers, know they don't have to be here the whole time because I usually have things handled. I shift the drink carrier to one hand and pull out my phone to take some pictures of the damage and text them with an update on how the morning is going. Once my message is sent, I make my way through the back alley of tents toward my booth so I can drop off the coffees and pick up the heavy-duty gloves, broom, and dustpan I have. We'll need to sweep up as much of the glass as we can before setting up the new booth.

It doesn't take me long to get everything I think Lane might need and head back to their booth. A couple of the volunteers I recruited are back from bringing the broken display to Lane's station wagon and are now taking away the broken table.

When they're out of the way, I get to work sweeping the mirror shards and broken frames into a bag that is placed into a box as an extra precaution. I hand the box off to another helper to bring to the trash and start to help with a basic setup. It doesn't take us long to put together once we have everything in place, and by the time we're done, you wouldn't be able to tell that this setup wasn't the original idea for the booth. I let myself momentarily bask in the feeling of community that we've cultivated over the past five years in this market before a voice interrupts my thoughts.

"Wow, thank you." A teary-eyed Lane appears in front of the small group of remaining vendors who pitched in. "I really don't know what I'd do without all of you."

The remaining crew give Lane their well-wishes for a good show, and I wait until everyone else is gone before checking in with them.

"Okay, so I swept up what I could, but don't let anyone in the back behind this table in case we missed any big pieces. I'm going to leave the dustpan and broom here with you in case you find anything as the day goes on." They nod as they listen to my instructions. "How does everything look? Do you need anything else?"

"It looks amazing. Really. I would be so lost without everyone's help. There's no one I trust more to have our back than you, Addison. You truly earned your badge today, Mr. Mayor."

I'm glad Lane is regaining some of their sense of humor.

I wait as they survey the setup and give it a once over in case they notice anything missing. "The only thing I can think of is a stand or something to prop up my booth sign. It was supposed to sit on the broken display, but that's obviously not going to happen now."

I carefully examine the thin wooden sign for a moment and realize that I have just the thing back in my booth to help keep it up.

"It looks thin enough to stand in a flower frog. Let me go see if I have one you can use. I'll be right back."

When I get back to my booth, I smile wide at the sight of my best friend and booth buddy, Gri, unloading her car.

"Hey, girl, hey," I call out as I approach, stuffing my work gloves in my back pocket.

"You're too chipper for the morning," she gripes.

"Good thing I have coffee for you, then."

She drops a box on the ground and immediately comes towards me. I laugh and unzip the tent flaps.

Gri's expression changes from exhausted to awestruck as she takes in my booth.

"Holy fuck, Ads. You had a busy off-season. This looks incredible." She walks around and takes in the new layout for my booth. I had a lot of fun constructing the new DIY bouquet station in the back that houses individual stems people can pick from a wire-covered wall to build their own arrangements. I also have a new showstopper piece front and center on a little display table in the center of the tent. My personal favorite bouquets are set up on a sideboard next to my checkout counter with a sign over them that reads 'Secret Message Bouquets.' I walk over and fiddle with a few of the explainer cards before picking up Gri's coffee.

"I felt the need to change things up this year," I say nonchalantly as I hand her the iced beverage. If I'm ever going to escape my stupid dead-end job as a dental office receptionist, I need to take a risk and go a little bigger in showcasing my talents.

"Well, mission accomplished." Gri takes a sip of her coffee and sighs, "Damn. Micah is good at what he does."

"That he is." I hold my own latte up to her in a pseudo-salute. I walk around the counter to my toolbox and open it to find that the large flower frog I usually keep in there is missing. Frown on my face, I try to think of where it might be, and as I scan the tent, I realize it's in my new showpiece bouquet. I put the toolbox away and step up to the large bouquet of mostly blue and purple flowers with pops of yellow that I have displayed on a small antique table in the center of the tent. I carefully remove the stems and tilt the vase over so the little spiky piece of metal that serves both as extra weight and a way to keep the bouquet positioned correctly tumbles out. I place the bouquet back in the vase and center it on the table.

"Stay," I command the inanimate object as I hold out my

hands like I'm instructing a dog. It doesn't move. Nodding at it in approval, I grab the flower frog and turn to my best friend. "I have to go run this over to Lane real quick. They had a bit of a disaster. I'll tell you about it when I get back."

"Already?! Geez, they're starting early," Gri remarks. As much as I love Lane as a person, they have a bit of a reputation as being the Market's resident disaster.

"It's going to be an eventful summer," I say as I head back out.

Gri mumbles something that sounds like "you have no idea," but I don't question it as I weave my way back through the maze that is the alley between booths.

Getting the sign up doesn't take long. Thankfully, it's made of a thin veneer, so it slides easily through the metal spikes that usually hold flowers in place. With a quick hug to reassure Lane that they're going to have an excellent show, I remind them about tonight's Vendor Dinner, and head back to see if Gri needs help with her setup.

As I get back to our booths, I frown as I see my center-piece bouquet has already tipped over on its table. Clearly, it didn't listen when I told it to stay. I pick it up and readjust it until it's sturdy and looking beautiful again.

I help Gri set up her popup tent and then go to finish opening the walls on mine. I tend to keep them closed until the show starts or Gri arrives so my stuff isn't out in the open. Makers Market has a great reputation, but that doesn't mean things don't happen. I tend to take extra precautions just in case. Being prepared isn't just the Boy Scouts motto. When I'm satisfied that everything is ready for customers, I head over to finish helping Gri with her booth setup.

"So what happened to Lane's?" Gri asks as I hand her another handwoven hoop to display.

"The foot stand on their back wall display snapped, and the entire thing crashed down, breaking a bunch of mirrors and taking out a table on the way."

"Yikes."

"Yeah, it was a mess. There was glass and splintered wood everywhere. Thankfully, they had some salvageable product, so they decided to stay and try to make up some of the cost."

"Geez."

I rephrase my earlier comment to see if Gri repeats what she said earlier. "It's certainly going to be an interesting summer." When she doesn't say anything, I turn to face her. "Gri?"

"Hmm?" She pretends like she hadn't heard me.

"I said this summer is going to be interesting."

"Oh, right. Yeah, definitely." She puts on a smile, but it doesn't reach her eyes.

I narrow mine at her. "Gri Tennant, what aren't you telling me?"

"Nothing. Don't worry about it."

I double down on my staring. "Gri, please," I plead.

"Okay, so you know how Jodie was having a bit of a shit year last year?"

I nod, thinking back to how Gri's girlfriend was experiencing increased pain and other weird medical symptoms last year and how Jodie and Gri had been trying to get her a diagnosis, but they kept getting the runaround from doctors and their insurance.

"Well, it turns out she has fibromyalgia. The diagnosis just came back last week, and we've been working with her new medical team to make a plan on how to help her manage it. It was really hard on her to come to so many shows last year, and I have a hard time doing them without her, so we were talking...and I decided to scale back a bit this year." She doesn't meet my eye as she says the last line.

"Geez, Gri, I'm glad she has a diagnosis finally, and I'm not surprised that it turned out to be a chronic illness, but that sucks. Though scaling back makes total sense. Everyone should reevaluate their business verses home life when they need to." And then it hits me what she's implying but hasn't said. "Wait. You're dropping Makers Market?" My voice cracks a little at the end of my question.

If I hadn't already been leaning against the table, I would have need to now. Gri has been my best friend and booth buddy since before this show opened. I don't even notice my breaths picking up faster and my hand scrunching up the tablecloth until Gri sets hers gently on top of it and grounds me.

"Addison." Her face moves into my eyesight. "Hey, I'm not really leaving. I'm just scaling back. I'm here today and then I talked to Seth and Lilly about coming back for the closing show at the end of the season, but in the meantime, I'm going to be focusing on my online shop. Jodie's doing okay now, but we're moving to a new place next month that will be a bit more accessible for her, as you already knew, and we're just trying to take this summer slowly so we can find our new balance."

My eyes soften as I force myself to meet her gaze. Her decision isn't about me. The logical part of me knows this, but every other part of me is having a hard time registering that fact.

"I know. I'm just going to miss having you around every month. You make these shows go by so quickly, and this is one of the only ones I get to do consistently. I do understand, though—Jodie's gotta be your priority." I try to summon one of my best smiles as I gather her in my arms and give her a reassuring hug, hoping it'll be just as effective at reassuring both of us that things will be alright.

"Thanks, Addison," she mumbles into my embrace. We stand there for a minute while I try to convince my brain that she's not actually abandoning me.

"Who's gonna be my booth buddy when you're gone? I can't trust everyone to know my spiel as well as you do."

"Oh, I'm sure Seth and Lilly will give you someone awesome as a new neighbor."

"As long as it isn't Bethany," we both say in unison. Bethany Cartwright-Jones is friends with my ex-boyfriend, and I swear she still reports to him about everything I do even after being broken up for almost a decade. It's unbelievably frustrating. We live in a big enough city to where we don't interact directly, but the art community is small enough that people in our circles overlap.

Even if she wasn't friends with my ex, I still wouldn't like her as a person. The first time we met, she was trying to intimidate a new vendor by insisting that they were set up in her space (they weren't) and that she had been in that same space every time she did the show (she hadn't). As one of the vendors who has been around since the Market's inaugural season, I was able to help clear things up, but she wasn't very happy about my involvement.

"Who died and made you the mayor of the market?" she had asked with a snooty tone. When I recounted the story at the Vendor Dinner that evening, everyone laughed, and the nickname stuck. Before she stopped regularly vending, Lilly made me a one-of-a-kind (un)official Mayor of the Market pin that I wear on my apron every time I'm here. I look down and adjust it now.

Another wave of sadness hits me as I realize our original crew of 10 vendors will have dwindled down to 3 when Gri leaves after today. I started making felt flowers 11 years ago as a temporary way to work on my arranging skills and save up money to open a flower farm with Liam, my aforementioned ex, after college. It was supposed to be temporary, but the universe had different plans—crueler plans, even, seeing as how I'm still making flowers and Liam is living my dream of being the area's most popular gay florist with his partner in life and business, Nick, also known as the man he replaced me with. When I found the craft market community, I started feeling better about how my creative plans had changed. These people have become my family, inspiring me and encouraging me along the way.

"Hey." Gri snaps her fingers in my face to pull me out of my head. "Don't go there."

"Go where?" I smirk, tilting my head slightly and trying to look as innocent as possible when I know she knows.

She glowers at me. "My darling dear demiboy, you can't fool me. I know you were thinking about everyone's least favorite local florist."

"Not everyone's," I mutter.

"Certainly *my* least favorite. And your moms', sisters', and Clay's, too. And we're the only opinions that count."

I laugh, and the smile returns to my face momentarily until I see that my centerpiece display has fallen over again. I look at it with a puzzled expression. Surely there's got to be a way to keep it up. I look in my toolbox and find some smaller items that might work as a weight, but I'm not going to hold my breath.

The show starts with a number of regulars coming in and chatting about how excited they are for this season's Market. I take out my phone at one of the first lulls, and after picking up the tipped-over bouquet again, I take a couple booth pictures to post on social media. I'm sure to snag one that has Gri in the background and tag her so we can convince any stragglers to come visit before she moves her sales online for the rest of the summer.

About an hour into the show, my centerpiece has fall-en over three more times, and I'm starting to internally panic. I check my box of tricks again but can't find any-thing else to use as a weight. I catch Gri's eye and wait for her to finish up with her current customer.

"What's up?"

"My bouquet keeps falling over. The vase isn't heavy enough. It's too top heavy."

"A lot like me," she jokes.

"Ha ha," I deadpan. "Can you watch the booth? I'm gonna go see if I can find anyone selling heavy vases."

"Go ahead. I'll cover you."

I grab my card and rush down the row, hoping Seth and Lilly found a new potter after our last one retired and mentally crossing my fingers they have heavy vases for sale.

CHAPTER TWO
Colin

An hour into this show, and I know I made a good choice. Committing to a full summer of shows just to save a month's booth fee is always going to be a gamble, especially in a market, but in this case, it's already paying off. Though, I wish I wasn't saddled next to the resident gossip. Her name is Bethany, and from what I can tell, she doesn't like anyone here. Why she's trying to buddy up to me, I don't know. The guy in the booth on the other side of her caught my eye early on and rolled his eyes, so I'm guessing she's always like this.

I do my best to tune her out and go back to restocking and reshuffling my already dwindling stock. To no surprise, mugs are a best seller right now; I'm glad I brought extras. The droning voice of my booth neighbor stops abruptly, replaced by a haughty scoff, and when I look up, the most gorgeous human I've ever seen is standing in front of me. The first thing that hits me is the constellation of freckles across the bridge of their nose, and then my gaze catches on a pair of shocking blue eyes behind thin-framed, round glasses, looking frazzled and anxious. I give them the slow head-to-toe once over before snapping into customer service-mode to see if there's something I can do to ease their obvious concern.

"Hi, how can I help you today?" I glance down at the apron they're wearing with an embroidered name tag that reads 'Addison (he/they)' and a pin that claims this beautiful human in the floral shirt is the 'Mayor of the Market.'

"Or should I say, how can I help you today, Mayor Addison?" I ask cheekily.

"Do you sell vases? Like heavy ones?" Their words come out rushed and slightly panicked. He glances back over his shoulder for the second time since we started talking.

"Sure do." I gesture over to the hard-to-miss row of vases that are sitting out. "They are indeed bottom-heavy, so I recommend not filling them up all the way with water if you don't have to. Though, if you're being chased and need something to throw at someone in self-defense, I'd recommend maybe a few of the mugs. They're easier to carry, and you can have a backup in case you miss the first time, but please spare my feelings and grab a couple from the B-grade stock section on the back table."

They look at me, puzzled. "What? Why would I..."

"You keep looking back over your shoulder like you're expecting an enemy to pop out of nowhere and attack you."

"Oh, no! Sorry. I just keep looking back to check my booth. My booth buddy should have it covered, but I think she might be getting a little swamped. It's hard to see from here." He turns his focus back to the vases and points at a tall, narrow-neck vase from one of my latest raku firings. It has a white crackle glaze on the top third of the vase that drips over the natural clay carved in a geometric pattern. I pick it up gently and hand it over to him to inspect. They hold it in their hands and kind of bounce it up and down to get a good feel for the weight of it.

"This is perfect. I'll take it." He says, stress melting off his face, replaced with a beautiful smile that almost knocks me off my feet. I get lost in it briefly but pull myself together long enough to take out my phone and complete the sale.

"Awesome." I clear my throat, hoping he doesn't notice my earlier pause. "That'll be $75?" The last part of my statement comes out as a question. I've been selling my pottery for long enough to be confident in my prices, but sometimes, with sales between vendors, things get negotiated depending on the show's protocol and general artist courtesy.

"The tag says $100, though. $75 isn't enough. Just because my pin might call me the mayor doesn't mean that I won't pay what your work is worth."

Damn, that smile is back, and when it crinkles his eyes like that, their whole body radiates with an unseen energy that could make poets weep and warriors ride into battle. They must have been a muse in a former life. Those blue eyes are like the water in the clearest ocean on the brightest day, and I'm being lured in by his siren song. *What the fuck? Where are these thoughts coming from? Weeping poets and muses? Who am I?* I look back to see them looking at me with a confused expression. Oh, shit. I stalled again. *Pull yourself together, Colin.*

My brain kickstarts itself back into gear, and I apologize as I take their card.

"Sorry, kinda spaced out there for a second. How about we call it even at $90?"

"$90 works," he lightly chuckles. "Thanks! You're a lifesaver." He takes his card back and picks up the vase from where he had placed it on the table when I was swimming in his gaze. Before I can even give my name, he's left the booth and is halfway back to his own tent.

Another scoff breaks me out of staring at his retreating ass and back into the present. I look over at Bethany, who is standing behind her table, arms crossed and rolling her eyes.

"Not a fan?" I ask with an eye roll, hoping the annoyance and rhetorical nature of the question get her to leave me alone.

"Calls himself the 'Mayor of the Market.' Come on, how cocky can you be?"

"I don't know, Bethany, why don't you enlighten us? How exactly did Addison get that nickname in the first place?" Samwise chimes in from the other side of the booth, clearly fed up with her bullshit. "Oh, that's right. You gave it to them. The rest of us, including Seth and Lilly, agreed it was an apt title, so we kept it. Lilly herself made them that button."

"Well, I certainly didn't vote for him." She sits back down with a huff.

"I didn't realize mayoral elections were contingent on a unanimous decision," I chime in, intentionally goading her a bit and smirking at her obvious annoyance.

Samwise shoots me some finger guns and turns back to the new person browsing his booth.

I try to see if I can catch sight of Addison's rusty red man bun and figure out what sort of items he's selling, but whatever booth he's at is just out of my eyeline.

A little while later, I'm cashing out the latest rush of ceramics enthusiasts when I see a notification pop up on my phone. 'Hairy Cow Florals has tagged you in a post.' Hairy Cow Florals? What the...

When the customers are gone, I open up the notification and see a beautiful arrangement of blue and purple flowers with pops of yellow sitting in the vase that I just sold Addison. The caption below reads:

A huge thanks to @ceramicsXcolin for the save today. This gorgeous bouquet would have been manure without your beautiful vase to hold it up. You truly are the hero of today's #MakersMarket. // Be sure to stop by if you're downtown. We're here until 5pm today!

Before I'm able to take any action, another group of potential customers comes up to the booth, so I close out of the app, making a mental note to go back and like the post later.

The day continues steadily after that. Around 1, my best friend, Trevor, and his boyfriend, Travis, swing by to say hi and give me a much-needed bathroom break. I walk in the direction of Addison's booth to see if I can catch their eye, but the booth is packed. The only thing I can really see is a wall with what I assume is a dwindling number of flowers in the back of the booth and the 2-dimensional cardboard head of a Highland cow wearing a flower crown peaking over the heads of the customers. Maybe I'll be able to say hi and properly introduce myself on the way back.

After the bathroom, I wander over to where the food trucks are and get myself a juice and a banh-mi. As I'm about to walk back toward Addison's booth, my phone vibrates with a notification of a new text from Travis:

TRAVIS
Hey man, there's someone here asking about your firing process and if you use a particular type of glazing. I told him you'd be right back, but the sooner you can get here, the better. I'm useless when it comes to the technical shit. Sorry.

ME
On my way.

I pocket my phone again and start to hustle back to my booth just in time to catch the curious collector. Travis and Trevor wave to me as they head off to go take a look around the rest of the market. It's helpful that I can rely on them to watch my stuff while I run out for errands and quick breaks during shows. Usually, I make nice with whoever is next to me, but the toxicity radiating off of Bethany shut that option down quick. I'm thankful that I told them about the show when we hung out earlier this week.

I don't see the guys again for another hour, but thankfully, I've had enough downtime to finish my lunch and do some quick browsing in the booths around mine. Samwise, the guy on the other side of Bethany, paints a bunch of fantasy-inspired art. One of his smaller pieces reminded me of the setting from my latest Dungeons & Dragons campaign, so we decided to do an art trade. Trades are one of my favorite benefits when I vend at new markets. It's always a boost to my ego when someone values my artwork enough to forgo a sale of their own.

When Trevor and Travis come back through to check up on me before they head out, I see that they have a small bouquet of flowers in one of their bags.

"Can I see those for a minute?" I ask, pointing towards the delicately wrapped flowers.

Trevor hands them over.

"Whoa."

"I know, right!? Each flower is handcrafted out of felt. I totally thought they were real when we walked by. There were even bees buzzing around some of them looking for pollen."

"No shit?"

"Honest. The artist seemed really cool, too. Says they've been doing these shows since the market opened."

"Cool." I rub the back of my neck and hand the bouquet back. "He stopped by here earlier to grab a vase. I hope it worked out for them."

"I thought I recognized your work in the booth. That piece is front and center right when you walk in. It's pretty cool." Trevor smiles, wiggling his eyebrows suggestively.

I roll my eyes in return. "Shut up, loser."

"Hey, we've gotta head out, but we're still on for brunch tomorrow, right? Did you want to go out this week or just chill at your place? We can bring the stuff to eat. Maybe do a board game day or something?"

Trevor, Travis, and I have been doing a bi-weekly Sunday brunch for years. We used to play Dungeons & Dragons with a couple other people from our LGBTQ+ support group, but they moved away at the end of last summer. The three of us have kept the brunch tradition alive, occasionally having a board game day or running two-player one-shots just to keep our skills honed.

"Yeah, my place sounds good. I might be too dead on my feet after today. Still have a couple more hours before it's time to load out."

"At least it looks like you won't have much to take home with you." Travis motions to the booth, which is significantly emptier than it was when I started this morning.

I chuckle. "True, but that just means I have to spend more studio time getting ready for the next one."

"I mean, it's not like this is your full-time job or anything," Trevor mocks sarcastically. "We'll see you tomorrow, C."

They each give me a hug and as I watch them walk off, hand in hand, laughing about whatever inside joke they have going on now, I feel a tug at my heart. There's a longing I haven't felt in a while, trying to break through and take root. *What. The. Fuck?*

CHAPTER THREE
Addison (he/they)

Today has been a good show, though it's a bit bittersweet knowing that I won't have Gri as my booth buddy next month. There's still about an hour or so left before we officially close, but the crowd has significantly dwindled, and most of the stock I brought today has sold. I still have the centerpiece, but I'm not upset about that not selling. This bouquet took probably close to 40 hours of active work to make. I work a full-time job on top of making art, so putting in the time to make new centerpieces for every show isn't feasible right now. Maybe one day, though.

As I'm looking at the centerpiece, I think about the new vendor who saved my setup with his fantastic vase. I'm so glad that Seth & Lilly added him to the roster this year, though I'll be having a word with them about his booth placement- next to Bethany? What were they thinking? Were they trying to scare him off? I should probably go check on him and let him know about Vendor Dinner before the day is over. As mayor, it's only fitting that I check in, though I'm not sure why I'm feeling so compelled to be the one to do it. Probably because he saved my day earlier. And maybe I should bring a little "welcome to the Market, thank you for saving my day" gift. That's normal, right?

Looking around my booth, I see that my DIY Bouquet

wall is pretty picked over, but I still have a few small arrangements in the "Send A Message" display. I spot the perfect small bouquet as I approach the grab & go section.

"Hey, Gri, can you watch my booth? I'm gonna go do a walk around and thank the ceramicist for saving my day." I call over to my friend as I grab the flowers out of the stand.

"Bringing a gift?" She raises her eyebrow at me.

"Definitely. His vase absolutely saved my display, and he's been stuck next to Bethany all day. I'm hoping this will convince him we're not all assholes and convey my proper gratitude."

"Suuure." She eyes me skeptically. "I walked past his booth earlier. He's cute."

"You think?" I ask genuinely.

"Definitely."

I conjure up a picture of him in my head. Aesthetically, his pastel lavender hair is pretty cool, but I don't really have the same 'attractiveness factor' calculator everyone else seems to. It was super isolating in high school when all the other people in my friend circles were trying to figure out who the hottest celebrity was, and I just didn't have anything to contribute. I understand beauty from an art perspective, but 'hotness' and immediate attraction are a whole different aspect that I generally just don't feel. It took me a while to really understand it, but I was able to talk about it with Mama a few years back, and she introduced me to the asexuality spectrum. The next day, she brought home a book from the library where she works, and as I was reading it, everything just started clicking. I've felt intense attraction to someone before, but it's very rare. I have a tendency to fall in love quickly and, to my own detriment, recklessly, but sexual attraction has never been a driving force behind my romantic head-space. Usually, I fall in love, and then I fall in bed, which can make finding a partner difficult.

Giving a little shrug to Gri, I head on down the path towards the Ceramics x Colin booth, and as luck would have it, he's not busy, and Bethany is nowhere in sight. I give a little wave to Samwise as I pass, but he's with a customer, and I'm on a mission, so I don't stop in. I'll see him later at Vendor Dinner anyways.

Colin is sitting in a chair with his head in a sketchbook. I stand at the entrance to the tent for a minute and watch him sketch out pottery forms, thinking back to the conversation I just had with Gri. The muscles in his arms and hands contract as his pencil moves across the page. His strong arms are covered in tattoos, and I find myself enthralled by the artwork. My eyes scan up to his face, where he's absentmindedly biting his lip, playing with a lip piercing. He has a short, well-maintained beard and somewhat thick eyebrows. I guess he could be considered attractive. Before I get caught staring, I knock on the table. He crosses out the sketch he was working on and looks up.

"Hey, Mayor Addison." His smile is small, but it reaches his eyes, grey like the sky at sea after a storm when the hope of safety feels assured and within reach. "What can I do for you? Did that vase work out okay?"

"Yeah, it was perfect. Thank you so much. I brought you a little gift as a way to say 'welcome to the Market' and also to express my appreciation for saving the day." I hand out the flower arrangement. "It's a gratitude bouquet. All the stems in there have a meaning that correlates to thankfulness."

"This is awesome. Thanks." He takes the flowers and inspects them further. "A couple of my friends stopped by earlier, and they said your booth was amazing. I wanted to swing by when I had a minute, but today was so busy, I didn't have the chance to take much of a breather until about five minutes ago."

"I'll be here all summer. Hopefully, you'll get to see it up close and personal next time. I'm so glad to hear things went well for you. I know breaking into new markets can be stressful, but I hope you'll find that most everyone here is accommodating and friendly." I look pointedly over at Bethany's empty booth.

Colin laughs. "Most people are. My neighbor, though? Not so much."

"Yeah, she's umm... an acquired taste?"

"A very diplomatic answer, Mayor."

"You don't have to call me that. Just Addison is fine."

"Alright, Just Addison." He smirks and sticks out his hand for me to shake. "You can call me Colin. I don't believe we did the whole name thing earlier."

I take his hand in mine. "Nice to officially meet you, Colin." I glance back over at his sketchbook. "What are you working on?"

He follows my eyeline. "Oh, that? There's an exhibit at the DART later this year, and I'm trying to figure out my concept so I can finally submit my application."

"That's so cool. Do you do a lot of gallery shows?"

"No, this would be my first. I've been thinking about trying to break into the larger art scene for a while, and this seems like a good first step."

"Awesome. Well, if you ever need a sounding board, I'm always up for it. Or, if you're wanting advice at all, Cal has been doing sculptures for a while, and I know he's exhibited at a few different gallery shows over the years. Have you met him yet?"

"No, not yet. What kind of sculpture does he do?"

"Mostly niche figures and a lot of custom work for people. It's all really cool and impressive. He'll actually be at Vendor Dinner tonight if you want to come. I could introduce you to him. I would have extended the invitation earlier, but I was a little stressed about my display."

"Understandable. What's Vendor Dinner?"

"Oh, right, Vendor Dinner is basically what it sounds like- a bunch of us get together after the show each month, grab food somewhere, and talk about art stuff. It's totally informal. Usually we're all pretty tapped after such a long day, but it's nice to commiserate or celebrate with people who are going through the same thing."

"That sounds cool. I can't make it today, though—I've got a thing. But I'll keep it in mind for next month."

"Cool." I smile at him as he fiddles with the pencil in his hands.

"So..."

"Yeah, umm, that was basically it. I wanted to extend the invite to Vendor Dinner and give you the gratitude nosegay as a thank you."

"Nosegay? Not bouquet?"

"I mean, you could call it either. Most people call them bouquets, but a nosegay is the technical term for a small bouquet of flowers. Actually, if we want to get really pedantic about it, this would be a tussie-mussie because it's meant to convey a message through floriography."

"You just said a bunch of words I have no reference for. What's floriography?"

"Sorry, I tend to ramble when it comes to my special interests. Floriography is the Victorian Language of Flowers. It's totally fascinating, and I could easily talk your ear off for a full day about the origins and how it's been adapted and how everyone is aware of it but doesn't really understand that that's where it stems from."

"Stems from," he snorts.

"Oh, ha," I say sheepishly. I can feel my cheeks turning red. "I didn't mean to make a pun there."

"Don't get embarrassed. It was fitting."

"Thanks," I can feel the redness cooling down, but only a bit. I wish I had something to fidget with so I could dispel the anxiety I'm starting to feel at my blunder. Increased anxiety isn't a typical response to unintentional puns, but trauma does weird things to a person.

"I'd love to hear more about floriography," Colin offers, snapping me out of my pending anxiety spiral. "What do these stems each mean?"

I can't tell if he's genuinely interested in learning more or if he's just trying to humor me, but either way, I'm thankful that he's giving me a way to move on.

I gesture for the tussie-mussie, and he hands it back to me.

"Okay, so sweet peas represent 'thank you for a lovely time,' but when paired with zinnia, it's seen as a token of appreciation. On their own, zinnias are for 'everlasting friendship.' The iris and clematis together indicate an admiration of ingenuity. Begonia is a tricky one because it has a double, contradictory meaning. In some instances, it is seen as a warning, but in this case, it's used to repay a favor. And finally, the greenery is laurel, which stands for 'glory, victory, and success'- all things I genuinely hope you find here at Makers Market."

"Wow. This is really cool. Seriously. Thank you. I love it."

I hand the flowers back to him. Out of the corner of my eye, I see Samwise starting to soft-close his booth. I've been here talking longer than I originally intended to be.

"I should probably get back and let you finish your day. But thanks again for the vase. It was perfect. I'll, uh, see you next month?"

"I'll be here."

I smile and head back to my booth where Gri is waiting. As she sees me, her face lights up. I'm barely back in the safety of my own space when she starts in on me.

"So... how'd it go? Well, I assume. You were gone for a while."

"It was fine. Good. He's cool. He let me ramble on about floriography for a few minutes, so that's always fun for me."

"He's into you."

"What? No. Why would you say that? He doesn't even know me."

"Ads. I love you, and I don't even let you go on about floriography."

I scowl. "I don't think he's into me. He was just being nice. Probably."

I step around her and start to soft close my booth, consolidating the items I have left down to one table and pulling down some of the now empty displays.

"Not everybody has to automatically crush or not crush on someone. And besides, I unintentionally made a pun and got wicked embarrassed, so even if he was starting to crush on me, it was probably gone after that."

"You're too hard on yourself. You realize people make puns every day, right. It's not a character flaw and definitely not something to get embarrassed over."

"I know. I just… Liam trauma."

"Fuck that asshole."

"No thanks." I try to lighten the mood, but I think she can tell that I'm starting to be in my head about it. Liam was a controlling asshole who tried to turn me into someone I wasn't. He'd police my language and make me feel unsophisticated and sophomoric whenever I made unintentional puns. It's been years, and I've talked about it in therapy, but every now and then, small reminders blindside me. I think being back at the Market and encountering Bethany earlier put me in a headspace I wasn't expecting. Logically, I know that there's nothing wrong with puns. My moms and sisters still use them like they're bilingual and puns are their second language, but I just can't. My grief over the tainted part of myself starts to build, and my nose starts to itch like it does before the tears come. Before I can do anything, Gri is right next to me, one hand around my waist, giving me a side hug and anchoring me to the present.

"Hey, Addison, I'm sorry that got dug up on you today. It'll be okay, though. Trauma sucks. Liam sucks. He did a number on you, and I'm glad you're in a better place now. You deserve the world and he deserves to be worm food."

I take off my glasses and let my palms rub over my eyes, circling them to massage my temples a little bit. Gri's presence and gentle touch help ground me and keep me from spiraling again. I take a minute to breathe deeply and get my bearings before slapping a smile back on my face and bringing her into a full embrace. If this mini breakdown had been in front of anyone but my best friend, this would have been a lot worse.

"Thanks, Gri," I mumble into her hair. "You're my favorite."

At that moment, a throat clears from behind us. We turn and find Gri's partner, Jodie, at the front of our tent. Her eyes are jovial and bright as she maneuvers her rollator into the booth towards us.

"Should I be concerned?"

"Not at all," I chuckle. "Your lovely wife was just reminding me that my past is in the past, and I'm better than my ex."

"Damn right you are," she winks at me before turning her attention to Gri. "And my wife? When did we get married?"

"Only in their mind, dearest," Gri responded. "Though if you'd stop being stubborn and let me make an honest partner out of you, I would in a heartbeat."

"Not one of your more romantic proposals," Jodie says as she leans in for a kiss.

"Ugh, you two are disgusting. Here I am pouring out

my relationship trauma and you two are sucking face like we're in high school."

"Um, excuse me? Sucking face? What is this, the 90s? Who even says that?" Gri mocks me.

"Whatever," I roll my eyes lightheartedly. These two have been some of my relationship inspiration for as long as I've known them together. Aside from my moms and my sister and brother-in-law, they're the healthiest relationship I know. I admire their dedication to each other, but it still makes me yearn for something I've always wanted.

"Where are we going for Vendor Dinner tonight?" Jodie asks.

"Mediterranean?"

"Sounds good to me," Gri enthuses.

Jodie offers to go inform the other vendors while Gri and I start fully closing down our booths. The mood is a little somber as we both know that we won't be doing this again together anytime soon, but I know that our friendship goes beyond the footprint of the Makers Market. I know we'll make time for each other as we always do, but it's still sad for this chapter to close.

CHAPTER FOUR
Colin

"I probably should have gone to that Vendor Dinner yesterday," I mutter out loud to no one in particular.

My body is exhausted from the adrenaline of a busy show day. I got home and crashed before fully unloading everything from my car, so I get to handle that fun task this morning. *Lovely.* Coffee first, though.

As I'm waiting for the French press to finish steeping, I check the time on the clock. It's almost 10, so that means Trevor and Travis will be over soon for brunch. If I time this right, I can probably enlist their help in getting the rest of the items out of my car. There shouldn't be much left. I brought in the essentials last night—cash box, the painting I traded for with Samwise, and the flowers that Addison brought me.

A rare smile creeps over my face when I look over to the table and see where the bouquet is now displayed in one of the smaller vases I made a few years ago. It's almost like this vase was made for that exact arrangement. The curves accentuate the shape of the bouquet, and the light is hitting it in a way that adds vibrancy to the handcrafted blooms, almost bringing them to life. I grab my phone off the counter and start framing a picture for social media. I'm trying to figure out the perfect caption when I hear my door opening.

"Knock, knock, fucker," Trevor calls from the front

entryway. The smile drops from my face. Not that I'm not happy to see my best friend, but I would have liked a few more minutes in the memory of yesterday's conversation with Addison.

The alarm goes off on my phone, and I rush to turn it off.

"Perfect timing. Coffee's ready." The two men come into the kitchen and set down the bags of ingredients they brought over.

"We lucked out. HeftyFeline had fresh challah, so we get to dine well today," Travis says as he pulls out a loaf of delicious braided bread.

"Excellent." I set my phone down and grab a couple mugs from the cabinet for our coffee.

These guys are the closest thing I have to family, and I'm grateful that we get to do things like this on a fairly regular basis. When your family is either gone or has abandoned you, you have to embrace the family you make or the one that makes you. Trevor's parents stopped talking to him when he came out as trans, but he was already out of their house and living his own life before he got up the courage. It's one of the things we bonded over. We didn't choose to be this way, but at some point, we stopped living our lives for other people and started to be our authentic selves, no matter the consequences. Some consequences are just more heartbreaking and traumatic than anyone should ever have to deal with. Travis might not be trans, but he still has dealt with his own share of tragedy for his identity. He grew up black and gay in oil country and was beaten up so regularly that his adoptive parents sent him to boarding school just to protect him, not that environment was much better. He doesn't ever go back, but his parents come to visit a couple times a year. They're supportive in their own way, and they love Trevor, so that makes a difference, but it's still not the same when he can't go home without fearing for his safety.

We move around the kitchen like a well-oiled machine, having done a regular brunch together every month for the past 7 years. Trevor takes over the music, Travis starts up the stove, and I get to chopping the fruit they brought from the farmer's market.

Trevor is setting the table when he notices the flowers that Addison gifted me yesterday.

"Ooh, these are gorgeous. Did you get them from that artist yesterday? What was their name?" He points a fork over at his boyfriend.

"Hairy Cow Florals," Travis answers, not looking up from where he's flipping the french toast over in the skillet.

"Uh, yeah. They came over to my booth at the end of the day and gave them to me as a 'thank you' gift for, and I quote, 'saving his show'."

"Well, that's adorable, and this bouquet is stunning."

"Umm, actually, it's not a bouquet. It's called a hurdy-gurdy or something like that."

"A hurdy-gurdy is an instrument," Travis corrects as he brings the first plate of food over.

"Okay, so not that," I think back on the conversation from yesterday. "A tussie-mussie. That's what it's called. Each stem represents something different. I forgot to write down each one, but they're all generally themed around thankfulness. It's from Victorian England, I think."

"Okay, that's cool. Secret message bouquet. Does one of them say, 'I think you're cute, and we should so totally bone'?"

"Bone? Okay, Rosa Diaz." I shove his head playfully to mess up his hair a little bit. We start to tussle a little.

"Now boys, if you make me spill this plate, you will be the ones going back to the market to beg HeftyFeline for a new challah loaf that I'm sure they sold out of hours ago."

Travis cuts through us with another delicious-smelling smorgasbord of cooked food.

"Yes, Daddy." Trevor innocently bats his eyes at his boyfriend. I huff and find my eyes rolling back in my head.

We all sit around the table, and there's one chair empty, as it has been for the past three years.

"To Colleen," Travis says.

We raise our glasses and toast to the woman who supported us all when our parents either couldn't or wouldn't, my grandmother. She's the reason we have this brunch tradition. After I met Trevor and Travis in our LGBTQ+ support group, she practically adopted them the way she did for me when my parents kicked me out. She had them over a couple times a month for a homemade meal, which turned into brunch on the weekends. Sometimes, we'd stay in and cook, but every once in a while, we'd take her out as a thank you. I'll tell you one thing, going to drag brunch with your grandmother is one of the most entertaining experiences a person can ever have. She was a hero. When she passed a few years ago, my own blood relatives didn't show up to send her off, but the drag kings and queens definitely did. It reiterated that she was a great person and the rest of my biological family sucks.

The food is mouthwateringly good, and I'm about to ask what game they want to play today when Trevor decides to pick back up on the conversation we were having before we started eating.

"Okay, so what's up with your new flower friend?"

"What do you mean?"

"He brought you a gift of flowers that have meanings. That's adorable and sweet and flirty as fuck."

"I don't think it was meant to be flirty. At least I didn't get that vibe from him."

"Honey, you've been out of the game so long, would you know a flirty vibe if it was waving in your face?"

"Yes, I have a number of flirty vibes in the top drawer of my nightstand. I'm well aware of what they look like," I bite back.

"Oooh, we've got a feisty one today."

"Seriously though, it wasn't a flirty thing. I think they just wanted to make sure that I felt welcome as a vendor. He invited me to a dinner with the other vendors, but I was so spent, I couldn't people anymore."

"Do you hear yourself? He wanted you to feel welcome and invited you to dinner, and you don't think he was being flirty? Colin, honey, please. You've gotta give this to me. Have you talked to them since?"

"Since yesterday? No. And how would I? I don't have their number."

"But you know his business name. You could easily reach out on social media." Trevor grabs for my phone on the table and opens it up.

"What's this?" he asks, eyebrows raised in amusement.

I look over to see what he's referencing and notice the screen is still on the page where I was going to create that post before the morning chaos ensued.

"I was going to post a picture I took of the tussie-mussie in the vase, but then you showed up, and I got distracted."

Trevor starts typing something out on my phone. I try to reach over from my seat to grab it, but he just twists his body and maneuvers the phone away from me. I look over at Travis for help, but he just shakes his head.

"It'll be easier if you just let him do what he's gonna do." With a pointed look at his boyfriend, he continues, "I'm sure Trevor wouldn't do anything torrid or inappropriate on your business page." He emphasizes 'business' to remind Trevor that this is my livelihood and anything off-brand could have a negative impact on the growth I've been trying to cultivate. It's bad enough that I can't use 'trans potter' as reliable search terms anymore because they tend to bring up a certain author's transphobic rhetoric. I don't need any other issues for my online presence.

Trevor sighs and deletes a couple lines of text but then goes back to typing. He finishes up, and I hear the whoosh of the picture being posted as he hands me back my phone.

NEW POST BY @CeramicsXColin:
I had such a great time at the Makers Market yesterday. Check out the way the morning light hits this stunning tussie-mussie from **@hairycowflorals**. I'm going to have to add more flowers to my collection if this is the type of gorgeous detail I can expect. Can you believe they're handmade? STUNNING ✨

"I also followed him and sent a DM. You're welcome."

"Trevor! What the fuck!?" I maneuver into the DMs and hope that whatever damage he's done can be fixed before I get blacklisted from the craft market community.

DIRECT MESSAGE FROM @CeramicsXColin to @HairyCowFlorals
Hey, I had such a great time yesterday and absolutely love the new tussie-mussie. It looks great on my table. You should come check it out sometime. 😘

"Oh. My. God. I am going to kill you. Try to be less subtle next time. I don't think he could pick up what you're trying to say," I hope the sarcasm in my voice is the appropriate level of dripping. Hastily, I type out a retort.

DIRECT MESSAGE FROM @CeramicsXColin to @HairyCowFlorals

I am SO SORRY. My idiot of a best friend stole my phone and wrote that last message. He's dead to me now. I promise I'm not that forward or creepy.

DIRECT MESSAGE FROM @CeramicsXColin to @HairyCowFlorals

But really, though, thank you for the flowers. They truly are gorgeous and they do actually look great when the sunlight hits the table. I'm so sorry again.

I put the phone away and turn to stare daggers at my former best friend.

"Now I just have to hope that he doesn't block me for being a creeper, you dipshit."

Trevor is practically cackling from his self-described sense of humor. I glare at him for a minute longer and then look over at Travis, who has just been observing the whole spectacle like it's a comedy sketch he paid money to watch.

"Thanks for all your help," I say, narrowing my eyes at him.

He raises his hands in a gesture that indicates innocence. "Hey, I kept him from posting that directly on your main feed. At least he kept it to DMs."

"Fine." I stab at a piece of bacon on my plate to let out a bit of my pent-up aggression.

Our conversation turns to the usual topics that we tend to discuss every time we get together- life, work, dream trips, hopes for the future. I tease Travis and Trevor about when they're going to finally get married, and Travis, surprisingly, is the one to snark back at me about how I have the hook-up with a florist should they need one. Our day eases into the comfortable familiarity we have every time we get together for these brunches. Eventually, we bring out the board games and let our competitive natures take over.

It isn't until they leave later that afternoon that I see the response from Addison.

DIRECT MESSAGE from @HairyCowFlorals to @CeramicsXColin

😊😊 Don't worry about it, Colin. I honestly didn't think that first message had your tone in it, but I'm glad your friend knew about tussie-mussies. That term isn't widely used. He was right about one thing though, it does look great on your table. The sunlight really makes it pop, and that vase is perfect for it. -Addison

JUNE

CHAPTER FIVE
Colin

For some unknown reason, I convinced myself to get up earlier than usual so I could make it to the Makers Market early and do some shopping. Okay, maybe the reason isn't technically unknown. I wanted to see if I could catch a few extra minutes talking to Addison. After our brief time talking at last month's Market and our online encounters in the month since, I'm hoping that I can figure out why he intrigues me so much.

We haven't really messaged much in the month since the last market, but they've liked all my new posts, and I've interacted with their content.

I pull my truck up to my newly designated booth space and unload as quickly as I can, hoping I'll be able to find a halfway decent parking space. Apparently, arriving early has some perks. I chug the rest of the coffee I brewed this morning and get to work setting up my booth. After years of trial and error, I've got my system down to exactly 48 minutes. It usually means I get to stay in bed and enjoy that precious sleep for just a little bit longer. Laziness is one hell of a motivator.

When everything is set up to my standards, I open up my email so I can take a look at the vendor map that was sent out for this month's market. I'm in booth A3, which is down the lane from where I was last month. I'm closer to the food trucks, so that'll be helpful if I need to duck out for a snack. Travis and Trevor can't make it today, so if I don't immediately click with whoever I'm next to, I'll at least be able to keep an eye on my stuff while I'm in line for lunch. I scan the list for Hairy Cow Florals and see that Addison is actually in space B3, directly across from me. I don't know how I missed that the first time I read through the email, but it makes me smile now.

I look up and across the way, and sure enough, there's Addison, opening the walls of his tent and talking to one of his booth neighbors. As the tent sides come down, a visual explosion of color greets everyone in the vicinity. Addison's booth is decked out like a pride flag. There's a back wall with flowers displayed in a rainbow gradient, a sideboard of arrangements in different pride flag configurations, a display of heads showing different flower crowns, and in the center of the tent, in the vase they bought from me last month, is a gorgeous rainbow gradient bouquet set on top of a pride flag tablecloth.

If you couldn't previously tell Addison was part of the community or at least the world's biggest ally, you certainly wouldn't be able to deny it now. I watch as they pick up one of the flower crowns from the table and places it on their head, adjusting it in the mirror until it sits just right.

I look around at my booth and feel a little disappointed in myself that I didn't even think of playing up the pride angle at all. I know I'm pretty stealth, but I'm proud of being trans. Now seems as good a time as any to remedy that.

I walk across the walkway, intent on picking up a trans pride bouquet if he has one or maybe building one of my own if he doesn't.

"Morning, Mr. Mayor." I knock on the edge of a table. He turns around from fussing with the flower wall, and his smile grows brighter. The freckles on their face seem to dance across their nose as it scrunches with his grin.

"Hi Colin, how are you?"

"I'm good." I gesture to everything. "This is stunning. You must have gotten here early to have everything set up already."

"I'm usually one of the first people here. I like having the extra time to meet with people and do a little shopping of my own when I can."

I nod. That all seems to make sense.

"Your booth looks great, too." They comment. "I'm glad we're across from each other this month. It'll make it a lot easier if I have any more display emergencies."

"Oh God, I hope not. Everything looks so perfect, I can't imagine a single change. But maybe you can help me rescue my display this time."

Concern laces his face.

"What's wrong? I have a bunch of extra supplies and stands. What do you need? I probably have something we could use." He starts to walk back to the other side of the flower wall.

"Oh, no. Sorry. Nothing's wrong or broken. I just forgot that it's June, and I don't have anything in my booth to represent my identity. I was hoping you might have a bouquet that would fix that."

The concern drops from their face, and his smile returns. "I can definitely help you with that."

He walks over to the display of pride flag arrangements. As he passes me, I get the whiff of a delicate floral scent mixed with dirt, like he's actually been out in a garden working recently. I let the scent wash over me and follow Addison towards the bouquets.

"So, which identity are you looking for?"

"Trans, preferably." I point to the pink, blue, and white arrangement.

He picks it up out of the stand and fluffs it before

handing it over. "This is a great one. All the stems are culturally relevant to the trans identity. The forget-me-nots are for remembrance of lost lives, the roses are an homage to the quote—"

"'Give us our roses while we're still here'," I recite.

The grin on Addison's face widens. "Exactly. The protea stands for change or transformation. There's some chamomile in there for 'energy in adversity,' and then the greenery is a bunch of oak leaves which symbolize bravery."

"You really could talk about floriography for a full day, couldn't you?" I smirk at them playfully.

A slight blush spreads across his face. "I really could. I used to try getting more people interested in it, but I could practically see their eyes glazing over when I really got going, so now I just do it subversively. Every once in a while, someone comes along who is genuinely interested in it and lets me go on, but most people just see flowers and go 'oooh pretty'."

"They are pretty, but I love the hidden meaning. What's the most bizarre accidental meaning someone has put together?"

Addison puts his hands on his hips and thinks for a minute. "Oh! I've got it. Okay, so everyone loves lavender, right? Well, historically it's been used as a symbol of 'distrust.' I once had someone grab a bunch of lavender stems and mix it with anemones, rue, datura, and wormwood. Which basically is a bouquet that says, 'I know what you did, you're going to regret it, and I don't trust you.' She bought it for her girlfriend because she loved the flowers and thought they looked pretty together. Turns out, she got home to find out that her girlfriend was cheating."

My eyes widened. "How did you hear about that?"

"You remember Gri, the weaver who was next to me last month?"

"I think so." I'm not sure I actually do.

"That was her before she met her current partner."

"No fucking way." I chuckle, "Well, I'm guessing that was a bonding experience for you both. Does she listen to your definitions now?"

"She did for a while, but her instincts have been pretty spot on for bouquets. When she met her new partner, Jodie, she asked me to double-check the bouquet she picked out, but she had chosen all good stems."

"Intuitive."

"Quite." We stand there, just looking at each other. It's a little awkward, and I'm about to say something when Addison starts talking again. "Did you want to get it? The bouquet, I mean. Or maybe you want a different one? I mean, you don't have to get one at all if you don't want."

"No." I reach out to briefly touch their forearm and stop their rambling. I feel sparks between us at the contact. "I absolutely want to get this arrangement. It's perfect and exactly what I'm looking for."

"Do you want it wrapped up?"

"No, I'm gonna put it directly in the vase. You can save the packaging."

"That makes it easy for me." He walks back to his check-out counter and pulls out a box of cards. "I'm still going to give you the care instructions and other stuff that goes with it."

"Perfect. If you throw in a couple business cards, I'll display them next to it." I walk over and watch as he grabs a couple extra business cards, putting them in a pile. "How much do I owe you?"

"This one is normally $150, but since you're a fellow vendor, it's $135. And I should say, a percentage of all my sales today are going to support a number of mutual funds for queer and trans people."

"In that case, don't discount it and add the extra to the donation."

"Are you sure?"

"Absolutely. This is technically a business expense for my booth, so please, take the money." I hand over the card I use for business purchases. "I'll just need a receipt."

"Easy enough to do. Just enter your preferred delivery method, and you'll be all set." He hands the card reader over to me, and I go through the steps, opt for an email receipt, and take my card back as the machine chimes.

I should turn back around and head to my booth, but I don't want to leave yet. We stand there looking at each other again, and the longer we do, the deeper their blush gets. It's adorable. I'm about to ask him about the flower crown he's wearing when he blurts out, "Have you met Lane?"

He starts walking over to the booth next to his, where another vendor with short black hair is hanging wood-framed mirrors on a heavily weighted and reinforced wall.

"No, I don't believe I have." I follow after him.

CHAPTER SIX
Addison (they/he)

I am making a complete and utter fool of myself in front of Colin. He just makes me feel all flustered and tongue-tied. Maybe introducing him to Lane will distract him from my awkwardness.

I turn back and see that he's right behind me, following me into the booth next to mine. I wait until Lane has finished putting a piece up on their display before speaking. They might be the only person I know who is clumsier and more accident-prone than I am, and after last month, I know they really don't want anything to go wrong today.

"Hey Lane. This is looking great. I can see why you wanted to go with the pallet backdrop." They look over at me and Colin, who has stepped to my side but slightly behind.

"Lane, this is Colin. He's one of the new vendors this year, and he's gonna be across the way from us today. He totally saved my show last month."

Lane walks over to us and sticks out their hand. "Nice to meet you, Colin. What do you make?"

"Ceramics- mostly functional ware like mugs, bowls, and, luckily for the Mayor here, vases, but I like doing some experimental forms and sculptures when I have the time." Colin produces a business card out of his pocket and hands it over to Lane.

"Cool. I'll have to check it out if I have the time today." Lane grabs one of their cards and hands it over to Colin. I let them talk for a little bit as I check out some of Lane's new creations. The wood is beautifully carved, and the mirrors are polished perfectly. I catch my reflection in one of the mirrors and see that the easily triggered blush I feel almost every time I talk to Colin has finally started to calm down. I don't know what it is about him that makes me blush, but I do know that I can blame my Scottish ancestry for the pale skin and auburn hair that enhances any sort of redness in my face.

I turn away from the mirror and decide it's probably time to head back to my booth. I wave at Lane and Colin and start to walk over when I hear footsteps following behind me.

"It was really nice to meet you, Lane. Good luck with everything today. I'll definitely have to come back by when I have some more time. Your pieces are fantastic."

Colin scoots around the table and follows me back to my booth.

"You didn't have to stop talking to Lane just because I was heading out."

"I know." Colin gives me a playful smirk that lights up his eyes. Dammit, here comes that blush again. I meet his smirk with a smile and turn toward my display wall. I give myself a minute to let my blush subside again by fussing with some of the flowers on my DIY Bouquet wall. When I turn around, Colin is still there, trying on a flower crown.

"That looks good on you." I come up behind him and help adjust the ribbon in the back. When it's secure, I step to the side and look at our reflections in the mirror. Colin's storm-colored eyes catch my ocean-blue ones, and a shiver runs through my body like a wave from my toes to the top of my head, where I'm wearing my own flower crown. We stand there for a minute, eyes locked through the mirror.

An intensity and longing I haven't felt in years starts to take the place of the shiver, and I'm trapped in his gaze.

A clattering from Lane's booth behind us breaks the building tension. We step apart and away from the mirror.

"That, uh, really looks great on you. I call those the 'car-GAY-tions' because it's the gay pride flag and they're carnations and..." I'm rambling. *Why am I rambling?* Oh, gosh. The blush is back with a vengeance now.

Colin chuckles as he takes the crown off.

"That's clever." He hands me the crown. "Maybe I'll have to get it for Pride. Will you have a booth there?"

"No, I used to vend there, but then I decided I wanted to experience the whole festival rather than being confined to a 10x10 foot section of it."

"Makes sense to me. What's your favorite part?"

"Definitely the eye candy," I joke. When he looks quizzically at me, I point to my pin. "I'm ace." I point to the pan-romantic/grey ace pin on my apron that I made earlier this week. He laughs and then his eyes flit over to the pronoun pin I'm wearing today.

"Did you change your pronouns?" He asks.

"Just their order. I usually change my pins out depending on how I'm feeling that day."

"That's cool. I don't think I know anyone else who does that." Colin's enthusiasm seems genuine. "So if I don't see you, is there a default you'd like me to use when talking about you?"

"Not really. I mean, I usually default to 'he' because most of the time I'm good with being seen as a guy, but sometimes I'm just not. I don't know how to explain it better, but it makes sense in my head."

He nods. "I get that. As long as your identity makes sense to you, that's all that matters. You don't need to justify yourself to anyone else if you don't want to. The world doesn't get to decide who you are."

I feel myself easing into a comfortable space with Colin. My gut is telling me he can be trusted with my friendship. We migrate back over to other parts of my booth and start talking about our experiences at past prides. He tells me about the time when his grandmother led the parade after the intended grand marshal got food poisoning and protesters were threatening to shut down the festival.

"So she said, 'Honey, if anyone has issues about an 80-year-old woman supporting her grandson, they can lick a donkey's ass because kissing mine is a privilege that no transphobic piece of shit will ever get the pleasure of experiencing.' The organizers overheard her and decided to let her be the new grand marshal. She became a bit of an icon that day."

"She sounds amazing."

"She was." His face becomes a bit more somber.

"Oh, I'm sorry."

"Thanks. It's been a few years, but she was the only blood family I had left."

I reach out, touching his forearm and giving it a reassuring squeeze.

"You'll have to tell me more about her." I smile softly but genuinely. "Oh, before I forget, I've got the perfect pride accessory for you." I squat down and start rifling through a box, emerging a moment later with a green felt carnation boutonniere in my hand. "I made these last year, but they didn't really sell, so I decided to keep them to hand out."

"Not many Oscar Wilde fans around?"

"You get the reference?" Not many people know their queer history enough to get the connection. I feel a bit of a flutter in my gut at his enthusiasm.

Instead of just handing the boutonniere to him, I walk around the counter so I can fasten it in place on his t-shirt. He closes his eyes, and a contented look comes across his face. I try not to fumble with the pin and accidentally stab him. Something about Colin has me nervous and completely relaxed at the same time. It's unsettling enough to where I step back. His foot takes an unintentional half-step forward as he opens his eyes and seems to hold himself back from invading my personal space.

"You smell like a garden." His voice is quiet, unnecessarily raw sounding. He clears his throat.

"Nature of the job. I spend a lot of time outside with plants and flowers. Every spare chance I get, I'm in the garden." My smile is soft. "You smell like dirt, too."

"Thank you?" His remark comes out closer to a question than a reception of my compliment.

"Different dirt, though. You smell like clay and campfire." My voice fades out, and the blush that seems to be making its appearance well-known whenever Colin is around returns with a fervor.

"Excuse me, how much is this?" A random person appears before us, holding a bouquet that is clearly labeled with the price. I practically jump away from Colin. I didn't realize we had gotten so close. I turn to the potential customer and snap into customer service mode.

"That bouquet is $65."

Colin looks over at his booth where a few people are browsing. He picks up the trans pride bouquet and gives me a little wave as he leaves to go over.

When I'm finished ringing up the customer, I check the time on my phone. The market started 15 minutes ago.

I shoot a text to Gri.

ME

Something weird happened. I lost track of time talking to someone and missed the first 15 minutes of the market.

Her response is almost immediate.

GRI

I'm sorry, what happened!? Is your booth set up? Are you feeling okay? Do you need help? I can be there in like half an hour if you really need help with setup.

ME

No, I'm set up and fine. We were at my booth and kinda lost track of time just talking. We didn't realize that the market had opened until a customer asked me about the price for a bouquet. I don't know how it happened. One minute we still had an hour to go and the next thing I know we're getting interrupted.

GRI

We?!!??!?!? Addison Baird, spill! Who is this mystery person? I leave and the next month interesting things start happening for you? Not fair. I want to watch. Maybe I'll convince Jodie to stop by with me and we can bring popcorn for the entertainment.

ME

Oh geez. That's just what I need. You two are worse than those Muppet critics.

GRI

Their names are Statler and Waldorf, put some respect on them.

ME

They're Muppets.

GRI

You're dodging the question. Who was the mystery person?

ME

Colin.

GRI

The ceramics artist who was next to Bethany?

ME

Yeah. He's across the way from me today. Seth and Lilly rearranged a few people since you abandoned us.

GRI

Hey, that's not fair. You know I'd be there if I could.

ME

I know. I know. Just giving you a hard time. 

I miss having Gri around, but if she was here, I probably wouldn't have had that time getting to know Colin. I glance over at his booth, and he's chatting with his new booth neighbors, Timms, a collage artist, and Cal, a sculptor. They share a laugh, and I shift my eyes away before he can see me staring.

The day picks up and I catch Colin's eyes a couple times. We wave, and I smile at him. The third time it happens, he makes a face at me, and I burst out laughing. I grab a whiteboard that I used to use for a sign and write out a message:

BUSTED

I hold it up to him with a sheepish grin on my face. He throws his head back in laughter before ducking behind his table, only to reemerge a minute later with a clipboard that has a sheet of paper on it. He's scribbled something in Sharpie, and I have to adjust my glasses on my face before I can read it.

SORRY NOT SORRY

The next wave of customers comes in, and I put the whiteboard down so I can help them. The day carries on like that until the afternoon. As I'm thinking about finally grabbing my lunch, I start to smell a burning scent, not a pleasant one like the smell of campfire that lingers on Colin, but almost like melting plastic. I look around, but everything in my booth is in order as much as it can be for half a day of being prodded. I take the flower crown off my head, and it's intact.

"Hey, Lane?" I call over to my booth neighbor.

"What's up?" they call back.

"Do you smell something burning?"

They sniff the air, and then I see it; the edge of their table is smoking.

"Oh shit, Lane!" I point at the table and rush over with my water bottle. I douse the table with some water, and it stops smoking.

"That was weird." The smell lingers and then grows, but this time, it's less plastic and more paper. We turn around and see some of Lane's business cards are starting to catch fire on a different table. I toss the remaining water on the burning cards before the flames get too large and cause serious damage.

"What the fuck!?" Lane exclaims. They go to pick up the burnt cards off the edge of the table and snatch their hand back. "Ouch."

I look at the bright spot on the table by the cards and then look back at the mirrors. The sun is hitting them at an angle that is causing things to catch on fire.

"Lane, it's the mirrors. We have to take them down or

cover them or something."

They shake their hand and follow me over to the display wall holding all the mirrors.

"Oh, this is a disaster." They look defeated.

"It'll be okay. Let's just take these down, and we can troubleshoot from there. Nobody got hurt. You just lost a couple business cards and have a couple melted table corners. It'll be okay." My metaphorical mayoral hat is on my head, and I'm trying to problem-solve before the situation gets dangerous.

We rush to get the mirrors turned upside down on one of the tables.

"This is so weird. That's never happened before. I do markets all the time. None of this makes sense."

"Have you changed anything since last time?"

"I got a new order of mirrors in, but I bought them from my regular supplier, so I didn't think to check them beyond the usual 'is it broken or not' system."

"You may need to check with them to make sure they sent you the right ones. This could have been really bad."

"I know. I would have felt awful."

"Lucky you're next to me. Wool doesn't catch on fire as easily as paper would, and I use the quality stuff." I smile to try diffusing the tension and panic. "Lane, have you sold any pieces with the mirrors from the new shipment?"

"No, I don't think so. I sold a few of the old stock, but none of the new ones."

"Well, that's good then. At least you don't have to worry about your customers' houses burning down accidentally." I chuckle, but I know I've said the wrong thing when I look at Lane's wide eyes.

"Oh, shit. That would have been the end of me."

"Don't panic. It didn't happen. Sorry I even put the idea in your head. Listen. Do you want to take the mirrors out now and try selling these at a discount as frames, or would that be too difficult with the construction?"

"I could try." Lane examines the back of one of the mirrors. "I don't have my tools with me, though. Any chance you've got needle nose pliers?"

"I do indeed, my friend." I clasp them on the shoulder and rush back to my tent to grab my toolbox.

Crisis averted—for now at least.

CHAPTER SEVEN
Colin

Today has been a busy market, possibly even busier than last month. People have been in and out of the booth all morning, putting a serious dent in my stock. If this keeps up, I might have to cancel one of the smaller one-off shows I'm signed up for just to make sure I'm able to restock for the next market. The bouquet I bought from Addison this morning has garnered a lot of attention, and I've been directing potential customers over to their booth after they've finished with mine. Not that Addison and Hairy Cow Florals need more. It seems like they've had a line all morning, too. I have no idea how we lost track of time earlier, but I'm glad I was able to get to know them a bit better.

Talking to them is easy, like we've been in each others' lives for years. Sure, we've had a few awkward moments, but for the most part, Addison puts me at ease, and something about them is so compelling. There's a bit of a lull in our corner of the market, and I'm considering walking back over to their booth to see if they want to grab some lunch with me when I notice a commotion in Lane's booth. I move to put my cash box in a secure location and am about to rush over to see if they need help when an older couple comes into the tent and starts asking about specific pieces. Trying not to convey any alarm as I don't know what's going on across the way, I do my best to be attentive and answer their questions while trying to keep an eye on whatever's going on over in Lane's booth at the same time.

Addison sprang into action, which is what made me realize something was going on in the first place. Watching Addison quickly move about Lane's booth is like watching a superhero get to work saving a town. They dart around the booth, removing mirrors and dousing tables with water, a blur of bright floral patterns and auburn hair. I finish with the customers who stopped by and catch Addison's eye as they're returning to their booth. I give a tentative thumbs up and put what I hope is a bewildered expression on my face.

"All good?" I mouth as clearly as I can.

I watch as Addison picks up the whiteboard they used to communicate with me earlier and wait as they write something.

'Sun + Mirror = Fire,' I read, and my bewildered expression morphs into one of shock. I quietly say, "Oh, shit."

Addison must be a pro at reading lips because they just nod towards me. They hold up a finger as they take their disheveled hair down and put it back up in a fresh bun. I notice that it's the same color as the highland cow in the logo on display behind them and chuckle a bit to myself. After a minute, the whiteboard has a fresh message.

"Okay now. No catastrophic damage or pending danger."

Well, that's good. I'm glad no one got burned. I grab for the clipboard I was using earlier to communicate with them.

"Need any help?" I write out with a dark Sharpie and hold it up for Addison to see. They smile and start writing.

"No, I think we're good. Thanks." It looks like they drew a little heart at the end of the message.

"Hungry?" I respond. "Wanna grab lunch?"

The smile from earlier this morning returns and lights

up their face.

"Yes, please." They put the whiteboard down and grab a 'Back in 5' sign from behind their checkout area.

I check in with my booth neighbors and ask if they'd be okay watching my booth while I grab lunch, and after they agree, I head over to where Addison is talking to Lane.

"Hey," I try to keep the anxiousness out of my voice when I reach them. "Get everything sorted from earlier?"

Lane looks a bit weary but tries to be upbeat as they respond. "Working on it. Thankfully, Addison has the nose of a bloodhound and caught everything before my booth fully caught fire."

"Thankfully, indeed. That really sucks. I'm sorry I couldn't help you two at the time, but can I bring you any sort of food or drink or anything? Sounds like a rough morning."

"Oh, uh, an iced tea would be great. Micah knows how I like it."

"That's an easy enough order to remember. You got it." I smile kindly at them and turn my focus on Addison. They're looking intently between us, lips upturned slightly at the corner in a smirk that would make the Mona Lisa proud.

"You ready?" I ask.

"Let's go." They turn to Lane before falling in step with me. "Thanks for watching my booth. We'll be back soon. Use whatever tools you need to finish up with the replacements. I'll help when we get back if you still have some left."

"Thanks, Addison."

We walk down the pathway, steps synchronized in silence until we turn the corner.

"I could see it," Addison blurts out like they've been having a conversation in their head without me.

"What could you see?"

"You and Lane."

I'm confused. Where is this coming from? Why is Addison thinking about me and Lane? We've had maybe 5 minutes of conversation all day, and a lot of that was shop talk or me listening to them gush about how great Addison is.

"Why do you say that?"

"I know Lane, and I'm starting to get to know you a bit better. I think you'd be good for each other. Besides, you were really kind to them in offering to bring them a drink."

"They're having a hard day, and I've had a good one so far. I'd probably do the same for pretty much any other vendor."

"Oh." They go quiet as we get into line for Sha-wing and a Miss, one of the food trucks that serves shawarma sandwiches and platters. "Sorry for presuming. I do that sometimes. I'm a big fan of romance and have a recurring daydream of being a matchmaker. I didn't even consider that you might not be looking."

"I'm not actively looking, but I'm not not looking, if that makes sense. But thanks. I don't generally hook up with the closest thing I have to coworkers, though. It can create too much unnecessary drama if things go bad. I was on the outskirts of a community that got torn apart by a bad breakup and losing people you consider family is really hard."

"That makes sense." I can't tell if their skin is red from blushing or from being out in the sun for longer than 60 seconds.

All the comfort and ease from this morning is gone as we move up the line in awkward silence.

"I'm not mad," I clarify after another minute. "I think it's kinda cool that you have a recurring daydream. Have any of your dream matches become OTPs in real life?"

"OTPs?"

"One True Pairing. It's a nerd term for characters people want to be end-game in media."

"I like it." They drums three of their fingers along their lips, and a pensive look comes over their face. "My oldest sister and her husband were best friends in high school, and I kept rooting for them to fall in love. Does that count?"

"Sure, why not?"

"I didn't exactly do anything to move them along towards each other."

"Is that a requirement you want to place on yourself?" I ask.

"You're sounding a lot like my mom. She's a psychologist who asks a lot of probing questions like that."

"I must have picked it up during my many years of therapy. Sorry if I'm coming across too clinical or traumatizing for you. Parents can be... tricky." I force myself to stay present in the conversation instead of letting my mind wander to my own traumatic relationship with my parents.

"They can, but I love my moms," Addison says nonchalantly as if having multiple moms is a normalcy for everyone.

"Moms? As in plural?"

"Yeah, my moms are lesbians. Mum, the psychologist, carried us, but Mama, who's a librarian, is genetically my parent."

"That's cool. It must have meant a lot that they were both able to contribute to your birth in their own way."

"Yeah, it's pretty awesome. It helped a lot when I was younger and people tried to bully me about how two women couldn't make a baby. I got pretty good at defending our family. All three of us kids did."

"So two siblings and two moms. Cool."

They point at their flower crown. "Yeah, I'm a demiguy with two sisters and two moms. Our family wouldn't exactly be on the poster advertising tradition or masculinity."

That makes me laugh.

"I was going to ask about the flower crown. I don't know if I've seen that flag before, but that's really cool. I think a couple guys in the LGBTQ+ support group I'm in identify as demi."

"You're in an LGBTQ+ support group? That's really cool."

"Yeah, it's actually how I met my best friends."

"Awesome." They smile at me, and I bite my lip ring to keep myself from smiling back too wide.

We've gotten up to the front of the line, and any semblance of awkwardness is gone for the moment. We both place our orders and step off to the side while we wait.

"What about your family?" Addison asks me. For the briefest of moments, I consider telling them all about my messed up family history, but it's not the right time, or place and I've been burned by being too open too quickly in the past.

"I was raised by my grandmother. Parents really aren't in the picture." I hope I say it with enough conviction that they don't pry.

"Your grandmother seemed really badass when you talked about her this morning." My body unclenches, and the tension leaves as I realize they aren't going to push the matter further. Hope starts to spark in my brain. Maybe one day, we'll be at the point where I can trust them with everything. I don't try to extinguish the spark, but I don't want to purposefully feed it either.

"She really was."

"So it's just you now? That must get lonely."

"I have Travis and Trevor, though. They're my chosen family. We're a weird band of misfits, but we work, and we support each other through everything."

"Are Travis and Trevor the best friends who stole your phone to message me last month?"

It's my turn to blush. "Yeah, sorry again about that. Trevor can be a bit much when he wants to be."

"I don't mind. It let us start talking. That's a win in my book." They smile at me and then step towards the food truck window as our names are called.

After our food is situated, I follow Addison as they start to walk towards a coffee cart a few spaces away. My Chemical Brewmance has a shorter line than the shawarma cart, but we'll still be waiting for a little bit to get our drinks. I go to take a bite of my wrap when a glop of sauce lands on the image of a cat on the front of my shirt, barely missing the carnation that Addison pinned on me this morning.

"Oh, shit." I put the wrap back in the container and look around for napkins. Before I can panic too much, Addison is there holding out a few for me.

"Thanks." I smile sheepishly and take the napkins from them. Without me asking, they grab the container that my lunch is in and hold it while I clean up the sauce.

"Dang, I hope this doesn't stain. I love this shirt."

"I have some stain wipes back at my booth. I'll give you one when we get back over there. Should keep your cat friend from any lasting damage. Who is Kat and the Hurricane anyway? I meant to ask you earlier, but we got interrupted by the market opening."

"How rude of it not waiting for us to be done talking," I tease. "Kat and the Hurricane is one of my favorite bands. They're a group of trans and non-binary musicians who make queer synth-rock/alt pop."

"I'll have to check them out. I'm always looking for more music. I'm surprisingly tame and basic in my musical tastes. Or at least that's what people tell me."

"What musicians make them say that?"

"Taylor Swift, Phoebe Bridgers, Kacey Musgraves."

"If you're considering 'basic' to mean 'mainstream and

popular,' then, yes, I guess your taste in music is a bit basic, but you're allowed to like what you like. Can I make you a playlist of some of my favorites?"

"Sure."

"Awesome." The grin on my face is probably the widest it's been in a long while. I love sharing new music with people, and Travis and Trevor are sick of getting playlists from me. "Any hard limits on style?"

"I'm not really into heavy metal. The constant yelling can amp up my anxiety. I'm okay with a little bit, like in screamo, but not when it's the whole time."

"Understood. I will leave death metal off the list."

We order our drinks, and Micah has them ready for us quickly. I carry the three of them back in a container, and Addison is still holding on to both of our lunches. We keep casually talking about music, and I discover that we both went through an emo phase back in high school. Though theirs evolved into more of an Americana and acoustic taste and mine branched into ska and pop-punk.

When we're back to the booths, things still seem quiet, but we've been gone longer than I typically like to be away. I hand Lane their iced tea, and when I go to grab my food from Addison, I realize they're with a customer. My food is sitting on the top of the checkout counter, and a stain removal wipe is sitting in its individual package on top of the closed container. I look up and meet their eyes as they're talking with the customer. They smile and bite their bottom lip.

It's then that I realize I'm in trouble. Addison Baird could easily make me break my self-imposed 'don't get involved with the community' rule. Before I can get lost in their eyes again and do something I regret, I grab my food and the stain removal wipe, nod at them in thanks, and rush back to the safety of my booth.

CHAPTER EIGHT
Addison (they/he)

Colin is gone by the time I'm able to finish helping the customer who wanted to buy a couple bouquets, and when I look over to his booth, he's busy with a few customers of his own. It keeps going like that, and we're only able to connect one more time before the end of the day when I quickly scribble 'Vendor Dinner?' down on my dry erase board, and he gives me the thumbs up. The smile on my face is a reflex. It's not that I don't normally smile, but with him, I'm smiling and blushing a lot more than I usually do. I haven't been this intrigued by someone since college when I first met Liam.

As it does whenever anything reminds me of my relationship with Liam, my brain starts to spiral, and I start feeling claustrophobic and trapped in my own body. It scares me enough that I pull out my phone and text Gri.

ME

So something weird is happening and I could use some advice.

GRI

Weirder than you getting distracted this morning and not being ready to go right at market open?

ME
I was ready… I just wasn't aware that the market had opened when it did. My booth had been set up and I had technically already made a sale.

GRI
So yes weirder?

ME
Relatedly weirder?

GRI
Explain…

ME
You know how I told you about when Liam and I met in college and there was a pull between us?

GRI
Yeah?…

ME
It's happening again.

GRI
LIAM IS THERE!?
<Gif of speeding car>

ME
Calm down, Vin Diesel. No, Liam's not here, but that pull is happening again.

GRI
You can't take him back.

ME
Agreed, but I'm not talking about Liam. I was just using that as a reference.

GRI
Ah okay, go on.

ME
Well you know the new vendor, Colin?

GRI
The ceramics guy and the reason this morning got jumbled for you?

ME
Yeah.

I put my phone down for a minute and take a deep breath before I continue.

GRI
<We're waiting gif>

<eating popcorn gif>

ME
Geez, Gri, chill. I'm getting there.

Anyways...

I'm feeling a pull between me and Colin. We've been talking all day and I'm a bumbling, blushing idiot around him. I even tried to connect him and Lane so I could ignore the weird vibe between us.

GRI
LANE?! Seriously Ads!? I love them to pieces, but Lane is a disaster. Why would you do that to either of them?

ME
I don't know, I panicked... He wasn't interested anyways. He said he doesn't "hook up with coworkers".

GRI

That's a little weird since you don't technically work together.

ME

I mean, he explained it a little better. I guess he's dealt with other close-knit communities where people got together, broke up, and it wrecked the whole place.

GRI

Makes sense.

ME

Yeah, he's definitely lived an interesting life. Dropped a few tidbits, but I didn't want to pry in the line for Shawarma.

GRI

<Go On gif>

ME

I'm not going to. It's not my story to tell. I love you, Gri, but you're addicted to any sort of drama.

GRI

Boo, you're no fun. Give me something? I'm boooooooreddddddddd.

ME

If you're so bored, you should come hang out and meet him yourself.

GRI

Maybe I will. Will he be at Vendor Dinner tonight?

ME

Yeah, I think so. Not sure where we're gonna go yet.

GRI

Let me know. I'll see if Jodie is feeling up to going out later.

ME

Okay. I should go. We've only got an hour left and today's been busy.

GRI

Have fun!

ME

Thanks, Gri. You're the best.

GRI

I know. 😊 Now go sell some flowers like a good little demiboy.

I let out a heavy sigh as I put my phone back in my apron pocket. I don't have the answers I was looking for, and I'm still feeling a bit amped up emotionally, but talking to my best friend has at least taken the edge off my anxiety, and I don't feel like I'm going to have a panic attack in the middle of my booth anymore.

Looking up, I notice Colin is staring. He holds up a sign. "You okay, A?" I nod, but the smile on my face feels tight. He doesn't look like I'm convincing him, but I don't want to really get into it, so I turn towards my back display wall and start to rearrange the remaining stems, trying not to let the negative emotions take over.

That's the thing about PTSD and trauma. You can be having an amazing day, and then one thing can blindside you, and you find yourself fighting to stay regulated and out of your own head. It's easier when you're in a safe environment, like being in my garden for me. Putting my hands in dirt or pruning my favorite rose bush helps my body get centered and stay grounded. But when I'm at a show, I usually have Gri around, and she knows every-thing. She's helped me through a few panic attacks either by coaching me through them or by giving me a way to hide out until things pass. Now that she's not here, I don't have that safety net anymore. I didn't think I'd need it so soon.

"You sure you're okay?" Colin's voice is behind me. I felt his presence before hearing his voice, but I didn't want to turn around because my face would give me away in an instant.

I almost lie, but then part of the truth falls out of my mouth.

"Not really, but I will be." My voice is strained.

I hear his foot take a tentative step forward, but it stops before he gets to me.

"A-Anything I can do to help?" he asks softly.

Still not looking at him, I take a centering breath before responding.

"Can you just watch my booth? I need to just not be on for a minute." What am I saying? Why can't I mask this around him? If it had been anyone else, I would have been acting normally.

"Sure thing, Mr Mayor." I can hear the gentle encour-agement and care in his voice.

I duck around the display wall to the area I have set up for storage and crouch down, taking off my glasses and putting them on top of a tub. The heels of my palm rub at my eyes, and I move them in circular motions while prac-ticing my grounding breaths. I don't know exactly how long it takes, but I'm able to get myself regulated and cen-tered again. I pull my phone out of my pocket and open the camera app so I can check my reflection before going back out to face people.

After redoing my hair and straightening my clothes, I plaster a small smile on my face, take one final deep, grounding breath, and step back to the front of my booth. Colin is still there, but he's not alone; Samwise is chatting with him. I'm simultaneously relieved that he won't be able to ask me questions and disappointed for the same reason. I shove that feeling aside; it's thinking like that which got me stuck in my spiral in the first place. I sidle up next to them and try to seamlessly insert myself into the conversation.

"Hey, Addison!" Samwise greets me with a smile.

"How's it going?"

"Great. I just wanted to stop by and find out if you were coming to Vendor Dinner tonight? Seems like we're planning to hit up the Korean BBQ buffet since people said it was overall a good day."

"Yeah, I'll be there. I've gotta text Gri and let her know, too. She and Jodie might stop by."

"Awesome. Well, I'll leave you to it." He turns to Colin, "Colin, it was great to see you again. I'm glad you got away from Bethany."

Colin chuckles, "Ha, thanks. Hopefully, she wasn't too miserable for you today."

"Nah, I'm used to it. I can handle her attitude. Reminds me of some of the people I went to high school with."

"You have the patience of a saint," I add. Samwise gives us a wave before heading over to Lane's booth.

I take my phone out and text Gri with the details for Vendor Dinner tonight. I'm not trying to ignore Colin, and I really should thank him for covering for me, but I also can't make myself meet his eye.

"So," he starts, and I try not to visibly wince as I wait for him to pry. "We can invite non-vendors to Vendor Dinner?"

"We usually don't, but Gri used to be my booth buddy, and she and her partner, Jodie, have been Market staples for years. Sadly, not anymore, though. Why? Was there someone you wanted to invite?"

"No, I was just curious… for future dinners. Usually, Travis and Trevor hang out with me and help me do a breakdown at the end of the night, and I like to make sure I feed them as a token of my appreciation. They're out of town this weekend, but in the future…" He trails off.

"Oh, I'm sure that would be cool." I bite the inside of my top lip and tentatively look over at him. "I can help you with tear down tonight if you want. It's the least I can do after you covered for me just now."

His inquisitive eyes meet mine, and I feel like my soul is being x-rayed. My breathing starts to shallow and speed up. I force myself to look away.

"If you say you're okay, I'll take your word on it, but you seem a little freaked out, and I just want you to know that I'm here to listen if you need to talk about anything. I know we don't know each other super well yet, but I have this gut feeling that we'll get there. I understand that trusting people is hard, and it's certainly not something I do lightly, but I see how you take care of everyone else at this market, and I want to make sure you're taken care of, too."

"Are you sure you're not a therapist? That was pretty textbook Dr. Siobhan Baird," I say. My natural defense mechanism is to joke about things, and the callback to our earlier conversation is an easy one to make.

He laughs, but it doesn't fully reach his eyes, which are still searching my face.

"Seriously, though. I'm around if you need me." He places his hand on my upper arm, and the touch grounds me in a way I wasn't expecting.

"Thanks, Colin. I'll be okay. You've already helped by giving me a reprieve and letting me get recentered."

"Does that happen a lot for you?" He sounds genuine in his question, but I'm still not ready to fully open up.

"Enough that I know how to handle it. Really, though, I'll be okay. I just needed a minute."

He gives my arm a reassuring squeeze before dropping his hand.

"Okay, Blooms. I believe you."

"Blooms?"

"Yeah, I decided you needed a nickname. Can't call you Mr. Mayor in every context, and like I said earlier, I have a gut feeling we'll be friends for a while. I thought about 'Flowers,' but that's practically Trevor's last name, and I don't want it to get too confusing. And, no offense, but 'Tussie Mussie' is too long for a nickname. A bit weird, too."

"Blooms it is, then." I relax a little bit more as he talks.

"Great." The smile reaches his eyes again, and I'm swept away by the grey irises looking back at me. Instead of looking like the sky after a storm, today, they look like a black and white photograph of the sun reflecting on water. I'm entranced. Once again, I find myself having to deliberately pull away from getting lost in his eyes.

"Well, now I'm going to need a nickname for you. I can't call you Clay—that's my brother-in-law's name. Vase just sounds weird. Let me think about this for a minute."

Colin stands patiently, examining some of the tussie-mussies and not pushing me to speak before I'm ready. I look at him again and really study him. His lavender hair and tattoo sleeves make me think of traditional Scottish thistles—enticing and beautiful but prickly if you go about getting near them in the wrong way. Between his band tee and torn jeans, he's wearing all black, which really makes the purple in his hair stand out. I look up at his face, trying to avoid being sucked into his eyes again. He's fiddling with his lip piercing as he picks up one of the tags, and his thick eyebrows furrow as he reads, a crease forming between them. My gaze traces down his body. He's built like a former athlete, but the real strength is in his arms. Not surprising for someone who slings mud all day.

That thought makes me smile, and the nickname is

solidified when I get to his beat-up black and white checkered Vans covered in clay mud from working in his studio.

"Alright, I think I've got it."

He puts the flower bunch back in its stand and looks at me, arms crossed and a playful expression on his face. "Okay, then. What is it, Blooms?"

"Mud."

"As in, 'your name is mud'?"

"Oh…" I sound a bit dejected. "I was going more for the 'clay equals mud'-slash-'mudslinger' aspect of ceramics. I didn't even think about the negative connotations."

He laughs, and my blush returns.

"You're something else, Blooms."

He winks at me, and my mouth drops. The awkward blush in my cheeks brightens, turning into something a bit more heated. *What the fuck!?* I don't get this way. My gut starts churning with want and desire. I recognize these signs. The ever-elusive attraction— this pull and longing that is leaving my body craving to slot right next to his chest and be held between those strong arms. It's a sure sign that I'm in danger of developing a crush, and an intense one at that. My brain is screaming at me to pull away, but my body is frozen in place.

"Yo, Colin!" a voice calls from across the way. He turns around to see Timms waving and pointing over to Colin's booth, where a couple people are holding mugs and staring at us.

"See you around, Blooms. I'll let you know if I need help breaking my stuff down tonight. Otherwise, I'll see you at Vendor Dinner." He smiles and leaves. I grip the counter behind me to keep myself from falling over because, for some reason I'm trying to not think about, my knees are a little weak at the moment.

Well, fuck.

CHAPTER NINE
Colin

The last hour of the show goes by quickly. I'm fairly close to being sold out again, and my teardown takes significantly less time than I expected. I actually considered going over and offering to help Addison finish packing up, but by the time the thought hits me, I'm already settling into my truck and letting my body relax a bit before I get ready to switch modes from customer service-centered to networking.

A big show like this usually has me completely drained at the end of it. I spend so little time around people during the week that it takes a bit of time for the adrenaline to wear off. Combine that with the exhaustion from constantly being on edge because I'm trans, and my instincts tell me to keep my head on a perpetual swivel. I'm ready to retreat to the safety of my little house, throw on some ska, and get to work slinging mud.

That last little thought makes my lips twitch into a small smile, and I think of Addison. I wasn't lying when I told them that my gut is telling me we'll be in each other's lives for a while. I had a similar reaction when I met Travis, though his wasn't as intense as what I feel with Addison.

I punch the address to the Korean BBQ place into my GPS and shoot a text off to the group chat.

ME

My phone starts ringing as I turn out of the parking lot. I hit the button to answer it.

"What's up? Scared I was being kidnapped?"

"That or body snatched. You're on speaker, by the way." Trevor's voice comes out of the tinny truck stereo. "What convinced you to not go back to your hobbit hole and voluntarily do more peopling. Cough twice if you're in trouble."

"What or who?" Travis's inquisition makes me glad that neither of them can see me. I'm pretty sure I've reached Addison-levels of blushing at the moment.

"No body snatching, no trouble. And I was invited last month but didn't go."

"What's the difference this month? Miss us too much?"

"Obviously."

"I am proud of you, C. You deserve to have a good community of people around you. I mean, we're great, but it's probably a good idea to have more than your coupled-up best friends."

"I have more than that. I've got the group." Our trans support group is great, but Travis and Trevor are the only ones I still hang out with outside of our monthly meetups.

"Sure, Jan." Trevor gives his best Marsha Brady impression. After a minute, he continues, "So today went well?"

"Yeah. I was in a different spot this time, but it didn't hurt me at all. I almost sold out completely."

"That's two months in a row. You weren't kidding when you said this market could be big for you."

They both know how nervous I've been about this year of my business. I've been stressed about making the ceramics thing a success. I originally gave myself five years of trying to find the balance, and this is year five. The last four years have been enough to keep the business paying for itself, but without enough to pay myself for the countless hours I put into it. I know I'm privileged in that I have my inheritance from Gram, which includes a fully paid-off house, but hiring lawyers to fight the contested will was costly and ate up a chunk of that inheritance. Being trans and not having health insurance through a job is also pretty expensive. I need this year to go well, to turn a profit, and to be able to start actually paying myself. Applying for the Makers Market has been a dream of mine, and the fact that they actually had openings this year felt like a sign. I still haven't met the organizers, Seth and Lilly, but from what my new booth neighbors, Timms and Cal, were saying, they're usually at the Vendor Dinners even if they aren't able to make it to the actual shows. Hopefully, that means I'll meet them tonight.

I continue talking to the guys for a few more minutes until I need to focus on the GPS directions so I can get to the restaurant. I don't know why, but something keeps me from telling them more about Addison. I share so much with them, but part of me wants to keep Blooms all to myself for a little bit. Nothing is even technically going on with us, just some light flirting and definite attraction on my part.

The restaurant parking lot is full of cars and trucks packed to the gills with signs of craft shows. I'm definitely in the right place. I give myself a couple more minutes to psych myself up before I decide I'm ready to go in.

I shouldn't have been nervous, though. As soon as I enter, I see Cal, Samwise, Lane, and Timms talking with a couple other people at a table. There are a few seats open, and they wave me over as soon as they see me. I pay at the entrance and head over to the group.

"Hey, y'all. Good day?" I ask as I approach, my Southern accent coming out a bit since I'm tired.

"Yeah, June is usually one of the better months. Lots

of people are excited about supporting queer artists, and the Makers Market has a high percentage of us," Samwise says, a bit like he's testing me.

"I'll drink to that," I say, tapping the green carnation that's still pinned on my chest in hopes that it assuages any doubts he might have about my inclusion in the community. I do a quick scan to see if Addison has made it yet. There's no sign of the burnt auburn-haired florist, so I situate myself facing the door so I can see whenever they come in.

"Ah, I see you've made a friend with the Market's mayor. They don't gift those carnations out to just anybody. You must have made a good impression," a woman observes. She looks familiar, but I can't seem to place her. I must have walked past her booth at some point. She's sitting with her arm around the waist of another woman. "Wait a minute...are you the new ceramicist?"

"Yeah," I confirm tentatively, the inflection in my voice making it sound a bit more like a question than a definitive statement. I hold out my hand to shake hers. "I'm Colin."

"Oh, I've heard about you. I'm Gri, this is my partner, Jodie." I shake Jodie's hand next. "Seems you've made quite an impact on my bestie."

My eyes go wide as I realize that the person before me is none other than Addison's best friend and former booth buddy.

"Ah, yeah." I start playing with my lip ring out of nervous habit. "They talk about you a lot. I really enjoyed hearing your friendship origin story."

"They told you about the doom bouquet?" she says, one eyebrow raising in slight disbelief.

"I asked what the most bizarre accidental meaning someone had put together was, and they told me about your combo. I was impressed. Remind me to ask you to pick out flowers I can send to my enemies next time."

Gri chuckles, "Ads would do it better. They'll be able to hook you up with the bouquet that will make the most cutting remark."

"I don't doubt it. They're a veritable encyclopedia of floriographic knowledge." I smile and hope I've passed whatever first impression test is being set.

"So… Ads tells me that you're the reason they were late opening for the market this morning."

"Ah, yeah. We kinda got caught up talking about Pride and exchanging our queer identity trading cards."

"Oh, so you are a card-carrying member of the queer community, too?"

"Oh, yeah. I'm a double dipper in the acronym: gay and trans."

"Fantastic. I've only got the lesbian bit covered."

"I've got dibs on the queer tag." Jodie, smiles and winks.

As if we've rehearsed the move before, we simultaneously turn to the other three guys who have been quietly watching our exchange.

"Gay and trans," Samwise says. We high five.

"Also gay," Cal says.

"I'm bi," Lane remarks.

"Sadly, I'm not a member," Timms says a bit dejectedly. I try not to be obvious when I sneak a curious look towards Gri & Jodie.

"Denial," Jodie mouths back. I bite back a chuckle.

"Well, looks like we've got the whole acronym. We'll have even more of it when Addison gets their ass here. That demiboy has so many labels, a CVS receipt would seem small in comparison," Gri says.

As if our talking summoned them out of thin air, Addison comes up behind the group, gives Jodie a peck on the cheek, rubs Gri's freshly buzzed cut hair, and slides into the chair next to mine.

"I like labels. They help me communicate things I normally wouldn't have the language to express. It's a lot easier to tell people I'm asexual than to explain that, no, I'm not interested in going home with them at the end of the night, and then having to give a whole host of reasons why not so they aren't dicks about it."

I try not to let myself feel like that comment is targeted at me and make a mental note that I should probably tone down the flirting.

"Alright, babe. I get it. Labels work for you," Gri resigns herself to defeat on this topic. She turns to Jodie. "What foods do you want me to grab you?"

It isn't until she gets up with Addison that I realize Jodie has a mobility device resting next to her at the table. I don't call attention to it, though. I know that I hate when people ask imposing questions about being trans. I can only imagine that having to rely on using a mobility device invites more invasive questions than I get these days from being pretty stealth. Unless they see me in certain lights with my clothes off, most people wouldn't be able to tell. My scars have shrunk and faded significantly after nearly 10 years post-top surgery, and starting testosterone at an early age really helped my body develop with more masculine qualities from the start.

With a nod of my head to the group, I stand up and make my way over to the bar to order whatever amber ale they have on tap. After I give the bartender my table number, they tell me they'll bring the drink over so I can go get food.

I find Addison at the sauce bar, where they've got a tray full of 5 different concoctions.

"Going for a record, Blooms?"

Addison drops the plastic container they were just about to start filling for sauce number 6.

"Geez, Mud, you startled me." They stick out their

tongue at me and pick up the container where it fell onto their tray. Their face scrunches adorably as they say, "You know, I don't think Mud fits. I'll have to think of something else."

"Fair enough. Sorry for making you spill. I didn't realize I was walking so softly."

"I don't think you were. The music is loud enough to cover your footsteps, but it's mostly because I was lost in my own little potion lab."

"Potion lab? Would that make you a witch or a mad scientist?" I grab my own sauce cup and start mixing in different ingredients according to the instructions on the wall.

"Neither? Both? Wouldn't you like to know?"

"Mysterious." I smirk at them. I see Addison subconsciously bite the inside of their lower lip. It reads more as a nervous habit than an attempt at seduction. "Hey, listen, I want to apologize if I've been overly flirty or made you uncomfortable or anything. I heard what you said about people not taking you seriously when you said you weren't interested, and I don't want you to think that I'm trying to pressure you into anything. I just don't spend a lot of time around people other than Travis and Trevor, so sometimes I can come across as..."

"Flirty?" Addison finishes.

"I was gonna say broody and awkward, but yes, sometimes when I find someone who I feel a connection with, I can lean into the flirty category pretty hard, and I just wanted to make sure that I didn't cross any lines with you or make you uncomfortable in any way."

Addison looks down at the sauce they're mixing. I start nervously playing with my lip ring and wait for them to speak.

"You really haven't made me feel uncomfortable, at least not in a way that would cross any lines. I embarrass myself pretty easily, and I've found that I jumble up words sometimes. In case you haven't noticed, I have no poker face when I feel strong emotions." They point to the blush creeping up their neck and deepening on their cheeks.

Glad that I could clear the air a little bit and get settled into a friendship track, I give a little friendly wink, trying not to come across as flirty, and head over to pick out my meats for grilling.

The dinner goes by really well. I'm introduced to a few other vendors, and I'm just getting to know Chris before he gets a sour look on his face as a punky-looking twink wearing a crochet crop top walks past and winks at him exaggeratedly. He storms off in the opposite direction from the twink, and I turn to Lane, who is standing next to me.

"Well, that was interesting," I muse.

"Oh, yeah. Chris and Sal have had a thing. They're the two fiber artists at the market—Chris does knitting, and Sal does crochet. Apparently, there's some sort of rivalry between the two mediums, and those two have been at odds for, like, three years now. I don't really have all the details. Addison might, though. You'll have to ask them." Lane responds nonchalantly.

"Or you could ask anyone else who was here when they first started," an alto voice says. Lane immediately smiles at the couple coming up to us and throws out their arms, almost smacking me in the face.

"Lilly! Seth!" they squeak.

Lilly and Seth embrace Lane. As their group hug disbands, Lane's arm is still around Lilly's waist. Seth reaches out his hand to me, and I shake it. It's calloused, like most artists or physical laborers, but surprisingly not as rough as I'd expect from someone who has made a living in the art world. Lilly also holds out her hand for me to shake. I notice her fingertips have a lot of healed small cuts, but from what I've heard, she works with paper a lot, so it makes sense.

"Hi, I'm Colin." I introduce myself. "I'm new."

"Colin..." I can see Seth running down a mental spreadsheet of vendors. "Oh yeah, Ceramics by Colin, right?"

"Yeah, that's me."

"Welcome to the Market. How is everything going for you? I hope moving you to a new location this month wasn't too much of a hassle."

"So far, so great. No complaints. I've done really well both months. Almost sold out today. I think I have like, half a box of stock that I'm taking home tonight."

"Fantastic. We love to hear it," Lilly chimes in. "Addison was telling us all about how you saved their show last month."

"Oh, well, I think that might be a bit of an exaggeration. I just had what they needed." I smile a bit sheepishly.

"It's never a bad thing to get in good with the Mayor of the Market. Especially right off the bat. We might technically be the organizers, but everybody knows that if you need help or have questions, Addison is the right person to ask." Seth says.

"They're pretty great."

"Yeah, they are," Lane interjects. "Did you hear that I almost burned down my booth today? Thankfully, Addison was there to discover the disaster before it got out of control."

"Honey, no!" Lilly chides. "What happened?"

"My mirror supplier fucked me over and sent me the wrong mirrors, so the sun's reflection started melting my tables and almost set a bunch of stuff on fire. I basically had to scrap my entire stock."

"Oh, shit!" Seth exclaims. "I'm glad you're okay. Do you have to worry about anyone accidentally setting their house on fire? Do you need us to help support in any way? We can put a message out on the official account."

"No, I should be good. I only sold my old stock before it all happened. I had just put out the new ones, and thankfully no one bought them before we discovered that they're death rays."

"I'm glad you didn't get hurt." Lilly hugs them.

"Me too."

"We'll have to figure something out for next month. If you're okay with it, maybe we'll move you to the other side of the row so your booth's back will be to the sun in the afternoon, and you won't have to worry about strong reflections."

"That would be amazing, thank you!" Lane exclaims. They turn around as someone from another table calls out to them and motions them over to where a group is gathered around two people looking like they're engaged in a one-on-one competition. Lane gives Seth and Lilly a hug before quickly going off to join the small crowd.

Lilly turns to Seth and places her arm around his waist. "You're thinking about the insurance liabilities, aren't you?"

"Yeah... that would have been a nightmare." His eyes close as he once again looks like he's going through a file folder of important legal documents.

"I'm glad Addison caught it when they did." I don't know why I haven't left the conversation, but I'm still standing there awkwardly, trying to make a good impression on the people who basically but unknowingly hold the fate of my business in their hands.

"For sure. Honestly, we love that one. The market

wouldn't be the same without them." Lilly beams. "I'm glad you're here tonight, Colin. We missed meeting you last month. I hope everyone's been making you feel welcome. We've worked really hard to make the market a safe place for our vendors, and for the most part, we've been successful. Everyone we've talked to has had nothing but praise for you and your work."

"Thanks," I respond.

"If you ever have any trouble with anyone- patron, vendor, whoever, please let us know. We take the safety and security of our vendors very seriously."

I nod, not wanting to sound like a toy preloaded with only the same phrase.

"Also, great shirt. Kat and the Hurricane is pretty badass."

"You know of them!?" I'm amazed. They're still relatively unknown, and I've never met anyone around here who's heard of them.

"Absolutely. I listen to as much queer and trans-fronted music as I possibly can."

"Me too."

"Have you heard of Laser the Boy?"

"Yes! I love him. How about JER? Are you into ska at all?"

"Not as much, but I have encountered JER's music a few times. Love their work."

Lilly and I fall into a conversation around our favorite queer and trans artists, and 20 minutes later, we've each got a list of at least 5 new bands to check out, links to our favorite online playlists, and a new friendship forming.

"It's great that you've cultivated such a safe place for queer and trans artists." I reflect on what Samwise mentioned when I first got to the restaurant. "Not all markets are like that."

"It was important to me as a trans woman that we

have a place for our community to really thrive. A lot of the Market's origins were inspired by 90s grunge and punk scenes. I'm started as a zine artist before I moved into teaching, and Seth might be an actuary now, but he started as a set designer for local theatre. We wanted to do it ourselves and DIY as much as we could. By the community, for everyone as long as you're not a fascist, racist, homophobic, ableist, transphobic asshole."

"Well, that rules out the majority of my family." I chuckle a bit darkly. Coping with humor is rare for me but comes out sometimes when I'm tired.

"Ouch." Lilly nods her head. "But understood."

I take her reassuring tone as a comfort that she truly does know what it's like to have a terrible family.

"I hate to leave it on that note because you've been awesome, but I'm wiped, and if I don't leave soon, I'm going to be camping out in the parking lot." I make my excuse to leave before I let more of my story slip to these people I just met.

"It was great to meet you, Colin. You've got our email, and our cell phones are listed at the bottom. If you need anything, Market-related or not, don't hesitate to reach out."

"Thanks, Lilly. I appreciate that."

I give her a tired nod, stifling a yawn, and start to head out to my truck. The majority of the parking lot is empty already. I'm just about to get into the driver's seat when I hear a familiar voice call my name.

"Colin, wait!" Addison comes rushing up to me. We stand on opposite sides of the open door, looking at each other. "I just wanted to thank you for an awesome day. I really enjoyed getting to know you better, and I especially wanted to thank you for helping me out when I needed a break. Gri is the only other person who has done that for me, and it means the world that you provided that safeness for me today. Anyways, I wanted to give you my number in case you ever wanted to talk or anything. Or if you want to meet up for Pride or whatever."

They hand me a torn edge from a sketchbook with "Blooms" written at the top and then a ten-digit phone number below it.

"Thanks, Blooms. I had a great day too. I don't know what my plans are, but if I'm able to go to the festival this year, I'll definitely let you know so we can meet up."

"Do you hug?" Addison asks, taking a step away from the door.

"Yeah, I can go for a hug." I softly shut the door and wrap my arms around their waist. They're a bit taller than me, but we fit together well. I try not to hold on longer than socially acceptable, but as soon as we pull away, I miss their warmth and how perfectly we fit together.

"Goodnight, Blooms."

"Goodnight, Nickname TBD."

I laugh.

They stand on the sidewalk outside the restaurant as I get into my truck and head home. I look back before pulling out of the parking lot; they've moved to their station wagon a few spaces away from where I had parked, but they're still watching as I drive off.

CERAMIXTAPE FOR BLOOMS

- Battle Dancing Unicorns (With Glitter) by Five Iron Frenzy

- Nobody Can Dull My Sparkle by JER

- blank space (feat. Suzie True & JER) by Skatune Network

- Sorry That I'm Like This by Kat & the Hurricane

- Glorious by Nur-D

- Garden by Meet Me @ The Altar

- Giving It Away by mae

- Last Hope by Paramore

- Pantsuit Sasquatch by Mollylele

- Jersey Never Seemed So Long by Element 101

- Snowbirds and Townies by Further Seems Forever

- Bloom (Bonus Track) by The Paper Kites

SPOTIFY

APPLE MUSIC

https://bit.ly/TDATT-playlists

JULY

CHAPTER TEN
Addison (they/he)

The best part about July is that my garden is in full bloom. I got up early this morning so I could prepare for the day and check on the bleeding heart heliopsis that is getting ready for its first bloom since I planted it. I can't wait until it's fully open, and I can study it in person. I'm excited, not just because it's a new flower in my garden but also because I'll hopefully be able to get enough reference sketches and pictures to use in replicating a felt version.

When I get out to the garden, it's barely dawn. I have a mug of tea and my sketchbook ready to go, and I sit on the moss patch under the old oak tree and listen to the world wake up around me. Honeybees from my sister's hive are starting to emerge, and I hear them buzz in the garden that I've been building up since I was 12. Each section is laid out and cultivated to bring as much harmony back to the earth as possible. I believe that we were set here to be stewards, not just to take whichever of Earth's resources humanity can extort.

My mind is starting to wander when a flash of orange catches the corner of my eye. A monarch is flitting and floating between the bees and lands near the center of a new bloom. The bleeding heart almost camouflages the butterfly, but the rhythmic movement of its wings allows me to watch as it takes the nectar it needs. I watch, mesmerized, my breaths falling in line with the beating wings. Moments like this are when my mind is clearest. I'm not bogged down by the anxieties that build or the failures that haunt me.

I'm a 32-year-old who still lives with their parents—not exactly a poster child for any sort of independence or success. I can feel the anxieties creeping in as the sun rises. Today is a show day, so I don't have a long time to stay out here. I finish my tea- a floral blend of chamomile, yarrow, lavender, lemon verbena, and rose that I grew, dried, and blended from last year's garden. When I get down to the dregs of the tea, I pour out the remainder at the base of the closest flowers.

I know I should be getting up and moving, but after last month's near panic attack, it's probably better that I do some extra grounding. Ideally, I'd weed, prune, or work on getting a new patch ready for planting, but I don't have time for that today. I put the mug down, spread my hands out wide, and place them palm-down on the moss. I close my eyes and let myself just feel. I never know what emotions are going to pop up when I do this, but it's always whatever I need. Slowly, I let my palms skim the surface of the moss and move over into the patches of clover surrounding it. My hands are damp with the morning dew. I focus on taking deep, grounding breaths and let myself take the extra minute or so of meditation to get my head ready for the day.

Once my body is starting to get antsy, I realize it's time. I pick up my mug and head back into the house. Today will be a good day. If I keep saying it over and over, I might even start to believe it.

I throw some Joy Oladokun on my phone, grab the rest of my supplies, and head off to the third market of the season. July's market isn't as fun as June's and historically tends to be one of the least busy during the summer because it seems to be peak vacation time, but that just means I get to spend more time talking to my fellow vendors and building those connections. I wonder if I'll have more time to talk to Colin again.

I'd be lying if I said he hasn't made regular appearances in my daydreams over the past month. Between being intuitively tuned into my moods, making me feel safe, and that hug after Vendor Dinner, I was already in dangerous territory of crushing hard. And we've been texting over the past month. Nothing too personal, but he sends me pictures of flowers he sees, and I workshop nicknames for him— still haven't found the right one.

It's a little terrifying to think I might be in danger of developing a new crush. When I meet someone who shows romantic potential, I can fall fast, and I fall hard. I get consumed with wanting to be part of their world. Just call me Ariel for that reason. And also because we both have red hair, though hers is more like a cooked lobster, and mine is reminiscent of a highland cow. I guess our hair reflects our heritage. ***Hair-itage***. I chuckle to myself as the tangent keeps me distracted.

Being romantically interested in a person but knowing that you rarely, if ever, feel sexual attraction to them is frustrating. It's a recipe for heartbreak, and I am no stranger to that pain. It basically rules out my use of any app because those are mostly used for hooking up, and I'm not usually looking for that. I need a connection with someone before I generally want to take that step. It's not because I'm prudish or because I'm trying to 'save myself for marriage,' whatever that means, but I just know that sex without an emotional bond does nothing for me. And if the emotional bond is one-sided, I get hurt. It's just easier to take care of myself whenever I need it than it is to risk being more broken than I already am.

I can tell that all the grounding I practiced this morning in the garden is in danger of being undone. Pulling into the parking lot, I decide to switch my music to something a little more upbeat and end up opening the playlist Colin sent me. Once I have my music going, I wait through a few songs until I'm feeling less trapped in my head and then start unloading the car. I'll have to thank him for the new music when I see him today.

Half an hour later, I'm fully unloaded, and my display backdrop is set up. There are only seven other vendors here, but since we still have close to two hours remaining until the market opens, I'm not surprised that people aren't here yet. I'm getting the flower wall loaded with new stems when Colin's voice cuts through my thoughts.

"Howdy, neighbor." He hops out of his truck and starts unloading his tent.

"Hey," I say, a little surprised. "I didn't know you were next to me today. I thought Seth and Lilly finalized the layout last month."

"Yeah, Lilly reached out to me after Vendor Dinner and asked if I'd be okay switching with Lane. She said something about how Seth didn't want to spend all day worrying about whether or not the market would go up in flames because the mirrors were misbehaving or something."

I laugh, genuinely laugh, and it alleviates the remaining anxiety I was trying to fend off.

"Well, I'm certainly not complaining. Now we don't have to worry about the long commute across the fairway to talk to each other."

"I know. But I was looking forward to breaking this bad boy in." He pulls a dry erase board out of one of the bins he's unloaded.

I smile wide. He was thinking about talking to me more. I'm really going to have a hard time protecting my heart when he's around.

I walk over to the truck bed and silently offer to help

him unload. We quickly get everything down and start working on getting his tent set up.

"Did you have time to get everything restocked?"

"Yeah. I almost had to pull out of a couple of my other markets to make sure I had enough stock for today, but that's not the worst thing that could happen."

"Oh, wow. Yeah, I've gone down to one show a month during the summer and then a couple popups in the fall because it's been hard to create as much as I want while working a full-time job."

"I can imagine. I'm fortunate enough that ceramics is my full-time job. For now."

"That's ominous." I look over curiously at him.

"Eh, art is tough. Bills are expensive. I gave myself five years to try and make it work enough to support me. This is the deadline year. I don't want to jinx anything, but if the rest of the year is like the past couple months, I should be able to go for year six."

We finish putting weights around the tent's legs and start on the tables, working in tandem like we've had years of practice. That comfort and ease seem to be recurring themes whenever I'm around Colin. I keep waiting for the other shoe to drop, some red flag to appear, but so far, my gut just has a warm feeling about him, like I've just taken a sip of my favorite tea on a cold day.

The rest of the setup goes by quickly, and the next thing I know, I'm looking around at Colin's completed booth and my half-finished setup. I start going back over to the wall I was working on when he showed up while Colin goes to park his car. Five minutes later, he's back and handing me flowers as we continue our conversation.

"I went to school for horticulture. My dream has always been to work with plants and flowers. Right now, though, I'm working a pretty dead-end job as a receptionist at a dental office. It's soul-sucking. I've always wanted to do something for myself."

"Like what?" he asks as he hands me a sweet pea.

"Well, I want to open a flower farm. Like real flowers, not just the felt ones. I mean, I'd still have those too, but I miss being around dirt all day. I worked on a flower farm one summer for an internship when I was in college, and it was the most exciting and energized I've ever been to go to work."

"What's stopped you?"

"Money. Space. Money. Student loans. Pick your poison."

"How much is the startup?"

"Probably close to $20,000. And that's not taking the land rental into consideration. Space around here is hard to get. Most of the developers snatch up any lots, and you really have to do a lot with soil prep and land surveys to make sure that you're not getting a space that will be toxic and kill everything you try to plant."

"That makes sense."

"Renting space is always a possibility, theoretically, but finding a farm that wants to lease part of their field for flowers isn't typically done. And again, conditioning that soil to work with flowers rather than other crops can be a costly endeavor. I'd be better off trying to buy my own house with a lot of land at this point, but college wasn't cheap, and I'll be paying that off for years."

Colin doesn't immediately respond the way I'd expect people to, so I turn to face him. "Don't tell me you're a trust fund kid and don't have any student loan debt."

"Okay. I won't tell you that I'm a trust fund kid with no student loan debt." He grins and cringes at me.

"Shut up," I playfully tease. "Hey, that's awesome for you. I'm glad you had that opportunity. As long as you're not against debt forgiveness, we won't have any issues." I wink.

He laughs. "Nope, not against that at all. If I was smarter, I would have gone with a computer science degree instead of an art one so I could hack in and wipe it all out."

"My hero." I clutch the bouquet I have in my hand and pretend to swoon. Joking with Colin is easy. I almost feel as grounded right now as I did this morning sitting in my garden.

We laugh some more. I'm enjoying this new soundtrack to my morning. Colin's laugh is deep and comes from his chest, but if he really gets going, he giggles. It's adorable. I could really get used to hearing it more.

"Hey, what do you think about putting this bouquet in that vase? I think they would pair well together." I look at the bouquet in my hand. The darker tones match the blues, reds, and blacks in one of the vases on the corner of Colin's display.

"Yeah, okay. That would be cool. Here, give me that one, and pick a couple more. I'll bring some vases over, and we can pair them up for both of our booths. I also have a couple smaller bud vases that would be perfect for individual stems if you wanted to try that." He gets up and grabs a couple vases from the table and a few more from a box below it.

I float around my booth, grabbing bouquets and stems that I think will fit well with the style and colors of vases he picked out. We work together, getting the flowers adjusted in their new homes, and when we're done, we have seven unique combinations. My favorite is a set of three bud vases that we've added nine stems to and intertwined a few of them to look like they've grown together. It's very 'nature taking over architecture' but subtle.

"What should we do with them?" I ask.

"Split them between our booths and try to sell them as collaborative sets?" Colin suggests.

"Sounds good to me. I should have some extra price tags we can use." I go around the table we've been working on and grab my toolbox. I plop it on the countertop with a heavy thud.

"Okay, Mary Poppins, that's an impressive toolbox."

"You can't be too prepared. I'm a bit clumsy at times, and I've been doing this show for a few years, so I've seen a lot of disasters that could have easily been thwarted if someone had just had a random thumbtack or extra tape or whatever, so I've amassed a collection of useful items over the years and bring them to every show."

"Smart move." Colin seems genuinely impressed. Most people tend to roll their eyes at my over-preparedness until they're the ones in trouble and needing something. "You really have earned your moniker and title. I may have to add 'Scout' to your growing list of nicknames."

I roll my eyes in jest and let out a breathy chuckle. I lay out the tags we need along with a fine-tip marker, string, and a single-hole punch.

"Grab me a couple of your business cards?" I ask, and he leans over into his booth, plucking a small stack of cards from the edge of the table.

I examine the cards when he hands them over. There's a blank corner where I'll be able to punch a hole without disrupting any of the design or text.

"Perfect. Do you mind if I punch a hole in these? I was thinking we could attach our business cards and the flower care card that I have, along with the price for the new items. That way, we don't have to worry about forgetting to include the other person's card when we sell these. And it'll emphasize the collaboration to anyone who's browsing."

"That sounds great to me," Colin agrees. He picks up the hole punch and gets to work preparing his cards. I grab my pre-punched cards and lie them out in front of each vase. Colin places his on top of mine, and we form a little assembly line to get the card stacks ready. We go back and forth on pricing a little bit and decide to offer a small discount for the bundled items.

Five minutes later, we have a tabletop full of gorgeous collaborations, labeled and ready for selling.

"Do you want to keep them all in one spot or spread them out between our booths?" I ponder.

"We can spread them out for better visibility. Then whoever's booth it's in can make the sale, and we can split the profits at the end of the day?"

"That sounds reasonable to me."

"Great." Colin beams at me and picks up two of the larger arrangements, taking them back to his booth. I quickly assess my setup and decide that I can feature the collaboration if I put them on my usual centerpiece table. I grab a couple platforms from my display supply box and bring them over. After moving the original centerpiece to the checkout counter, I remove the tablecloth, arrange the platforms, and create a new display layout that highlights the bouquets and vases. Colin joins me as I'm standing back and surveying my work.

"It needs something else. Maybe a sign?" I muse.

"That might help, but honestly, Blooms, that's a gorgeous layout. You really have a talent."

I blush a bit at the mention of my nickname. I don't know why I expected him to forget about it in the last month, but I'm glad he didn't. The warm feeling I had this morning grows in intensity, and the swoopiness feels a bit more like butterflies. I realize I've been staring at the table without responding for an awkward amount of time.

"Thanks," I mumble and then clear my throat. "I'll go see what I have."

Retreating to the safety of the storage area I have set up behind the wall display, I pull out my phone and text Gri. I know it's early on a Saturday, but I need help from my best friend.

ME

Gri, Help. I think I have a crush.

I throw my apron on and tuck my phone back in the top pocket instead of waiting for a response. Crouching down, I grab a chalkboard-style sign, a stand, and a chalk marker from the tub I keep my extra display items in. Bringing it over to the counter, I look over at Colin, who is chuckling at some of the tussie-mussie descriptions, and figure out what to write.

MUD & BLOOMS: A Ceramics X Colin and Hairy Cow Florals collaboration

I bring the completed sign over to the small table and place it in the center with the bouquets and vases around it. Colin comes over to look. His eyes dart to the pronoun pin on my apron before he glances over to take in the newly finished display. His smile lights up those gorgeous grey eyes in a way I haven't seen before, and the butterflies stir some more. I try not to let their fluttering turn into a nightmare. I've only had one other crush since my relationship with Liam ended, and that one ended with more heartbreak and an even more reduced feeling of self-worth. But Colin feels different.

"Do you think it's still missing something?" Colin's voice reaches through my spiraling thoughts like a safety line in the middle of a storm.

"I didn't. Do you?"

"No, but you've got an expression on your face like you're trying to work out a problem. I wanted to help if I could."

Like gulping a breath of fresh air after being stuck inside a stale room, I'm feeling slightly lightheaded by his kindness.

"I think we're all set."

Who is this guy? My inner voice is once again trying to

figure out what it is about Colin that is drawing me in at an alarming rate. I've known him for two months, but we've only interacted for less than a week during that time. That's not enough time for me to be feeling this way. It's confusing, disorienting, and a bit terrifying, but there's also a small spark of excitement and hope. I've been alone for the past seven years, and I miss the comfort of being in a relationship. Having someone to come home to and talk about our days, our hopes, our dreams, our problems. Someone to comfort me after a spiral and someone I can care for when they need it. The longing is an ache that keeps growing in power as I spend more time with Colin. I feel a vibration in my apron pocket and instinctively pull out my phone to see that Gri has responded.

I hold up my phone towards Colin. "Sorry, I've gotta take this real quick."

"No worries," he responds. "I'll just finish getting stuff set on my side. See you when you're done." He smiles and walks over to his booth.

GRI

It's Colin, isn't it? What's going on? He seemed pretty awesome. What's your holdup?

ME

Gri, I can't.

GRI

You can.

ME

I'm scared.

GRI

It's been nearly ten years since dick-for-brains (Liam) and 7 since shitface. You've grown. You know who you are. You're much more secure in your identity. You can allow yourself to have something good.

ME

You think he'll be good?

GRI

I've really only met him once, but Ads, the way he looks at you. *chef's kiss*

<biting fist GIF>

ME

How does he look at me?

I sneak a peek over at Colin, who is drawing in a sketch-book. He looks up at the flowers in the vase in front of him and then back at his sketch. I only look away when my phone vibrates with Gri's response.

GRI

Ads, that man looks at you like you're the only person that matters. He comes across as gruff and reserved, but when you walk into a room, he softens. His whole being changes because you're near him.

ME

That's a little unsettling.

GRI

Not in a bad way. It's not like he's acting or putting on a persona... it's more like his body reacts to your presence in a way that lets him lower any guard or defenses. I don't even think he realizes it, but there's definitely something there. I met him before you showed up to Vendor Dinner last month and his whole face lit up when he talked about you.

ME

It's too fast.

GRI

So go slow. Just be sure you go. Get to know him better. I'm not saying you should jump into bed with him right now. I know you don't work like that, but don't shut yourself off from something that might be just what you need and what you deserve. Because you deserve great things, Addison Baird. And if Colin feels like he could be one of those great things, then you should go for it. At your own pace and in your own way, but have some courage and faith. If he pushes you past your boundaries and hard lines, that's on him. You've got me and Jodie in your corner. As well as the majority of the market. We all want you to be happy.

ME

Was that on the last vendor meeting agenda?

GRI

<eyebrows raised gif>

You aren't supposed to know about those meetings. ;)

ME
But I'm the mayor :P

GRI
Yeah, yeah, Mayor. Go lord over your dominion and let me go back to sleep. It's early.

ME
Thanks Gri. I love you.
Enjoy your mid-morning nap.

I slip the phone back in my apron but don't get up just yet. I look at the small bud vases that remain on my check-out counter. I picked some wildflowers to put in the simple black containers- a dandelion, a thistle, and a clover. Three misunderstood flowers with meanings of hope and desire. Could I really do this? Could I actually open up my heart again and try, knowing that if history repeats itself, I'll be even more broken than I already am?

I hear Gri's voice in my head yelling at me for the negative self-talk and repeat the mantra she made me recite after she heard about my last breakup: "I am not broken. I am whole and perfect as I am. I am exactly who I need to be."

CHAPTER ELEVEN
Colin

Addison sits in their booth, staring blankly ahead for a few moments after they put their phone away. Everything in me wants to go over and make sure they're okay, but I don't want to overstep. This morning has been amazing so far, and I don't want to do anything that will jeopardize that. I'll give them whatever time they need and be here to listen if they want to vent about anything.

I look down at the sketch I've been working on. It's still missing something. The concept is eluding me. Aside from the 'make enough money to pay myself' goal, the one thing I want to accomplish this year is to break into the gallery scene. One of the local art galleries has a show every fall for new and upcoming artists, creatively called the New and Upcoming Artist exhibit. A few artists have been discovered there and have gone on to exhibit in larger cities like New York and Los Angeles. If you get in, it could be a game changer, and that's exactly what I need this year.

Creating art for markets is great, but once people own a piece or three, they don't always come back for more. And there are usually so many ceramicists at markets. It's one of the reasons I love the setup of Makers Market. They only allow a limited number of vendors from each category here. So while I may be the only one who sells vessels and vases, there are other ceramic artists here creating other pieces. Our styles are unique. Seth and Lilly really did their research when they curated vendors.

I look around at the other vendors setting up their booths and then back at the pieces that Addison and I put together this morning. They really did a great job choosing stems that would pull colors from my vases and accentuate the forms. My pencil returns to the page below it, and I start sketching the flowers in front of me. Maybe there's something with those forms that I can use to inspire this piece. The show is meant to feature autobiographical pieces, and I know that I want to highlight my transition. Maybe I can recreate the growth of a flower, though I'm not sure it would be entirely accurate. Before Gram stepped in, I wasn't exactly given the room to take root and blossom.

As I'm crossing out my newly abandoned concept, Addison steps into my peripheral vision.

"What are you working on?" They ask tentatively. An artist's sketchbook is an insight into their inner working- sharing it is like letting someone read your diary. Reflexively, I drop my pencil in the middle and shut the cover before dropping it on the table next to me.

"I'm trying to figure out a piece I want to do for the New and Upcoming Artists show at the DART."

"Oh, that's cool. I've been a few times. Gri was in it last year. Some of the work is really impressive. What do you have for a concept so far?"

"Well, this year, the theme is autobiography, so they're asking artists to pull from their personal journeys."

Addison wears an expression that looks like they're trying to raise an eyebrow, albeit unsuccessfully. "Isn't that basically the premise for the majority of art?"

I chuckle. "Yeah, pretty much.

I wait for a minute to see if they want to respond before I go on.

"Anyway, I've been having a hard time coming up with

how I want to execute my piece. I have the subject's concept nailed down- I want to showcase my transition, but every time I sit down to develop and build out an idea, the whole thing just falls apart."

"What were you trying just then?"

"Well, I was thinking about your flowers and thought of maybe documenting a flower's growth from seed to full bloom, but the more I thought about it, the less original of an idea it seemed, and it didn't feel fully authentic to my experience."

"What part of it is different from your experience?" They ask cautiously.

I open my mouth to answer, but something holds me back from answering. I feel comfortable with Addison, but I'm just not ready to go there yet. I shut my mouth and grab the pen out of the sketchbook to start fidgeting with it. Addison, to their credit, doesn't push me for an answer. They just sit there with me and wait.

"You don't have to tell me. It's okay," they softly reassure me. A hand reaches out and gently rests on my forearm. "I'm sorry for asking."

"No, it's okay." It's my turn to reassure them. "You're welcome to ask; it's just hard for me to talk about, and this doesn't seem like the right setting to get into all of my history." I smile sheepishly at them but avoid meeting their eyes.

"That's okay, Colin. I get it."

"Colin? Who's Colin? I thought I was Nickname TBD," I jest, grabbing onto the lifeline of changing the subject.

I pinch their side in the way I do with Trevor when we get into brother-mode. They bristle a bit, and I freeze.

"Addison, I'm so sorry. I forgot who I was with. That's something I do with Trevor when we're playing around, and I just forgot. I promise I didn't mean to touch you without consent."

Addison looks like they're dealing with some internal debate for a moment before looking at me and cracking into a shit-eating grin. "Addison? Who's Addison? I thought I was Blooms," they mockingly parrot back my earlier phrase. "But seriously, thanks. I appreciate your concern. Touch can be weird for me, but you're right that the Market isn't the right setting for getting into history. I'm generally okay with playing around, but you just caught me off guard. Though we probably shouldn't go too hard with it here next to all your beautiful and breakable creations. Knowing me, I'll shift slightly wrong and knock over the whole thing, and I can't afford to buy everything no matter how much I want to build a collection that's just your work."

I preen like a goddamn peacock. Addison likes my work and wants to own a piece—multiple even.

"Which one is your favorite?" I ask coyly.

Addison looks at me and then at the pieces laid out on tables. They get up and walk around before picking up a round mug with ridges and a handle. The glaze for that mug is two-tone. The bottom has a black underglaze that subtly shows off the speckles in the clay. The top is a drip effect glaze in a lavender and blue color known as purple aster. It suits them. With the way they're holding it, I can see them curled up next to a fireplace with a mug of tea and a blanket, being cozy and adorable. I shut my eyes tight and blink them open in rapid succession to keep myself from falling too deep into that daydream. I am not going to daydream about my new friend in a way they probably wouldn't appreciate. I realize that I'm not as familiar with the asexual spectrum as I thought I was, and I make a mental note to do some research when I get home.

"This is the one." My gaze snaps back to their face, and I nod.

"Good choice. What about it stands out to you?"

"It's not too heavy that filling it with tea will make my wrists hurt, but it's also sturdy enough that I don't feel like I'm going to break it if I put it down too hard or at a weird angle. And the ridges are spaced in a way that it's comforting to hold but not too awkward to drink from. I've had a few ribbed mugs that dribble when you try to drink from them. When I picked it up, this mug just felt right. It's hard to explain."

I nod some more. I know what they mean. I made that form because I imagined someone who likes holding something warm with both their hands, but if you fill up a mug with boiling hot beverages, it can be difficult to hold, so I put a handle there for good measure and safety. I also really appreciate the way the top glaze plays on the ridges.

I make a gesture for them to hand it to me. I weigh it in my hands. I don't remember every piece I've made, but I remember this one. It's the only one on the table that has this color combination. From the construction of the ridges to the application of the glazes, the whole thing was an experiment that I haven't replicated. I considered putting it in my discount pile, but I wanted to give it a chance. Instead of handing it back to them immediately, I wrap it up, put it in a bag, and then hold it out.

"It's yours."

"What? Why?"

"You helped me set up this morning. And you've been really great and welcoming. It's refreshing. Also, I want you to have it."

"But I can't," they start.

"You can." I cut then off. "Please, Blooms. I want you to have this mug. Your critique just proves that that mug was meant to be yours. Consider it a 'thanks for being my friend' gift. Besides, you gave me a thank you gift in May, so I can give you one in return."

"But..." they stammer.

"No buts, Blooms. Well, I mean, I like a good butt, but we don't need to talk about that right now."

They blush, and I grin. I love when the color tints their cheeks. They still haven't taken the mug, so I softly shake the bag in their direction. They stare at it for a moment and then take it out of my hand. The smile stretches across my face.

"Thanks, Colin."

Addison brings the mug back to their booth and places it securely in a tub below their checkout counter.

"Hey, I was thinking of going to grab some coffee. Do you want to come with, or want me to bring you anything back from Micah's?" they call over to me.

"I should stay here and watch things since we're getting close to market open, but I'll take a coffee."

"Cold brew, black with agave?" they recite my order from last month.

"Yeah, that exactly." I'm taken aback. It's an easy order to remember, but I still didn't expect them to do so. "Let me grab you some cash."

"No, Col. This one's on me. It's not a direct exchange, but it'll make me feel better about taking your mug."

I shake my head and sigh, but the smile still stuck on my face conveys levity. I watch as they walk off and I grab my sketchbook again.

I continue working on brainstorming ideas when Addison comes back 20 minutes later with the drinks.

"Micah, Samwise, and Lane say hi." They say as they hand me the cold brew.

"Well, hi back to them." I take a sip of the coffee, savoring the smoothness and sweetness of the caffeinated beverage.

"Any luck with the ideas?"

"A bit. Right now, I'm trying to narrow it down between a vessel and something purely sculptural. I'm leaning towards vessel, but that's a bit more abstract than most people will expect. Though abstract isn't necessarily the wrong path to take, especially in a show that is meant to be representative of the artist."

"What about combining the two? Like a vessel that resembles sculpture in some way." Addison ponders. They take a sip of their iced lavender latte.

"That could work." I put my coffee down and let my hand start to sketch out some basic forms that I use as a base when throwing.

"Are you thinking of wheel throwing or hand building?"

"I'll do a bit of both, especially if I'm combining the idea of a sculptural vessel. I'll start with a thrown vessel and then manipulate and hand build as much as I need to to get it in the right form."

"What's the story you want to tell?"

"I want to show how my transition took me from being a dying shell to a fully thriving human," I respond without thinking. My hand pauses. "Wow. Okay. Apparently, the twenty questions helped."

"Pretty sure it was just three." Addison winks and sits back in their chair, taking another sip of coffee.

"Irrelevant, your honor." I stick my tongue out at them. "Regardless, it helped. So thank you."

"Gotta earn that mug somehow." It's their turn to stick their tongue out at me.

"Brat," I chuckle.

"It's pronounced 'Blooms'."

I shake my head and force myself to look back at my sketchbook so I don't get lost in those gorgeous blue eyes like I have every time I've spent time with them.

CHAPTER TWELVE
Addison (they/he)

Colin is engrossed in his sketchbook, and the Market is about to start, so I head back into my booth and do a once-over to make sure everything is ready to go. I still can't believe he gave me a mug, no trades, no purchases, just a gift. I honestly don't remember the last time someone did that for me just because. I check the tub I put it in earlier just to make sure I wasn't dreaming. It's still there, wrapped carefully in the bag with the Ceramics X Colin logo stamped on it. A small smile grows on my face, and I bite my bottom lip to keep it from growing too big. Despite my best efforts, I can feel the heat rising, and I know my cheeks are becoming flush. I swear, this constant blushing is inconvenient and the reason why I can't wipe out my debt by winning at poker. That and I don't actually know how to play poker...

I finish my iced coffee just as the first customers are starting to come through. The morning goes by quickly. There's always a bit of a rush from the post-farmer's market crowd, but July tends to be when most people are away, so the crowds aren't as busy as they were in May and June. Usually, that would make my anxiety kick up a notch, but I find that I'm enjoying the slow moments this month. Most of that is because I have a new friend to talk to. I love Gri and Jodie, but it's nice not to feel like a third wheel in the conversation for once.

Colin and I talk about everything and nothing. I tell him about the garden I've been cultivating at my moms' house since high school. He tells me more stories about his grandmother. When we talk about our families, I notice that he only ever mentions his grandmother, never his parents or any siblings. I figure it's a painful subject, so I don't ask.

Around noon, we have a bit of a lull, and Colin asks me to watch his booth while he goes to the bathroom and picks up lunch for both of us from one of the food carts. I decide to take advantage of the slow traffic to work on tidying up the flower wall.

Out of the corner of my eye, I notice a couple lingering around Colin's booth. I do what any good booth buddy does and turn around to greet them.

"Hi, I'm Addison. The artist for this booth, Colin, just ran out to grab lunch, but I'd be happy to answer any questions I can and help you out if you find something you'd like."

"Thanks, Addison," the one in the flowy maxi dress says. "I'm Gwenna, and this is my partner, Bean." Her hand is resting on the waist of the other person, and she gives them a little side squeeze and a kiss on the top of their head.

"Nice to meet you both. Is this your first time at the Market?"

"Yeah. We just moved back. Well, I moved back. She moved with me," Bean responds without looking up from the mug they're holding.

"That's awesome. Welcome home."

I let them browse for a few minutes while I go back to rearranging the flower wall. Gwenna leaves Bean to look at the mugs and wanders over to my booth.

"These are beautiful," she says, picking up one of the

tussie-mussies.

"Thanks. Each stem is handmade, and those arrangements have secret messages coded in them."

"Secret messages? How?"

Oh, buddy, you just triggered my special interest.

"What do you know about Victorian England?"

"Not much."

"Have you ever heard of floriography?"

"Can't say that I have." Her eyebrows crinkle in a way that feels familiar, but I can't place it. She seems genuinely interested, though, so I continue.

"Well, Gwenna my new friend, have I got something cool to tell you about." I rub my hands together and grab one of the tussie-mussies from the stand. "Okay. These arrangements, because they are small and each one has a meaning, are technically called tussie-mussies. In Victorian England, people would use flowers to send coded messages from secret admirers. Many of the meanings have now been centralized and are still popular to this day. When you think of a flower that represents love, what do you think of?"

"A red rose."

"Yes! Exactly." My enthusiasm is building. "The origin of floriography is a bit hazy, but it was popularized in Victorian England, and that's the era and location it's mostly associated with, So much so that it's often called Victorian Flower Language, but it could have origins all the way back to Turkey- a fun story, but not one for today. Now, aside from the origins, the definitions could get confusing from time to time because some of the flowers had different and even contradicting meanings, depending on who you talked to. There were published guides in France and London, so you really had to trust your florist to know what was popular in your location. If you were in London, you probably used *Floral Emblems* by Phillips, whereas in

France, you probably were using Latour's *Le Langage des Fleurs.*"

I look up to make sure that Gwenna's eyes haven't glazed over, but she's still with me, hanging on my every word. The last person to let me gush about flowers like this was Colin, and he had the same rapt attention. Maybe more people are interested in floriography than I thought.

"There's even an American list, but that was heavily influenced by some of the British lists. Anyways, most of the flowers have very similar meanings between the French and English, but there were a few stems that might cause confusion or the wrong sentiment being portrayed. For example, in France, Virginia jasmine meant 'separation,' according to Latour, but in England, Phillips designated that it meant 'amiability,' but it's highly unlikely that you'd be sending a bouquet of just one flower if you intended to send a message. The cool thing is that certain combinations of flowers could mean a completely different message. Look at this one." I point to the flowers in my hand pointing at each stem as I explain, "The clover on its own means 'good luck,' but when it's paired with the dandelion and apple blossom, the three are meant to 'show hope that the recipient's wishes will come true.' It's a fun arrangement to give for a birthday."

Gwenna reaches out and gently takes the tussie-mussie from my hand. "That's amazing. So each of these arrangements have different meanings?"

"Yup. They aren't as popular now as they were back then, but I love it, and even if someone isn't looking to send a message, they can still grab an arrangement. The meaning really only has importance if it's meant to have importance."

"That makes sense," she says with a chuckle. Her laugh even sounds familiar.

"I'm really sorry, but have we met before? You just seem

really familiar."

"I don't think so. Well, not unless you're a fan of visiting Texas."

"Can't say that I am."

We look at the rest of the arrangements, and I point out the meanings of a few of them.

"Hey babe, this artist has the same last name as you," Bean calls over, interrupting us. They're holding up one of Colin's business cards.

Gwenna turns back to me. "What did you say the artist's name was again?"

"Colin. Colin Jameson. He's a fantastic artist."

Her eyes go wide, and I swear she stops breathing for a second. She sways, and I hold out a hand to steady her.

"Are you okay? Do you need to sit down?"

She shakes her head but then says, "Maybe? I'm not sure. Do you know when he'll be back?"

"Anytime, probably." I look around to see if I can see Colin anywhere. "He might have gotten caught up in the lines for the food trucks. Do you know him?"

"I- I don't- I'm not sure."

I grab my chair from behind the counter and guide her to it. I reach back into my stash of emergency goodies and grab a cold water bottle from the cooler.

"Here, drink this in small sips" I say, handing it to Gwenna. "You look really flush. I'd say it was the heat, but if you're from Texas, you're probably used to worse than this."

She takes little sips of the water and laughs, some of the color returning to her face. Bean has made their way over to us and is crouching down next to their partner.

"We should probably get some food into you, babe." Bean squeezes Gwenna's hand and raises it to their lips.

"You can stay here as long as you'd like. I'm sorry I don't have any snacks to offer, but I can always see if Colin can run back to the trucks when he gets back."

"No, that's okay," Gwenna replies hastily. "We've already taken up so much of your time today. We should probably just head over and get stuff ourselves. I have some food allergies, so I'm particular, and Bean is vegan, so we always like to double-check everything."

"Okay, if you're sure. Is there anything else I can do for you right now?"

Gwenna starts to shake her head, but Bean interrupts, standing and throwing their arm over my shoulder, but they're so much shorter it's a bit of an awkward stretch, "Actually, Addison, my ma"—they start and then see the pronouns on my name tag—"my fellow-them, apologies. I would like to buy a few of these fine mugs." They put pressure on my shoulder as we walk back to Colin's booth. I bend and lean over so they can whisper in my ear. "Also, if you've got one of those fancy message bouquets that says, 'I'm so glad you moved here and we got away from your awful family, you are the love of my life,' I'll happily take that."

I laugh and lower my voice. "Well, I've got an 'I love you' arrangement and also a 'I hate you/warning' arrangement, but you'd have to send that to the awful family, and honestly, doesn't seem like they're worth it."

"I'll take it. The first one," they clarify. "Not the warning one. Though that does give me an idea for a gift if we ever have to go back to visit."

I sneak back over to my booth to grab the tussie-mussie from the display. I use my card reader and Colin's to complete Bean's purchases. By the time I wrap everything up securely and hand it off, Gwenna is back on her feet, looking better, and comes over to us. She picks up one of Colin's business cards and looks at it with an expression I can't place before pocketing it.

"Addison, thank you so much. You're right; it must have

been the heat. The humidity here is unparalleled."

"Take it easy. Get some rest when you get home, and don't hesitate to come back if you're still at the market and need another break. It was really great talking to you. Most people don't let me ramble on about my special interest, so when I get the opportunity, I can go on for a while."

"Well, it was fascinating. I'm a big fan of history, so it was right up my alley."

Bean slips their hand into Gwenna's, and after a brief goodbye, they head off down the row towards the food trucks.

I'm just putting my chair back in place when a bag plops in front of me with a pinkish-purple lemonade beverage that has very little ice.

"Long lines today?" I ask, looking at Colin, who has quietly walked over to his chair.

"Not really, but I, uh, took the long way back." He's not quite meeting my eye.

I look at him skeptically. "Is that so?" He can probably tell that I don't buy his excuse because he looks sheepishly up at me.

"I mean, technically, I took a really long way around, but yeah..."

"Everything okay? Did you overheat, too?"

"Too?" He looks at me, and his evasiveness completely drops. "Oh my God, are you okay?"

"Oh, I'm fine, but the couple that was in here last, the woman got overheated or something and needed to sit down for a minute. It was weird. She said she's from Texas, but it must be a different kind of heat."

"Huh." He goes back to not meeting my eye.

Maybe just outright asking him will work. "What happened? You're acting weird."

"Oh, I thought I recognized someone I knew from a while ago, and I didn't want to run into them. It was a bad, um, separation."

"Is this your way of telling me you've been married before?" I joke, trying to lighten the mood a little bit. It works.

"No," he laughs. "But it kinda feels like it was a divorce of sorts. I'll tell you about it another time. Right now, we have food to eat."

Right on cue, my stomach grumbles loudly, and I decide not to press him for more than he's willing to share. He'll tell me when the time is right. We sit and eat our banh mis in silence, and by the way his eyebrows are furrowed, I can tell he's thinking hard about something. Seeing that expression on his face clicks things into place. He knows that couple, or at least the one that has his same eyebrows. As much as I want to ask, I respect that he said he'll tell me later, so I give him space to think and keep an eye out for anyone who might interrupt him while he's working through whatever is going through his head.

A few people come up after we've finished eating, and I can tell he's still not in the right headspace to deal with people. Before they start asking questions, I move my chair to a clear space behind my flower wall and gently direct him toward it.

"You look like you've seen a ghost. Whatever happened must have done a number on you in the past." I hand him another of my water bottles. "Drink this and sit there. I'll take care of the booths, and I'll check back in on you in a few minutes."

CHAPTER THIRTEEN
Colin

Oh my God, I can't breathe.

How did she find me?

I've gotta get out of here.

I need to punch something.

No.

I can't.

I can't risk them finding me again.

I go to pull my phone out of my pocket, but it's not there. My vision is tunneling, and I can see it over by my sketchbook in the other booth. My hands feel weird. I go to flex them, and something drops. Was I holding something?

She shouldn't be here.

She'll tell them.

They'll find me.

I need to run.

I need to...

I need...

I need to talk to someone, but the only person who truly knows the danger is dead. Gram would know. But I can't... She can't... Oh god. The tears start streaming down my face. Whether they're from fear or rage, I can't tell. Please don't let anyone be able to see me. I try to scoot the chair back as far as I can go and knock into some boxes. I don't have control of my body enough to turn myself around.

FUCK!

Therapy was supposed to help all this.

It was, you idiot, but you stopped going. What was it that they told you to do?

I can't remember. I can't... I can't...

My breathing is shallow and short. I'm hyperventilating. The vision in my eyes is blurred from the tears, and there are floating orbs swimming around in it, making it hard to focus on anything.

What's that smell?

It hits me. Dirt, flowers, moss—familiar and comforting. I close my eyes and breathe it in. Breathe them in. I feel a hand on my chest, right in the center, near my heart. A voice that isn't my own cuts through the noise in my head.

"Colin. I'm here with you. It's okay. You're safe. No one can see you. Can you try breathing with me? In for three."

The voice takes a deep breath, which I mirror.

"Hold for three."

I hold my breath.

"And now a deep breath out for 5. You got this. Do it again for me. In for three."

I follow the voice's commands until things start to calm down. The tears leave my eyes, the feeling returns to my hands, the dancing orbs and tunnel vision fade away, and there's Addison, kneeling down in front of me, one hand grasped in my hands. I was clinging to them, and I didn't even realize it.

"There's my Cluaran." They smile at me, not moving out of my space and letting me take the lead. "Feeling better?"

"What happened?" I ask cautiously. I think I know, but I just need it confirmed.

"You, my friend, had what I like to call an Addison Special, but most people refer to it as a panic attack. Looked like a pretty serious one, too."

They slowly reach down to grab the water bottle I dropped earlier.

"Here. You need to drink this. The whole thing. Trust me, it'll help. Small sips."

I take the bottle from them and sip the best I can with a shaking hand. I'm still clinging to their hand with one of mine, and I'm grateful that they haven't tried to remove it yet. Feeling their touch is grounding. Their other hand moves, and now they're enveloping my hand. It's a move I know well. Gram used to do the same thing. The nostalgia of the comforting gesture makes me smile a little and I put the water bottle down next to me. Instinctively, I do what I did with her—place my other hand on the back of their neck and pull them towards me until our foreheads touch. I stop myself before kissing them on the forehead like I would do with her. I don't want to make this moment any more uncomfortable for them than it probably already is, but I need the extra contact right now, so I selfishly let myself connect with Addison.

They take my clasped hand and hold it to their heart, squeezing it. We stay in that position for what seems like an eternity, but the rest of the world doesn't matter right now. The market doesn't matter. The only thing that matters is being in this moment with someone who makes me feel safe in a way I haven't since the only person who has truly loved me died.

When I'm finally feeling grounded and steady enough, I drop my hand from their neck and sit back in the chair. Somehow, I've been turned around so I'm not facing the booths.

Addison settles back into a squat, resting on their feet so they're still eye level with me.

"Not right now, but maybe someday," I say preemptively.

"What?" Addison asks, confused.

"I'm guessing you were going to ask if I wanted to

talk about it, so I was trying to beat you to it and give my response, but I guess context would have been helpful."

They chuckle. "You're not wrong. And that's okay. You don't have to talk to me about it at all if you're not comfortable. I'd just encourage you to tell someone at the very least. Trevor? Travis? A therapist? Someone you trust."

"I trust you."

"You do?"

"Yeah. I mean, I don't know. There's just something about you that makes me feel... safe?"

They go to sit back further and almost fall. Our hands are still connected, so I'm able to steady them in the moment.

"Thanks, Colin. You make me feel safe, too. And not just from falling over." They smile softly at me. "Can I ask a question?"

"I guess?" I respond warily.

"You don't have to answer if it's too personal or if you don't want to, but I just want to know, from one anxiety-ridden human to seemingly another, does that happen a lot to you? The panic attacks?"

I breathe out. "It used to. I haven't had one in a while. I had them a lot as a kid, but then, with therapy, they stopped for a while, and then when Gram died, I had them for about a year before they went away again. Today was... unusual."

"Okay. Thanks for trusting me with that. I know it's not exactly the same as having your grandmother around still, but if it happens again and you ever need someone to talk you through it, I'm here for you. Even if not literally. You can always call me or whatever."

They're rambling, and the blush is starting to creep back up. We're getting back to normal because I'm noticing things again. I start hearing the noise of the market again, like someone is slowly cranking up the volume of the background noise.

"Thanks, Blooms. I mean it." I look up to meet their eyes and really try to put all the sincerity I can behind my words. "I don't have many people around, but it's reassuring to know that you want to be there for me."

"You might have forgotten, but you were there for me first."

"I was?"

"Yeah, last month, when you came over to check on me, I was on the verge of a panic attack. You being there and allowing me to step away for a minute gave me the chance I needed to get grounded and avoid a nasty one."

"Wow, I had no idea." Knowing that Addison suffers from panic attacks weirdly settles me further. I don't feel as alone as I did before.

"You didn't? I thought you had my number, for sure."

"No, I just figured you were having an overwhelmed moment and needed an escape for a bit."

"I mean, I was, but there was more to it than that."

They don't go on, and, honoring the way they didn't press me earlier, I don't press them now. I just nod and squeeze their hand. We sit there for another minute before a noise at the front of Addison's booth causes both of us to turn our heads.

"Guess we should probably get back to it," Addison says and starts to stand up. Their hands fall from mine with one final squeeze, and they walk around the corner, giving me an extra moment to gather myself before facing people again. I pick up the water bottle and take a few more sips.

While Addison is busy with a small group of teens, I go back over to my booth and pick up my phone. It's only been about 20 minutes since I got back with lunch, so my whole episode probably lasted about 8 minutes rather than the hours it felt like.

Putting the phone down again, I pick up my sketchbook. My pencil is still marking the page I was working on before I went to grab lunch. Opening it up, I look at the concept I was working on. My almost run-in with my past has me rethinking things.

I am strong. I am a man. My family can deny it all they want, but I am thriving in my life without them. They can abandon me all they want, but I've grown. I've bloomed. As I'm thinking through my personal growth, I realize my concept isn't going to be complete with just a vase. I need to tell a more complete story, and for that, I'm going to need Addison's help.

CHAPTER FOURTEEN
Addison (they/he)

"Hey, Blooms?" Colin calls over after I'm done helping a group of girls put together friendship bouquets for each other.

"Yeah? What's up?" I look over at where he's got his pencil tapping on his sketchbook.

"I have a question to ask. A favor, really."

I walk the three steps over to his booth and wait.

"Okay, so I think as terrifying as that panic attack was, it ended up giving me some clarity."

"Clarity? About what?"

"About my showpiece. The concept I've been trying to embody really won't be complete with just a form. The form might show the physical transformation I've gone through, but I need something to represent the mental transformation and just how much I've grown as a person and come into my own."

"Okay..." I try not to sound too excited, but I think I know where he's going with this, or at least I hope I do.

"I was wondering if you would be willing to collaborate with me."

"Yes!" The phrase is out of my mouth before he even fully finishes asking. "What do you need me to do?"

"I was thinking I'd build a series of vases that represent my changing body—like a three-quarters torso sculpture hollowed, out and then in that, we could use floriography to show the internal growth I've gone through. I'd love if you could help me figure out which flowers to use, and maybe, if you have the capacity, either teaching me how to make them or, if you'd be open to making this a true collaboration, maybe you could make the arrangements while I work on the vases."

He sits there and looks at me with the most adorable anxious expression on his face. Yeah, I would do almost anything to help this man. That thought scares me a bit, but not enough to say no.

"That sounds brilliant. I would love to help. Let me grab my chair." I walk back over to my booth and pick up the chair that is still behind the flower wall. I also snag my own sketchbook, pen, and the small floriography reference book that I like to keep on hand at events.

"Okay," I say, sitting back down next to Colin. "What have you got for me? Walk me through the stages."

We sit there and talk for the rest of the day, only pulling away from our discussion to engage with customers and other vendors who stop by. It's about a half hour before close when a familiar-looking Black man about our age wearing a 'Protect Trans Kids' tank top walks up, holding hands with a heavier set man with a golden brown complexion wearing a jean vest adorned with a number of patches. They walk up with a purpose, like they know exactly where they're headed and why they're going there.

"Hey, boo," the one in the jean vest says, coming around the opposite side of the booth to me and giving Colin a clap on the shoulder.

"Hey, guys, thanks for coming. Have you met Addison?" Colin stands to greet both men and gives them hugs.

"Maybe?" he responds. "I think we stopped by the booth last time we were here, but it was pretty busy that day, so I don't think we got an official introduction."

"Addison, this is Travis and Trevor, my best friends and pains in my ass," Colin says, pointing to each of them in turn.

"Nice to meet you both. Colin told me that you usually come by to help him pack up when you can." I stand and shake both of his hands.

"Yeah, we help when we can. We've gotten pretty good at packing up the pottery. Our average breaks are down under 5 a month, if I remember correctly," Trevor says.

My eyes go a little wide at that. I try not to calculate the lost revenue, let alone the hours of work that go into each piece.

As if he can sense my thoughts, Colin leans over and whispers, "It used to be much worse. I used to lose 20 pieces a month because they weren't wrapped properly."

And then he laughs. The thought of losing hundreds of dollars in revenue terrifies me. It's why most of my products aren't easily breakable. Drop one of my bouquets on the ground, and you'll pretty much only have to dust it off before putting it back in place. Colin must really love his friends if he still lets them help with everything.

"We're gonna do a lap before we come back to help you tear down," Travis says. "If you need help with the teardown, Addison, we're more than willing to help. Any friend of Colin's is a friend of ours."

"Thanks. I appreciate it. My stuff is a little less fragile, so I might take you up on that offer." I smile politely.

The guys walk off, hand-in-hand, to go explore. Colin turns back to the page we've been working on, trying to figure out the best way to make the concept come to life.

"Do you want to get together this week and go over things more?" I ask, mentally crossing my fingers.

"Yeah, that would be awesome," Colin responds. My blush, which has been dormant most of the afternoon, makes its return at his enthusiasm.

"Would Thursday work for you?"

He pulls out his phone to look at his calendar. "Sadly, no. I have group that night. What about Wednesday?"

"I have family dinner on Wednesday. We should be done by like 7:30 if you wanted to meet up after, or..." My voice fades, and I bite my thumbnail.

"Or?" he asks cautiously.

"Or, well..." I let my confidence take over and take the leap. "Or you could come to dinner? It's me, my younger sister, and my moms. My oldest sister and her husband won't be there this week. No pressure. You don't have to if you don't want to."

He looks like his mind is fighting a battle he doesn't want me to see.

"Really, it'll be okay. You don't have to come. We can meet after. I won't be offended, and neither will my family because they don't know the invitation has been extended." I'm rambling again.

"No, Blooms, it's okay. I think I want to come. I have no reason to think that the rest of your family won't be as welcoming as you are, but I just need to think about it. Can I look at what my week looks like before I commit?"

"Of course. If you decide to come, I can show you my real-life garden, but that's the last bit of convincing I'll try to do. Take all the time you need. Well, it'll probably be good for Mum if you make a decision before noon on the day so she'll know to prepare enough for one more."

"I can definitely do that. I was thinking more along the lines of give me a night to recover from today." He waves his hand around in an all-encompassing manner.

"Right, that makes sense. Yeah, no problem. And again, no pressure. It's just a thought." I hope he doesn't think that I'm trying to back out of the invitation. I really do want to spend more time with him, and I think it would be good for Aisling to have another trans person in her life.

Not that Colin knows my sister is trans. It's not my place to out her. Community is important, and I know she's still looking for hers. Maybe she'll feel as safe with Colin as I do and trust him with that part of herself.

I sit there for a few minutes with him, a weird, inexplicable tension creeping into the air around us. Colin's the one to break the silence.

"Before they get back, I just want to thank you again for your help earlier. It means the world to me that you helped me get through that. I was sure it was going to be the end of everything, but you... you pulled me out of that spiral and got me back to where I needed to be. No one else has ever been able to do that for me before. Well, not since Gram. I usually have to go through it alone."

I reach my hand over to the top of his and squeeze near his wrist. "Anytime, Colin. Really. I've learned a lot of tips and tricks over the years. Kinda hard not to when one of your moms is a therapist."

"Right, I think you mentioned that last month."

I'm surprised he remembers. Just as we're settling back into the normal rhythm we had earlier, Trevor and Travis come back from their walk around.

"Guess we should start closing up shop," Colin says as Trevor starts bouncing on the ball of his feet. "This one gets anxious if he has to stand still for long periods of time."

Trevor glares at his best friend. Colin sticks his tongue out in response. They act the same way I do with my sisters, bratty and teasing in a familiar and loving way.

"Looks like it." I turn to Colin. "If they get too destructive, you can send them over to me, and I'll have them work on taking down the flower wall." Their playful banter encourages me to be bold. I give Colin an over-exaggerated wink that I'm sure both Travis and Trevor see.

I head back over to my booth, chair in tow, and start

to pull out the boxes that I keep behind the flower wall. Starting with the grab-and-go bouquets, I work my way around the booth, carefully taking things down and wrapping up any fragile displays I have out.

As I'm finishing with the tussie-mussies, Colin comes over with two bouquets in his hand.

"These are the two that I didn't sell today."

Oh, right. The collaboration from the beginning of the day. That feels like so long ago, I almost forgot. I usually save my centerpiece table for last, just in case some big spender decides to buy whatever showpiece I'm displaying right at the end of the show.

"Oh, awesome, thanks!" I say, taking the bouquets from him and putting them into their appropriate bucket. I turn around and go to the centerpiece table, which has the three bud vases and one large vase holding a bigger bouquet. "I guess I should return these to you. Did you want to split the money now or take care of it later when we meet about the collaboration?"

"Let's do it when we meet this week. It'll give us time to figure out who owes what without having to worry about rushing to do it now."

"Sounds good to me." I smile.

Travis and Trevor return from what I assume was a trip bringing tables and tubs to Colin's truck. All that's left over from his booth is his tent.

"Okay, boss-friend, put us to work. How can we help?" Travis asks me.

"Oh, umm." I look around at what's left. "If you want to start pulling down flowers from the flower wall, that would be extremely helpful. I have the bins separated by color, so it's pretty easy but still organized."

"Welp, that rules me out," Trevor says, giving Travis a little love tap on his butt. "It's all you, boo."

"Listen, just because you're colorblind doesn't mean

you can't help. You pull them off the wall, and I'll organize them." He pulls his bear of a boyfriend into his arms and walks him over to the wall where I already have the bins out. They start making out like Colin and I aren't there. A small squeaking sound leaves my throat.

"Hey!" Colin snaps his fingers at them. "Enough of that. Save it for later when you get home. I thought you wanted to help."

Travis and Trevor pull apart.

"Only because you feed us," Trevor quips.

"Brat." Colin scoffs. "You won't be getting any food if you don't help my Blo- my friend finish tearing down this booth."

Trevor cocks his eyebrow at Colin, looking back and forth between us, and I unsuccessfully try not to blush as my brain comprehends what he was about to say.

My Blooms. His. That does not help me squash this crush I'm developing.

With Travis, Trevor, and Colin helping, we make quick work of the rest of my tear down. Instead of having them lug my stuff all the way over to the parking lot, I go and drive my car over to the booth. Enough people have left that there's space for me to access it now without blocking traffic or endangering people.

"Are you coming to Vendor Dinner tonight? We're getting wings and pizza," I ask the group.

Travis and Trevor look towards Colin for direction.

"Not tonight. I think I need to go home and decompress for a while."

I understand why he would decline additional socialization tonight.

I start to nod and let him know when Trevor starts whining.

"But Daaaaad," he playfully pouts.

"We can still get pizza and wings if you want, but

you've gotta help me unload the truck at home first," Colin reassures them both. "Today was a day, and I'm all peopled-out."

They don't argue with his reasoning. That's the thing about best friends, they know where the lines and limits are. Clearly, these guys are close.

"Sounds like a plan. We'll meet you back at your place," Travis pulls his boyfriend into his side, and they start to walk off, giving me and Colin a chance to say a private goodnight before going our separate ways.

I rub the back of my neck with my hand. My blush is back... again, though if I'm honest with myself, I don't think it ever really went away. Why does this moment feel like the awkward end of a first date rather than two friends going home after a long day at work? Colin doesn't say anything as he pulls me into his arms and gives me a strong hug. I melt a little in his embrace. He might have been the one who needed comfort earlier, but being in his arms relaxes me in a way I normally associate with being in my garden.

Too soon for my liking, he's pulling away. It might be a warm July evening, but I feel a chill as his body steps away from mine.

"I'll text you tomorrow about dinner. Have a fantastic night, Blooms. You deserve it."

I watch as Colin jogs off to meet up with his best friends and let out a full-body shiver before getting in my station wagon and heading to grab food.

Later, after Vendor Dinner, I get home, and my phone pings.

COLIN
Hey Blooms, I'm in for Wednesday. Tell your mum to set that extra seat. Sleep well and have sweet dreams.

The smile on my face is still there as I drift off to sleep.

FROM ADDISON'S SKETCHBOOK

Colin's Bouquet

- Chamomile: Energy In Adversity

- Olive: Peace

- Larkspur: Levity

- Ivy: Fidelity; Attachment

- Narcissus & Clover: Hope for Change

CHAPTER FIFTEEN
Colin

After talking to Trevor and Travis on Sunday night over pizza and beers, I'm feeling better about going to Addison's house for dinner with his family.

The near-miss of a run-in with Gwenna took a lot out of me, and I actually slept longer than normal on Sunday. Addison checked in with me throughout the day to make sure I was doing okay. I feel bad not telling them about what triggered my panic attack, but I just wasn't ready, and I'm grateful that they didn't push.

Monday was a slow day for me in the studio. I still felt a bit hung over from the emotional whiplash, but I read through old notes that Gram left me and took some time to connect with the family that chose me.

By Tuesday, I was feeling back to normal. I spent the morning in the studio, trying to make up for the missed day of work on Monday. I'm not beating myself up about it because I know that my mental health is important. Therapy taught me that if I neglect my brain's needs, the rest of my body will suffer. From experience, I know that when that happens, my work will be shit.

It's Tuesday, and despite it being the evening, I brew some coffee and get to work reviewing my social media from the weekend. The stories people posted on Saturday are long expired, so I can't see them unless people send me the pictures separately or tag me in an actual post.

I'm able to salvage 3 posts from different people. I'm about to close out of the app and move on to my next computer-oriented task when I see it. A notification for a message request. My heart falls into my stomach, and I'm filled with dread. I pull out my phone and text Addison.

ME

Hey Blooms, what were some of those grounding techniques you were talking about when you had your panic attacks?

Addison's reply comes in almost instantly.

BLOOMS

The one that helps me most when I catch things early is the 5-4-3-2-1 method. Identify 5 things you can see near you, 4 things you can touch, 3 things you can hear, 2 things you can smell, and one thing you taste. Are you okay? Do you need me to call?

ME

I'm okay. Just felt an anxiety spike and wanted to be prepared if it got worse. Thanks ♥.

A heart? I'm not a heart guy. Maybe I am for him.

I put my phone down and go through the steps he sent over. Five things I can see: my computer, my pen, my notebook, my cash box, and my hands. Touch four. I reach out and run my hand across my desktop keyboard before moving it to the handle of my coffee mug. From there, I run my fingers through my hair and finish the step off by rubbing my face. Next step: three things I can hear. The most prevalent sound is Nur-D's song '20 Cha' streaming from my Bluetooth speakers. After letting the music flow over me for a moment, I realize I can also hear my breathing and the squeak of my chair as I tap my feet enthusiastically to the beat of the song. Two things I can smell: my coffee and the ever-lingering presence of clay. One thing I can taste: I take a sip of my coffee and breathe in deeply after I swallow.

I'm feeling much calmer and more settled when I click the button to show the message request. Before I can psych myself out, I open the message.

DIRECT MESSAGE from @GJamesyXO to @CeramicsXColin

Hi. I don't know if you'll see this or if this is even the right person because I didn't actually meet you in person, but the coincidences were too much for me not to reach out and try.

My name is Gwenna Jameson, and I think I'm your cousin. My grandfather's name was Leon Jameson, and he had a sister, Colleen. When I was 12, my parents told me that my cousin ran away. Something about that never sat right with me. Shortly after my cousin left, my great aunt Colleen stopped talking to anyone in the family. I gave up looking for my cousin, but if you're him, I just want you to know that I love you and I miss you.

Please know that I don't expect a response back, but you should know that your courage all those years ago helped me come out. I don't talk to the rest of the family anymore because they're still bigots, but I'm not.

I'm sorry for not trying to find you sooner.

And if you're not my cousin, I'm so sorry for this weird exchange. My partner, Bean, and I love your work. They've been using the mug they bought every

morning since we brought it home.

-G

I put the phone down and take a deep breath. Closing my eyes, I lean my head back against the chair and let the tears fall.

Any doubt that may have been lingering is gone. It was Gwenna. My childhood sidekick. Closer to me than any of my siblings. The one I confided in. She's here in my town. She was at the market on Sunday.

I click through to her profile and look at the first few pictures in the feed. There's a picture from Pride last month. She's holding a lesbian flag, and the person next to her is holding a non-binary flag. There's a picture from a few weeks ago where she's with the same person, kissing them on the cheek in front of a 'sold' sign and a cute little blue house.

Holy fuck. She's here to stay. It wasn't a fluke. My cousin is here. A tiny spark of hope and a whole lot of longing come rushing in and start to consume me. It's been three years since someone I had a blood connection with actually tried to connect with me in a positive light. It's all too overwhelming. I put my phone face down on my desk and walk out of my office and over to the couch. Laying down, I pull a heavy blanket over me and snuggle one of the throw pillows in my arms as I put on one of my comfort shows.

I don't want to think. I let the sounds of *Heartstopper* fill my brain and only let myself think about Nick, Charlie, and their friends.

I wake up a few hours later, and my TV has turned off from being in power saver mode. I go to check the time on my phone before remembering that I left it in the office. The rest of the house comes into focus, and I hear my playlist coming through the still-connected speakers.

I get up off the couch, hugging the blanket to me, and shuffle into the office. I go through my routine: turn off the speakers, stop the music, disconnect my phone, and head into my bedroom where I will hopefully get restful sleep, but seeing as how it's already 3:30am, I'm doubtful.

This whole week is going to be a wash. Maybe I should cancel seeing Addison tomorrow. Today? Later. But no, I'm actually looking forward to it. And I won't be the only queer person there. Addison has two moms. If there's anywhere I can feel safe, it should be with them.

The small voice of doubt is loud at this ungodly hour, but I do my best to ignore it as I crawl into my bed and fall back to sleep.

When my alarm goes off a couple hours later, I turn it off and let myself sleep as long as I need. Around 10, I'm finally crawling out of bed. My body is sore, my mouth tastes disgusting, and I desperately need a shower.

When I'm finally feeling human again, I decide to get out of my head the best way I know how- slinging mud and rocking out.

I head into the studio and grab one of my old Five Iron Frenzy CDs to throw in the boom box I keep in the corner. For the next few hours, I'm like a wedging and throwing machine. I get into a rhythm, stopping only to change discs. After the fourth album finishes up, I check my phone. It's 3:30, and I have a couple missed texts from Addison.

BLOOMS

Hey, just wanted to touch base about today. I'm really excited that you're coming. The last person I brought home was Gri and well, that's a story for me to tell in person.

I mean my family knows we're just friends, but yeah... Hopefully I didn't scare you away. You're still coming right?

Right?

Col?

Colin? Are you okay? It's been a few hours. Let me know you're getting these texts when you get the chance.

Oh, you're probably busy in the studio. ☹ Sorry for blowing up your phone. Text when you can. No rush or pressure.

Hey, just checking in with details for tonight (assuming you haven't been attacked by any sentient clay monsters). Dinner is at 5. Text me back and I'll send the address.

That last message is from 20 minutes ago. I wipe my messy clay hands on my apron and text back.

ME

Hey, Blooms, sorry for the lack of communication today. Last night was a rough one, so I kinda blocked everything out and focused on studio stuff today. I've just finished a marathon throwing session.

I look around at the three boards full of drying mugs, vases, and plates.

ME

I'm looking forward to tonight. I'll bring my sketchbook so we can talk after.

BLOOMS

If you're not feeling well, you can totally bail. I won't be offended. I'm not trying to get rid of you, but I'll totally understand.

ME

Nice try, but you're not getting rid of me that easily. I was promised a home-cooked meal that I don't have to make.

BLOOMS

Oh, no one told you? You're cooking tonight.

ME

cough *cough* I think I'm coming down with something. Definitely feels contagious.

BLOOMS

Poor baby. Gonna miss out on Mum's marmalade chicken.

ME

Oh look, I'm miraculously healed.

BLOOMS

It's a Festivus miracle.

I laugh out loud at that. I love that our banter can range from serious to lighthearted as easily as it does.

Addison sends through the address, and it's about half an hour away. I look at the time. I should probably start cleaning myself up if I intend to make it there on time.

An hour later, I'm ready to go. I do a mental check before I walk out the door: keys, phone, wallet, packer, sunglasses? All good. Confidence? A little shaky but still present at the moment. Time to go.

I stop myself just before walking out the door. Gram would probably flay me alive if she knew I was going to someone's house as a guest for the first time without bringing a gift.

I turn around and rush into my studio. Looking around, I grab the first appropriate piece I can find: a ceramic cheese board and coordinating toothpick holder.

Hopefully, they like charcuterie.

I arrived at Addison's house with about 5 minutes to spare. I would have been a lot earlier, but I pulled into a parking lot down the road to give myself 10 minutes of panic and pep-talk time. Remembering a practice one of my child therapists taught me years ago, I voiced all my fears and visualized them evaporating like steam. Just getting them out of my head helped clear my brain and get me ready to face a family dinner. I haven't been to one of those in almost 15 years. Sure, I'd been to and hosted plenty of dinners with Gram and my found family, but a "proper" family dinner with parents and siblings, I haven't done that since my parents kicked me out and abandoned me.

I look up at the house with its brick exterior and golden yellow front door. There's a Little Free Library decorated in the art style of the Madeline books in the front yard, and a couple apple trees are planted over on the side opposite the driveway. Everything looks normal and inviting, but my father's actions taught me that looks can be deceiving. I almost turn my truck back on so I can leave when I take a deep breath and remember that Addison lives here, and he is not my father.

When I open my eyes again, I notice the flag that I missed before. Right next to the golden yellow door is a progress pride flag waving in the summer breeze. It's not a new one either, judging by the way the colors have faded. Seeing it gives me the courage to get out of my truck. I grab the gift I brought and head out.

Walking up the path, I see some of the stones lining the walkway are painted and have different sayings and affirmations on them. It's nice to see the values of the family laid out here for everyone to view.

Addison must have heard me approach because by the time I've stopped reading the stones, I look up and there they are, leaning on the doorway, arms loosely crossed in front of them, a warm and inviting smile on their face.

"Hey," I say with a smile of my own stretching across my face. I hold out the cheeseboard. "I brought something for your moms. As a thank you."

"You didn't have to do that."

"Pretty sure Gram's ghost would come back and haunt me if I didn't." I put on a bad impression of my Southern grandmother, "'Colin Jameson, I raised you better than that. Just because we don't live in the South anymore doesn't mean we forget all of our Southern hospitality.'"

Addison laughs. "Well, thank you. Come on in. I'll let you give it to them yourself."

I follow behind him and kick off my Vans when I see the pile of shoes at the front door. We walk towards the back of the house, where I hear music playing. Right before we enter what I assume to be the kitchen, Addison turns and faces me.

"Look, I just want to preemptively apologize for the ridiculousness you're going to see and experience tonight. Mum likes to play up Scottish stereotypes when we have new people over and may lay the accent on thick." He pauses, listening. "Ah, yes, bagpipes."

I listen too and hear that bagpipe music has replaced whatever was previously on the radio.

"Good to know," I chuckle.

"And Mama will probably just want to interrogate you about your favorite books, so I'd recommend picking a couple you know well and having them ready to go."

"Geez, Blooms. You couldn't have given me warning and told me ahead of time," I tease, winking and suppressing the urge to pinch his side.

"Sorry, I'm just really nervous. It's been a while since I've brought someone home who isn't Gri and Jodie."

"It'll be okay. I'll be on my best behavior," I promise.

"It's not you I'm worried about," he mumbles and then

pushes the door open, revealing a kitchen bustling with activity. A woman with red hair is cutting up pieces of cheese—score one for me for bringing the cheese board—and using the handle of the knife as a microphone to serenade another woman with curly jet-black hair and a nose that look just like Addison's.

A third member of Addison's family sits at a small table on the other side of the room. She has the same black hair as her mom and the same blue eyes as Addison. I'm guessing she's one of his sisters.

The bagpipe-heavy song switches to one I recognize. 'I'm Gonna Be (500 Miles)' by the Proclaimers starts. Addison's mom with the red hair dances her way over to us and grabs both of Addison's hands, urging him to move his body with the music. Thankfully, she put her knife/microphone down before approaching.

"Dance with me, ma wee lad," she urges in a thick Scottish accent. Addison rolls his eyes before indulging his mother. I watch and feel the fullness of love that permeates the kitchen. It's almost overwhelming. I shift my weight from foot to foot.

"Did you want to dance, too?" a voice asks. I look over to see Addison's younger sister is now standing next to me.

"Nah, I'm good. I'm a terrible dancer."

"Can't be worse than Addison. He has two left feet, as the saying goes."

We watch as their mother, who I'm guessing is the one Addison refers to as 'Mum', spins Addison, which causes him to get tripped up on his own feet and stumble towards us.

"Whoa, hey there, Blooms." I catch and steady him, all while somehow holding on to the gift I brought.

He's tangled in my arms now. Addison's blush is fully taking over his face and neck. My mind wonders just how far it goes. If this were any other circumstance, I'd want to kiss him right now, but not without knowing that he wants it too, and definitely not while his family is in the same room. Watching us.

I subconsciously lick my lips and bite at my lip ring before helping him right himself. Addison's mom with the black hair has turned the volume down on the stereo, and the three women are standing by the kitchen island opposite us, just staring and watching this whole thing unfold.

I can barely take my eyes off Addison until I know he's okay. When I feel his weight shift from relying on me to relying on himself, my body starts to tense. Apparently, having Addison in my arms took away some of my apprehension about being in a new location with strangers.

"Mama, Mum, Aisling," Addison starts, "this is Colin. He's my new booth buddy, and we're working on a collaboration together."

"Hi," I said a little awkwardly and tentatively. "Thanks for having me over for dinner."

"Hope you're hungry for Haggis and black pudding."

"Ignore her," Addison's black-haired mom interjects, rolling her eyes adoringly at her wife. "Siobhan, I thought I told you to behave. Don't make me get your ball gag out in front of our guest."

Aisling snorts laughter while Addison groans beside me. When I turn to look at him, he's bright red. Can someone actually die from embarrassment? If it's possible, Addison is probably a prime candidate.

"Okay, that's it, we're leaving." Addison takes my hand and pulls me through the room towards a sliding glass door that leads out to a stone patio, never mind that I'm not wearing shoes. Before we get through the doors, his mom calls out.

"Sorry, honey. We'll tone it down."

"Thank you." Addison turns to face the rest of his family. "Colin, this is 3/5 of my eccentric family. My Mama,

Lolli Stamp-Baird." He points to the woman with the black hair. "My sister, Aisling." He gestures to the younger black-haired woman. "And finally, the menace that is Mum, Dr. Siobhan Baird. Believe it or not, some school out there gave her a PhD and she's actually a licensed psychologist."

"It's nice to meet y'all," I say, and then remembering the cheeseboard that I have been holding since I arrived, I hold it towards his mothers. "I wanted to bring a gift as a thank you for your hospitality."

"Suck up," Aisling mock coughs. Lolli playfully hip-checks her out of the way before coming over to me.

"Thank you, Colin, it's gorgeous." She turns and brings it over to the sink. "It'll be perfect for the cheese course Siobhan is attempting not to butcher. Honey, the meat is already dead; you don't need to slay it further."

Siobhan had been attempting to cut some salami-looking meat into small pieces, but either the casing or the knife was making it difficult to cut smoothly.

"I'm going to have to talk to Dauphine about cutting slices for me so I don't have to do it next time." Taking the freshly washed board from Lolli, Siobhan puts it on the counter next to her workstation.

"Who's Dauphine?" I whisper to Addison, but apparently, I'm not quiet enough because it's Lolli who responds.

"She's our cheesemonger. Works just down the street about 5 minutes away. It's a dangerous thing, having such quick and close access to some of the best cheese in the area. She even imports some from the UK so the good doctor here can have a little taste of home."

"She's a gentlewoman, a scholar, and a pure cheese wizard. I wouldn't recommend anyone else. You need cheese, you go see Dauphine. She's the best at what she does," Siobhan agrees with her wife.

"I'll have to go visit her at some point. I didn't know we had a cheesemonger in the area. Most of my cheese comes from the grocery store."

"Blasphemy!" Aisling shouts.

"Sacrilege!" Lolli exclaims.

"Inconceivable!" Addison jokes, smiling and winking at me.

"I will be sure to repent and make absolution for my sins by visiting the cheese shop this week."

"As you should," Siobhan says seriously.

"We take our cheese very seriously," Addison warns.

"So I can see," I smile back at him.

"Come on, let's go out back. I want to show you the garden." We head back to the front door real quick so I can put on my shoes. When they're on, Addison grabs my wrist and leads me out the sliding glass doors. We step out onto a paved patio area, and as Addison leads me down the steps, my breath catches. We're surrounded by one of the most gorgeous gardens I've ever been in. It's laid out like a story. There's a narrative and flow to how things are planted. I follow Addison in reverent silence as he leads me through it and explains the purpose behind why each plant is where it is and some of the floriography he used when planning the layout.

We're about halfway through when Aisling comes up to us.

"Hey, dweeb, stop showing your boyfriend your garden; dinner's ready."

"He's not... We're not... Shut up Ash," Addison sputters. His blush has returned and matches the tea roses he's just finished showing me. Aisling looks satisfied at successfully embarrassing her brother.

"Come on, Blooms," I say softly to him, my hand on his forearm. "Let's head in."

He nods and leads the way back up to the house.

CHAPTER SIXTEEN
Addison (he/they)

I'm trying not to be stuck in my head as we head towards the delicious-smelling dinner my moms have prepared. Aisling was just being the bratty little sister she is, but once again, it's weighing heavily on my mind that my last non-Gri and Jodie dinner guest was Steve, and before him, Liam. Apparently, I've only brought home boyfriends or best friends. Not to say Colin couldn't be a best friend, but like I mentioned to Gri, it feels more.

Right before we go inside, Colin stops me, a contented grin on his face tinted with a look of concern in his eyes.

"Thanks for showing me your garden. I really loved getting to see where your inspiration comes from."

"If we have time after dinner, I'll show you my favorite spot."

"Awesome, maybe we can work on the project out there."

Oh, right. The project. Colin is here to work on the collaboration. Not because he's my boyfriend or even wants to be, but I don't date, so why am I slightly disappointed?

"Yeah, that sounds like a great idea." I try to sound chipper as we head inside, but one glance at his face shows that I was unsuccessful.

Dinner starts just as I expected it to. We're munching on the charcuterie board Mum put together when the interrogation starts.

"So, Colin. Tell us about yourself," Mama asks. I groan.

"I, um, I'm an artist. I make ceramics and pottery," he stammers, sounding a lot less confident than he usually is.

"That's great. We love artists." I can tell Mum has picked up on his trepidation. I give her a warning look not to go into therapist-mode. She ignores me. "Did you make the cheeseboard?"

"Yes, ma'am." The southern lilt to his voice comes out. He's wringing his hands under the table. Instinctively, I reach for his forearm and give him a reassuring squeeze, hoping he takes it as the sign of support it's intended to be.

"How long have you been doing ceramics?" Mama continues the interrogation.

"Since college, ma'am. I majored in art, and my grandmother encouraged me to keep going with it after I graduated. She was my biggest cheerleader."

"Was?"

"Yes." I give another squeeze and try to sneak him a small, encouraging smile. "She passed away almost three years ago, now."

"Oh, I'm so sorry to hear that, Colin," Mama genuinely says. "I lost my mother shortly after college. It can be hard. What about the rest of your family? Do they live around here?"

Colin's forearm slips out of my grasp and is replaced with his actual hand gripping mine so tightly it could cut off the circulation to my fingers. Squeezing his hand won't be felt, so I opt to move my thumb in what I hope are soothing circles.

"No, ma'am. They, umm... I believe they're back in Texas. We don't— we aren't close."

Before Mama can continue with the conversation, I decide it's time to step in. "Hey, Aisling, did you ever hear back from that game shop?"

"Yeah," she says somewhat dejectedly. "They said they didn't have any open tables for girls like you." She puts the last few words in air quotes.

"That's frustrating. What do you play?" Colin asks.

"Dungeons and Dragons."

"Seriously?"

"Yeah?" she confirms hesitantly.

"Well, my group is down a couple players, and we'd love to have you if you're interested. We meet a couple times a month and do a whole brunch thing. It's a lot of fun." Colin's offer comes with a genuine smile.

Aisling's eyes go wide. "Umm, yes. Absolutely. Definitely interested." She pauses, and her voice gets a little soft. "So I don't know if Addison told you, but I'm trans. Will that be an issue?"

"Not at all. We all met through an LGBTQ+ support group, and seeing as how I'm also trans, it would be hypo-critical of me to exclude you on that basis."

Aisling's smile lights up the room. I knew introducing her to Colin was a good idea.

I bite back my smile as I watch the two of them talk about their favorite classes to play and different stories from adventures they've played. I look up at Mama and Mum to see them both smiling at me. Mama nods subtly and squeezes Mum's hand, who winks at me and raises her eyebrows. I roll my eyes in return and go back to devour-ing my marmalade chicken.

The rest of dinner continues on without too much tor-ture or embarrassment on my end. I see Colin visibly relax as the evening goes on, and it makes my heart full to see just how quickly and easily my family has embraced him.

"That was absolutely delicious. Thank you, Dr. and Mrs. Baird."

"Technically, dear, it's Stamp-Baird for me," Mama gen-tly corrects him. "But you can call us Siobhan and Lolli.

Or Mum and Mama."

"Sorry." Colin forces a smile, a bit of tension building back up in his shoulders.

"An honest mistake, dear. Don't worry," Mama replies softly.

"Hope you saved some room for dessert. I made Fern Cake," Mum mentions. "But it still needs a little while before it's fully set, so you can go get a start on whatever it was you were planning on doing tonight. Give you all a chance to digest dinner."

With that not-so-subtle hint from Mum, I take our cue and run with it.

"Did you want to go back out to the garden for a bit? I still have to show you my favorite spot." I nudge his arm with my elbow.

He nods at me and gets up, following quietly as we go back outside to where we left off. Instead of continuing my tour from earlier, I head straight to the moss patch under the old oak tree. Sitting down, I pat the space next to me and wait for Colin to take the hint. He does, and we sit in silence for a few minutes. I'm almost about to break with some non-sequitur when he starts.

"I'm not used to that."

I don't respond, letting him take his time to say whatever he needs to get out now.

"My dad was an angry man. He was controlling, quick to anger, and believed that he was the ultimate authority in all matters pertaining to our family. We were a very religious family— my dad was in a position of authority in the church and my mom was heavily involved in the childcare. We were taught from the beginning that the greatest commandment wasn't about treating others the way you want to be treated, but rather about submitting to the authority of our parents, but even that was weighted. Dad's word was second only to the Bible."

He pauses and his face scrunches as he tries to find the right words. I shift my hand closer to his, ready to reach out and grab it if he needs me.

"No, that's not quite right. His word was an extension of the Bible. If we did anything that went against my dad's will or wishes, we were treated like we committed grave sins akin to murder. Mom played into it, too. Her submission and subservience inflated his ego and self-righteousness. When my brothers reached their late teens, she started to cave to their authority, too. My sister and I were expected to follow our mother's lead and let them control us as they practiced to be the men of their own households one day. My sister went along with it. Her dream was to be a housewife like our mom one day.

"I never wanted to be like that. I knew that I wasn't going to be able to be myself fully around them. I might have been young, but I was observant. I heard the things my dad said and the lies my brothers would make up to control my mom. I saw how my parents treated me and my sister, raising us to be obedient, brainless, spineless servants of whatever future husband they selected for us."

Tears are streaming down his face, and my heart is breaking for the trauma he experienced at the hands of those who were supposed to love him unconditionally. I place my hand on his and he puts his head on my shoulder.

He wipes his free hand across his eyes and continues. "When I first started realizing that I wasn't a girl, I thought maybe I was just jealous of the treatment my brothers were getting, but as time past more and more, I didn't want what they had either. Ignoring all that privilege, I started paying a bit more attention to the other girls around me. I wasn't like any of them. I was much more of a tomboy, but even beyond that, I felt weird whenever anyone referred to me as a girl or started talking about my future as a mother and a wife. It made my skin crawl.

"I had two shining lights in all of this. My secret best friend, Benji, and my cousin, Gwenna. They were the first two I confided in about not wanting to be a girl. They both also accepted me right away- using my preferred name, sneaking me boy clothes, letting me just be myself when I was around them. And Benji gave me the ultimate piece of hope when he told me that his dad used to be his mom. The three of us would play together whenever Gwenna's parents brought her to my family's house for Bible study. We'd go out to the woods and I'd get to change into my stashed clothes and then we'd go meet Benji by the creek. When Gwenna wasn't around, I still met Benji there as often as I could. There was a fallen tree that we fashioned into a fort. It was where I stashed my clothes and a diary..."

The hairs on the back of my neck start tingling and I can tell that we're getting to a heavy part.

"You don't have to talk about this if it's too painful, Colin." I assure him in a whisper.

"No, I- Blooms, I trust you and I want you to know. It's just hard to relive."

Colin takes a moment to breath and adjusts his body so he's in contact with me. He picks up our joined hands and starts playing with my fingers. I ignore the chills running up my arm from where he's touching me and wait for him to continue his story.

After a few more minutes, he exhales and continues. "Everything came to a head the summer before I was supposed to start high school. I had gotten into a big fight with my parents again about not wanting to be homeschooled like my sister and stormed out of the house. It was a Sunday, so I was wearing nice church clothes. I got to our fort and Benji was there with a backpack of clean clothes for me. He waited outside the entrance to our fort while I got changed. I was telling him about the shit my parents were trying to pull and got stuck trying to pull my dress off. Benji was always a gentleman. He knew I had a crush on him, but he wasn't gay, so he had let me down gently and we were able to stay friends. He became closer to me than my actual brothers..."

Colin smiles at the tangent and memory of his friend.

"Anyway. Benji helped me get my dress off, but that's also when my brother found us. He thought I was about to have sex or something and he just raged. His anger was like my dad's. He wouldn't listen when I told him that I was just changing into play clothes. He started berating me and yelling at Benji. He tried to hit Benji, but I stepped in the way. He got me right across the face."

Colin points to a small scar at the edge of his eyebrow. I shift so I can look into his face and see where he's pointing. Without thinking, I lift my hand and gently brush it with my thumb. My hand moves down the side of his face and my palm cups his cheek. He leans into the touch and my whole body shivers when our eyes meet. I quickly pull my hand away and adjust my body so we're back to sitting side by side. Colin takes my hand again and continues his story like the moment we just had didn't happen. It takes me some effort, but I'm finally able to tune back into what he's saying.

"-ted at him to run away, but he was practically frozen to the spot. My eyebrow was bleeding and I was pleading with my best friend to run away. It was the most terrifying day of my life and it just kept getting worse. Benji finally recovered from the shock of seeing me hit and ran away. People might try to blame him for not jumping in to fight, but Benji and I were both smaller than my 18-year-old brother. We wouldn't stand a chance against him on our best days. The most I could do was try to be as much of a dead weight as possible and give Benji the best chance to get back to his house before we got back to ours.

"My brother pulled me away from the fort and through

the woods to our house. My clothes were still half off and I was clutching the backpack Benji had brought me. I don't know what I planned to accomplish with a bag of boy clothes, but surely it would have been better than the narrative my brother was going to spin about me being a slut, a harlot, a jezebel, or any of the other words he was spewing in my direction as he dragged me home.

"We got there and the rest of our family was there—still in their church clothes. Greg Jr practically dumped me on the ground in front of our parents and the backpack spilled open. My diary slid across the floor and my sister picked it up. I was trying to silently plead with her to ignore it, but she opened it up and started reading it. I missed the entire explanation my brother was giving my dad and watched in horror as my sister's mouth dropped and she handed the diary to my mother. Mom read a bit and then interrupted my dad and brother to show them what she found."

I take a sharp breath in, my heart breaking further for the fourteen-year-old kid Colin was. I can't imagine having your entire family turn on you like that.

"I watched as my father's face turn the darkest shade of violent I've ever seen." Colin shudders. "He pointed at the page and told me to explain. When I couldn't find my voice, he slapped me and quoted scripture. It was his favorite method of punishment. If he was the right hand of God, he was going to dole out God's justice and wrath against the disobedient, starting with his own family. I was crying, not so much from the hit but more from the shock of the events. I looked at my mother, but she was no help. Her face was stoic and blank; she looked right through me. My father ripped the pages out of the book and told me to get out of his house. I'll never forget the words he used. 'Freak. You are a disgrace to this family and an abomination against God. You are no longer welcome to live in this house, girl. Get out or face His wrath.'"

"Oh my God," I whisper nearly inaudibly. Tears are streaming down my face now. I squeeze Colin's hand.

"I did the only thing I could do. I ran. The only place I could think to go was to Benji's. I wanted to make sure that he made it home okay. At that point, it was starting to get dark, but thankfully, I knew the woods really well. My vision wasn't great from all the crying and the blood, and my body was weak, so I was stumbling along and got scratches and scrapes, but I eventually made it to Benji's house, where I heard some loud voices on the other side of the front door. I almost didn't go in, but Benji saw me and ran outside. He wrapped me in a hug and brought me in. I was able to tell Benji's dads that my parents had kicked me out, and they helped me get cleaned up and told me I could stay with them. One of his dads was a nurse who worked in the ER and with trauma victims, so he made sure that everything was documented, just in case. I didn't even know he had done it until later.

"I was able to stay with them for a couple days before the confrontation happened. My parents had decided that they couldn't have a daughter out in the world pretending to be a boy. Think of what the church would say. So my dad and my two brothers came to take me home. Benji's dads didn't let them in the house. My dad threatened to come back with the cops and accuse them of kidnapping, along with some other horrible falsities. Benji stayed with me, hidden in one of the back rooms out of sight, and even-tually, my family left. Unfortunately, that meant that I wasn't going to be able to stay with Benji for much longer. His dads asked if there was anyone else in my family who might be able to help, and that's when I gave them Gram's name. They had to use the phone book or 411 or something to find out her number, but they got ahold of her, and she was there half an hour later despite living an hour away.

"I found out later, but she'd had her suspicions for a while about me being a boy. Since I was really young, actually. It's why she let me sleep in a different room than my sister when we visited and read me stories that weren't on my parents' approved list. She'd been leaving me little clues about being a safe person. I'm glad I realized it when I did. I can't imagine what would have happened if I didn't have her. She fought for me. We met with her lawyer the day after Dad showed up, and I had to tell my story again—all the neglect, the abuse, the night they kicked me out, everything. It was a strong case made even stronger by the documentation that Benji's dads had provided the night everything went down.

"She was able to win custody of me easily. I don't know what happened with my sister and younger brother. I lost touch with everyone after that. Gram cut my parents and siblings out of her will for their being complicit in my abuse. My aunts and uncles were technically my dad's cousins and weren't in the will either, but since they belonged to the same school of thought as my parents, she cut off contact with them. I never got to talk to my cousin, Gwenna, again after that. She was almost 12 when all this went down. So it was really just me and Gram after that. We didn't stay in Texas long after that. We moved around a bit and eventually settled here so I could go to college.

"Benji and I eventually lost touch as the years went on. I've thought about trying to find him or his dads to thank them again for everything they did for me, but I haven't been able to find any of them on social media. I don't know where they ended up."

The sound of crickets, frogs, and faint music from the house is the only thing we can hear. I squeeze Colin's hand and lean my head on his this time.

"Thank you for trusting me with that. I can't imagine it's easy for you to live through it again."

I feel the warm wetness of a tear hitting our hands.

"And I'm sorry if my family or I did anything to bring back that horrible experience for you."

He's quiet for a while before he objects. "You didn't do anything wrong. Your family is great. It's just so much the opposite of what I'm used to from parents and siblings. Gram and I would have dinners that eventually were filled with love and joy, but there was always that sadness encroaching, even after Trevor and Travis joined our little found family. We were brought together by pain, but y'all are bonded together with love. It's amazing to see. And your moms are so accepting of your sister. I'm sure she had a rough go of it for a time, we all do, but I'm so thankful she didn't have to go through it alone."

My heart is breaking for this man. We sit there in silence for a few more minutes. My phone buzzes in my pocket. I pull it out to see a text from Mum.

MUM

Dessert's ready if you want it. Though I can always pack it away to go if you need me to.

She can see the oak tree from one of the windows in the kitchen. Knowing her therapist senses were tingling at the end of dinner, I'm not surprised that she's been keeping an eye on us.

"Mum says dessert is ready if you want some now, but she can also pack it up to go if you're not in the mood to do any more peopling tonight."

"Thanks. That might be a good idea." He pauses for a moment, neither of us moving. "So much for working on that collaboration tonight, huh?"

He chuckles and wipes his eyes, finally breaking the connection we had.

"Ahh, why am I such a mess?" he calls out to the night.

"Trauma and the patriarchy?" I supply.

He turns and smiles at me. "Fuck yeah, that's right. Trauma and the patriarchy. Toss religion in there, and you've got the baddies for any D&D campaign."

He rubs his eyes, stands up, and shakes out his body, releasing any remaining tension being held there. He turns around and holds out his hand to help me up. When I'm on my feet, he pulls me into a hug.

"Thank you, Blooms. I feel better talking to you about all this."

"I'm glad I could be a safe person for you to get it all out." I wait a moment, enjoying being in his embrace. "Come on. You've gotta try this Fern Cake. It's my favorite."

FROM ADDISON'S SKETCHBOOK

Colin's Bouquet, continued

- Dandelion: Tell Me I Am Wanted

- Clover: Think of Me

- Queen Anne's Lace: Sanctuary

- Mistletoe: Surmounting All Difficulties

- Lily of the Valley: Return to Happiness

- Snowdrop: Hope After A Dark Time

- Eucalyptus: Protection

CHAPTER SEVENTEEN
Colin

It's been a week since the dinner with Addison's family and a little longer than that since I first read the message from Gwenna. I've read it at least five more times since then.

My phone is heavy in my hand as I take it out to read through her message again. How our family reacted wasn't Gwenna's fault. She kept my secret. She didn't betray me. She loved me. I've missed her.

Fuck, am I really considering this? I haven't had any contact with that part of my family in a few years. Not since my sorry excuse for a father tried to contest Gram's will. But even then, that was him, not Gwenna. And her message said that she doesn't talk to my family anymore either.

I open up the message and start typing before the adrenaline wears off.

DIRECT MESSAGE from @CeramicsXColin to @GJamesyXO

Gwenna-

Hi. You've got the right me. I'm sorry we didn't see each other on Sunday, but I couldn't find the strength to face you after all these years.

I didn't run away back then. I never would have left

without telling you. It's a long story, but I promise whatever my parents or siblings said was a lie.

My parents found out and then kicked me out for being gay and trans. Gram saved me, and we never looked back. I'm sorry they lied to you.

I don't know if I'll be ready to meet anytime soon, but for now, maybe we can message?

-Colin

I back out of the message before sending it. I don't know if I'm ready to send it yet, but at least it's written. I just need a little bit of bravery or encouragement to actually hit the button.

Looking at the clock, I realize that Addison is coming over in half an hour to talk more about our collaboration. Since he knows the whole story and actually met Gwenna and her partner, maybe I can find the strength to talk to him about this too and get some feedback on what to do.

Needing something to busy my hands and shut off my brain a bit, I head into the kitchen and start putting together a small charcuterie board. I visited the Baird's favorite cheese shop earlier this week, and the team was able to give me some recommendations. Lolli and Siobhan weren't kidding when they said they were on a first-name basis there. It seemed to get me some sort of VIP treatment with the cheesemonger.

By the time I've put the finishing touches on the selection, there's a knock at my front door. I don't even realize I'm smiling for the first time in a couple days until I see the face of the person I'm growing addicted to being around. It should scare me, but it doesn't. Addison is strong and safe and has been checking in with me every day since I told him my tragic backstory. They haven't pushed for any more details, but they've made it clear that if I need to share it, they'll be right there to listen.

I realize we've been staring at each other for a moment without speaking. I mentally shake myself from my stupor and gesture them inside.

"I'm glad you could make it," I tell them as I give them a hug. "Welcome to my house. It's small, but it's just me here, so I like it."

My house isn't anything special, but it's where Gram and I lived since we moved to the area when I went to college. It's the perfect size for two people, but it doesn't feel too overwhelming with just me.

I show Addison the basics—living room, bathroom, office, kitchen/dining area, and then the converted garage I use as a studio.

Shelves line most of the walls—a small one containing reference books and more industrial ones with unopened glaze containers and boxes of clay. A converted tool bench is set up next to a utility sink with my basic tools and a glazing station. A bisque kiln is situated in one corner, with a few rolling racks blocking it from view. There's a stack of six-foot-long boards I use for my initial drying process stacked vertically behind my wheel. A couple sawhorses hold a few of the boards and some pieces I've been working on this week.

"It's not much, but it's mine," I say, proud of the work I've put into building my safe haven.

"Not much? Colin, you have a dream setup here. I work out of a desk in my bedroom. You have a full studio. This is amazing."

I start playing with my lip ring and try to see my setup through their eyes. It certainly has come a long way from the $20 thrift store shelving unit and refurbished pottery wheel I found on an online marketplace. I don't have the shelf anymore, but I've kept the wheel working well with proper cleaning and regular maintenance.

"We can work in here, or we can work in the house. The seats might be a bit more comfortable in there, and I have cheese."

"From the grocery store?" They tease me with a wink and a nudge.

"I'll have you know that I went to visit a certain cheesemonger this week." I stick out my tongue and nudge them back. I forget that Addison is tall, lanky, and not one of my former rugby opponents. They find themself off balance and trip over their own feet. My reflexes aren't quick enough to grab them before they stick out their hand to catch themself and send a board of drying pottery flying.

"Oh, shit!" they exclaim as they fall to the ground.

"Blooms, are you okay?" I rush towards them, any regard for the pottery ignored. All my focus is on my friend who has maneuvered into a sitting position, head in their hands.

I slide to the floor in front of them, checking them over for any scrapes or worse injuries.

"Blooms, I need to see your face and your hands. Did you get cut at all? Did you hit your head?"

They don't immediately show me their face, but when I gently tug on one of their wrists, I see bright red splashed along their freckled face.

"Blooms," I coax. "Addison, please." My use of their first name gets them to look at me finally. I don't see any cuts, but their glasses are a little askew. Reaching out, I go to right them on their face, but Addison flinches. I pause and slowly withdraw my hand.

"Are you okay? Are you hurt?" I ask again, slowly and calmly.

"Only wounded thing is my pride," they respond and try to put a smile on their face, but it feels forced- not like the genuine smiles that light up every room they enter and make the butterflies in my stomach start doing somersaults. They look around at the mess of smashed clay and start to breathe quickly.

I react before thinking, clutching their wrist in my hand, not letting go when they instinctively try to pull back.

"Addison, look at me. Please." They do. "Don't worry about any of that. I'm sorry. I shouldn't have nudged you so hard."

"It's not your fault. I should have been steadier on my feet. All that work."

"Blooms, I promise the fault is indeed mine and mine alone. The work can be redone, pots can be thrown again, but there's only one you. As long as you're okay, everything else will be too."

They look at me, their eyes searching for any sign of insincerity. I try to put as much honesty and truth into my expression as possible, but something doesn't sit right. I've had enough trauma in my life to recognize signs of PTSD, and right now, Addison is ringing all my alarm bells.

I feel their pulse slowly come back to a normal rhythm and start to stand up. I offer my hand to help pull them up, fighting every urge in my body to instinctively pull them into a hug and secretly vow to retaliate against whoever made them react like this to a mistake that wasn't their own.

Thankfully, they stand up without issue. I was a little worried about their ankle.

"Come on, let's get you inside to a more comfortable seat than the floor of my garage studio."

That gets a chuckle out of them, the hint of a genuine smile peaking out on their face. My clenched muscles relax slightly after seeing that.

I lead them back into the living room and then head back into the kitchen to grab the charcuterie board and a couple seltzers.

They still look a little dazed when I get back, but after we eat some of the food, they loosen up a little bit.

"I'm sorry again, Addison. I shouldn't have nudged you so hard. Are you sure you're okay? You didn't hit your head or anything, right?"

"Colin, I promise. I'm okay. Like you said, it was an accident. And no, I didn't hit my head." Their smile this time is a little more believable but still not back to its full brightness.

"Good. I wouldn't be able to forgive myself if I'd let anything happen to my Blooms." I wink, trying to bring back the playful mood we were in before the disaster in the studio.

A familiar blush creeps up on their cheeks, and they relax further into the couch. I smile. My Blooms is back.

"Now, about this collaboration. I know we talked at the market about the concept, and I just want to make sure we're on the same page. Honestly, now that you know my story, it might be easier for you to help me pick out the right flowers to use."

"Yeah, I was thinking about that. What if we started with one or two stems and slowly built up the bouquet from there. Are there any specific flowers you want to use or words you want to express?"

I think for a few minutes. Addison pulls a couple books out of their bag. I recognize the floriography reference book we were looking through the other day and their sketchbook, but they also have a book with pictures of flowers that can be used as a guide.

"Can I look through the picture guide?" I ask. "Maybe I can find something in there that speaks to me."

"Sure." They hand it over and open up their sketchbook to a new page, poised and ready to take notes.

I flip through the pages in silence before stopping on one that catches my eye.

"What's the meaning behind this one?"

Addison smiles when I show them the purple flower on the page.

"Well, it depends on the type," they respond. "A Scottish thistle like this one represents retaliation. It would actually be a fitting one to include, in my opinion."

I'm a little taken aback. I've worked really hard to keep my anger and resentment under control. My worst fear is being anywhere near as wrathful as my father and brother. That Addison would associate me with a seemingly negative flower is disheartening.

"In what way? What about me says that I'm a spiteful, revenge-fueled person?" I notice my tone comes out a bit prickly.

"No, it's not that," they say a bit defensively. "It's... it's more like you living your authentic life to the fullest is the best retaliation you can take against your family or anyone who's ever doubted you."

"Oh..." I play with the tab on my empty seltzer can. I'm still not sure I like the association, despite being drawn to the flower. "That's not something I've really considered before, but I'm not who I am to get back at them."

Addison is thoughtful before responding, like they're really taking his time to think on the words they want to say.

"I know. You are who you are for you, not anyone else." They pause. "I don't think I'll ever be able to fully understand how your family could turn their backs on you like they did."

"Brainwashing, ignorance, and no willingness to grow." I give the default answer I've told myself over the years. Reaching out, I touch Addison's hand and look into their eyes. "But I get the connection you were trying to convey. Sometimes, I want to be the best me to spite them, but my old therapist told me that wouldn't be a healthy motivation. You're right; I have to be me for me, not anyone else."

Addison's eyes light up. "So let's change the meaning."

"What do you mean?"

"For the thistle. Let's change what it means."

"You can do that?" I'm dumbfounded. "I thought there were rules. You have books with lists."

They pull out one of the books that has a column of multiple definitions.

"I mean, we can't officially change the meanings that have been used for centuries, but if you look at the lists, they aren't always consistent. Depending on what list you use or where you were located, the meaning could change. So let's make the thistle our own."

I smile. It's all I can do with my heart in my throat. I'm in awe that this beautiful human, with their wild, untamable hair, their freckles and constant blush, would throw out hundreds of years of tradition just for me.

Addison continues, "So let's think. Thistles are prickly motherfuckers, but they're beautiful and grow in almost any environment, like dandelions. And the blooms are purple, like your hair."

They reach over and ruffle my hair, pulling me out of my daze. A laugh bursts from my chest.

"So prickly beauty?" I bat my eyelashes.

"I was thinking along the lines of 'worthy of effort.'"

Their hand drops and cups my cheek, and I see their eyes drop to my lips. Oh my God, are they going to kiss me? My breath hitches, which seems to startle Addison. They pull their hand away and start fiddling with the pen that was laying on their sketchbook.

"You know, because they can be a bit intimidating when you first see them, and then if you take the time to really get to know them, you get the opportunity to really appreciate them and see their beauty."

Addison finishes their explanation, and we sit there,

looking forward and not touching. Eventually, I clear my throat.

"Yeah, a thistle sounds like it would be a great inclusion. Maybe for the last bouquet in the series? I was thinking of doing a set of five forms. One of me as a kid before I was able to come out, one after Gram rescued me, one after starting testosterone, one after I was able to get top surgery, and one of me now."

"I think those would be great stages. What if, along with the growing bouquets and the meanings behind each flower, we also represent them in varying states of health. So the earlier blooms could be a bit more withered, and then they could be buds, and finally finish in full bloom. I think instead of showcasing different flowers in each vase, we build it up. So we start with one or two stems in the first form, add a few more in the second but keep the same types. Does that make sense? So you'll have a throughline. Some things might have changed as you've grown, but ultimately, you've always been you."

"That's a great idea. I think it makes a lot of sense. What if we incorporated an element of weeding in there? Because I had a lot of poor self-worth when I was a kid, and I still do, but it's not as prevalent. So if there's something in there that would represent how miserable I was, maybe we have those in full bloom in the early vase, a few less in the next, and then gone or seriously reduced by vase 3 or 4."

"Oh, we could try that." Addison pulls the floriography reference book into their lap. "Think about what words or feelings you want to portray for the first one, and especially think about that one you want to have as the throughline."

"How about the thistle?"

They smile at me and nod their head before turning back to their pile of books. "Okay, so we use the thistle as our focus flower in each bouquet. Give me a couple words about how you felt for the first form."

"Silenced. Sad. A little deceptive, like I was living a double life. Afraid. Jealous of other families, like Benji's, where people could just be themselves."

"Okay, let me see what I can come up with."

I watch as they flip through the books and writes down a couple notes in their sketchbook. After a couple minutes, they show me what they've got.

"So we have belladonna, or deadly nightshade, which could represent silence. It's also a toxic plant, which plays into the toxic environment you were forced to be in. For the jealousy element, bramble would be a good choice. It means envy, but that works. For sadness, we could use wolfsbane. Dogbane or datura could be used for the deceit, whichever one you like better. Or both. We also have a choice for fear—either a yellow acacia or red columbine. Either would go well with the other flowers we have picked out, but the columbine has a secondary meaning of 'foolishness' which you might find relevant."

"I like it. I think the columbine is a good choice. My parents certainly thought what I was doing was foolish, and even though I know it wasn't, that was certainly part of the fear at the time."

"In that case, I recommend we go with the dogbane for deceit. It has reddish undertones that will help tie it together with the other flowers."

"Okay. Wow. We have our first bouquet planned out." I'm quiet for a moment, stunned by the surreality of our situation. This might actually happen. "And you're sure you don't mind working on this with me?"

"Honestly, I'm honored that you would choose me to help with this."

"Blooms, you're amazing. I hope you know that, and I hope I can continue to remind you of it at every opportunity.

I don't know what I did to deserve your friendship, but it's been one of the best things to happen to me in a long time."

They blush, and I smile at the familiar reaction. We're sitting as close as we were in the garden the other night, sides touching at multiple points. It's comfortable and electrifying. I don't know who moved into that position or if we're just naturally gravitating towards each other, but it feels right.

We pull out our sketchbooks and work side-by-side on forms and shapes for the piece. Before either of us realizes, the cheese on the plate is gone, and it's starting to get dark outside.

"Do you want to work on another one tonight?" Addison asks gently. "I'm sure just going through that one was a bit of an emotional toll, and I don't know if you're still feeling a bit raw from the other night."

"A bit." I smile. "This was a good start, though. Maybe we can grab coffee or something and go over the next one this weekend? I have a show on Saturday, but I'm free on Sunday morning if you've got time."

"Yeah, I could do that." They slightly lean into my shoulder, and goosebumps shoot down my arm and leg.

Not wanting the night to end there, I pull out my phone.

"Hey, can I ask you for some advice? While everything's still raw, that is?"

"Sure. What's up?" They stop packing their stuff away and turn to me.

I take a deep breath before starting.

"So, at the last market, I told you I took the long way back from picking up lunch, but what I didn't tell you is the true reason why I did that."

They doesn't say anything, just sit there listening, a gentle expression on their face.

"I was almost back at the booth when I saw a familiar face. Someone I haven't seen in almost 15 years— my cousin, Gwenna."

Addison nods in understanding. "I thought she might have been related to you, but I didn't want to push. You have the same eyebrows. For what it's worth, she didn't seem like a bad person when I met her, but if she's one of the people who hurt you, I can have her banned from the next one. Say the word."

I love how they're willing to go to whatever lengths to protect me. I reach out my hands to calm them.

"Calm down, Mr. Mayor. There's no need for that. She was the cousin who I trusted- my best friend. Apparently, our family told her that I ran away. She sent a message to my social media. And look at this."

I show them her profile, clicking on the pictures of her and her partner at Pride and ending on the one where they've bought a house.

"She lives here now. She's queer. Her partner is non-binary, if the flag isn't just an ally signifier." My voice is starting to sound a little excited.

"Are you going to message her back?"

"Do you think I should?"

"Do you want to?"

"Yes? It's been so long. I just don't want her to resent me for never keeping in touch. I just didn't know how to do it safely. I feel so guilty for leaving her there. I wish I could have taken her with me."

"Those are all completely understandable thoughts, but she reached out first and didn't tell you to automatically fuck off, so I'm guessing she's not that resentful. What did she say?"

I show them the message she sent last week and see that my drafted response is still there. I start playing with my lip ring as Addison reads that as well.

"So, should I send it?"

"I would, but it's not my decision to make."

"Can't it be?" I ask, only slightly joking.

"No, Cluaran. This one has to be all you, but I'll be here for you if you want to send it now or if you ever decide to meet up with her in the future. You don't have to go through this alone."

That was the courage I needed. I hover over the send button for a brief pause and press down.

"Hey, Blooms?"

"Yeah?"

"What's 'Cluaran'?"

"It's Scot's Gaelic for 'thistle'." They smile at me and hoist their bag over their shoulder.

"I like it." I smile back.

THISTLE Be A Good One (I Hope)

- Thistle by Hundred Waters

- Thistle by Vincent & A Secret

- Belladonna by Fitz and the Tantrums

- Flowers (from Hadestown) by Eva Noblezada

- Roses / Lotus / Violet / Iris by Hayley Williams

- Queen Anne's Lace by Sorority Noise

- Queen Anne's Lace by Walking Medicine

- Flower by Amos Lee

- Dandelions by Hawthorne Heights

- Dandelion by Kacey Musgraves

SPOTIFY

APPLE MUSIC

https://bit.ly/TDATT-playlists

AUGUST

CHAPTER EIGHTEEN
Colin

Gwenna got back to me less than twelve hours later, and we've been talking pretty regularly in the two weeks since then. I wasn't sure how long it would take me to be ready to meet up in person, but I talked to Addison about it, and he agreed to be there just in case.

That's how I find myself in a coffee shop on a random Thursday afternoon. One of the benefits to having the meeting now is that it's happening during Gwenna's lunch break, so we're on a bit of a time limit. Working full-time as an artist allows me to make adjustments in my schedule, and Addison took the afternoon off even though I told him he didn't need to.

My leg starts to shake, and I'm restlessly tearing at a straw wrapper while playing with my lip ring.

"We can leave any time you need," Addison reassures me. He presses his leg into mine and gently places his hand on my upturned forearm.

"Thank you." I put my head on his shoulder.

"Say the word, and we're out. Ooh, maybe we should come up with a phrase or code so I know you want to go."

"Like a conversation safeword?" I lift my head up and look at him with amusement.

"Exactly!" His eyes brighten with the widening of his smile.

"Hmm...how about 'Cheesemonger'?" I say in jest.

Addison laughs, and the butterflies in my stomach start doing some real intense parkour. They've been making their presence known every time I interact with Addison. Addison texted me? There they are. Addison and I get together to hang out and work through our collaboration? There in abundance. If nothing else good comes from today's meetup, I know I can at least have a good time with my Blooms.

"I'm not sure 'Cheesemonger' would be a good one considering how passionate my family is about cheese. What if you claim to love your least favorite pottery technique?"

"That could work. It's either sprigging or burnishing—both have gorgeous results, but they take forever to execute. Gah, my wrist hurts just thinking about burnishing. I had to make this piece one time in college that was a set of 6 identical burnished eggs. I swear I thought I was going to develop carpal tunnel at 19. It sucked."

"Burnishing, it is." Addison takes a sip from his iced lavender latte.

"Hey, before they get here, I just wanted to thank you again for being here for me. Other than Travis and Trevor, I really don't have people in my life I can rely on to be there for me when I need them. And they're both busy with work a lot of the time."

Addison sets down his drink and looks at me. I notice the compassion emanating from his eyes, not pity, but just a kindness I haven't seen directed at me much in the past few years.

"I'm glad you feel safe enough with me to rely on me. I think we're starting to make a really great team." He places his hand on my forearm again and squeezes.

"Me too."

I look up as the door chimes. Addison's hand doesn't move, grounding me as I see my cousin walk in. She looks great. Her hair is dark brown like the Jameson side, but she's got curls like her mom's. She looks a little apprehensive but excited. There's no shrieking embrace like there would have been when we were little, but as she and her partner walk over to us, I can feel the excitement of my younger self seeing his partner-in-crime again after nearly 15 years of separation.

Addison stands up and greets Gwenna and her partner, Bean. They all hug like old friends, the way I should be with Gwenna, but our hug is a little stiffer at first. Despite that, I can't make myself let go, and we cling to each other in the middle of this cafe for longer than is generally expected for a standard greeting.

When we pull apart, I'm surprised to see that my eyes are damp. Hers are too. Bean and Addison hand us tissues. Of course Blooms would have brought tissues. He's such a demiboy scout.

We sit down at the table, and Bean excuses themself to go grab theirs and Gwenna's drinks.

Addison's words break the silence that has fallen. "So, Gwenna, I saw the post of your bouquet the other day. Thanks for tagging me in it."

She turns her focus from me to him. "Thanks, Addison. I absolutely love it. You are so talented."

"Thank you." He starts to blush a little, and that familiar sight helps me relax slightly.

"You look great," I say, my voice raw from the emotions of earlier.

"Thanks, Col." The familiar nickname she used to call me softened my heart a little more. "You do too. You look like you."

I have to hold back the tears again. She's known my true self almost as long as I have.

"Thanks, Geeje."

She laughs at the nickname she used as a kid.

"God, how did it surprise anyone that we turned out queer?" She laughs some more.

I smile, not quite able to laugh just yet. Maybe I do need to go back to therapy. Addison's hand finds mine under the table, and he interlaces our fingers. The queasy feeling in my gut is immediately replaced with those butterflies, and the smile on my face reaches my eyes. I look at him with a soft expression and squeeze his hand. I don't know how he can read me so well already, but I don't hate it.

Bean comes back with their drinks.

"A dirty chai for my lady," they say with a kiss to the top of Gwenna's head. She closes her eyes, content at the gentle touch of her partner.

"Thanks, babe," Gwenna sighs. It's a familiar and comforting expression.

"You look just like Gram whenever I'd bring her tea."

She smiles at me.

"I miss her."

"Me too."

We sit there silently for a minute. Addison's thumb has started making soft circles on my hand.

"So, Bean," Addison starts the conversation back up. "What brings you both to town? You said you're from here originally?"

"Yeah," Bean responds, grateful to break the awkwardness that was falling over the table. "I grew up here, and my parents still live on the East Side. Gwenna and I met in college and decided to move here after she finished her Master's."

"Oh, that's awesome." I perk up a bit. "What did you study?"

She looks at me sheepishly before answering. "Counseling and Psychology. I want to work with kids who have dealt with religious trauma and abusive homes and help them get to a place where they can thrive and live authentically. Especially queer and trans kids."

I'm choked up. I don't know how to respond. I play with my lip ring and nod at her. I can feel the tears pooling at the edges of my eyes again.

"That's fantastic!" Addison enthuses. "My mum is a psychologist. Are you planning to get your PhD? The schools around here have some really great programs. I bet my mum would love to talk to you about that. Working with the LGBTQIA+ community is one of her primary focuses and has been for a while."

"Really? That would be fantastic. Thanks, Addison." Gwenna smiles at him before looking back at me. "Don't worry, Col, I won't use any of my Jedi mind tricks on you."

I chuckle.

"I'm sorry, Gwenna, I'm really bad at this. I..."

"Colin, you're okay. If this is too hard, we can always go back to talking through texts and messages. You went through a hell of a lot more than I did."

My heart plunges at the thought of her leaving.

"No!" I quickly respond. "I want to be here. I want to do this. I've missed you so much; I just don't know how to not be awkward and shy."

"It's a trauma response."

"I thought you said no Jedi mind tricks," I deadpan.

"It's our mostly shared trauma, dipshit."

"Gwenna Marie Jameson. Language!" I say in my best impression of her mother.

Some of Bean's drink sprays the table as they snort in surprise.

"Shit, that was terrifying," they say. "You sounded just like her mom."

Gwenna starts laughing and wiping away her partner's mess. "Damn, Colin, that was impressive."

"Thanks. So you've met Vanessa and Shawn?" I ask Bean.

"Yeah... it was awkward. They were so confused by me. Knowing what I did about their bigotry, I might have played into the androgyny a bit."

"Dad didn't know how to address them. He kept stumbling over honorifics until Bean put him out of his initial misery by telling him to address them as Doctor, which made him even more confused and flustered."

"Because a woman's place is in the kitchen, but a doctor is a respectable position for a man, and he couldn't figure out which one I was. Spoiler: it's neither," Bean says with a little wink.

Addison and I laugh at that. I could absolutely see my uncle getting increasingly frustrated trying to figure Bean out.

"So you have a doctorate?" I ask.

"Yeah, I'm a pediatrician. I mostly work with kids ages 8-15, and my emphasis is also focused on queer and trans youth. It's part of the reason we moved back here. It was getting a little too dangerous to explore practicing in Texas as a non-binary physician."

We all quietly acknowledge the sad reality of my home state.

"So, is that how you met?" Addison asks.

"Kinda. We met at a conference for LGBTQ+ healthcare workers," Gwenna answers.

"I was presenting on a panel about how to recognize signs of trauma in trans youth, and Gwenna had some insightful questions. We met up for coffee after so I could pick her brain a little more, and we hit it off."

"And then we found out that my school was close to where they were in a residency program, so we just kept meeting up for coffee, and things went from there."

Addison sighs next to me. I glance down at our still-entwined hands and give him a little squeeze. He looks at me with a dreamy expression on his face.

"I love a good love story," he says.

"Me too." Gwenna agrees. "So how did y'all meet? And how long have you been together? You make a cute couple, and this is turning out to be a fun double date. We should do it more often."

At that, Addison's body tenses, and he lets go of my hand.

"Oh, we're not..." he starts, the words trailing off.

"We're just friends. But we did have a really great meet cute."

"Oh, I'm sorry for assuming." Gwenna blushes slightly.

"It's fine," Addison says, but his smile is tight, and his hands are wringing the bottom hem of his shirt, similar to how mine were before Gwenna and Bean got here.

I stifle the urge to grab his hand and instead just press my leg into his. He moves it away slightly. I get the hint and try to focus on my cousin and her partner rather than on the person I really want to pay attention to right now.

"Uh, we met at the Makers Market earlier this year, actually. Back in May. Addison was in desperate need of a heavy vase for one of his bouquets that kept toppling over, and I had just the one for him."

"Aww, that's a cute story. I'm glad y'all are friends." Gwenna says cheerfully.

"Me too," Addison responds, but it's lined with an air of sadness I haven't experienced from him before.

We keep talking, and I'm as tuned in as I can be, but I'm also a bit distracted because something with Addison has changed. He's here and participating in the conversation, but his words seem a little short, and the light I generally associate with him isn't as bright as it usually is. It makes me a little worried, and I want to check on him, but I also don't want to miss out on reconnecting with my cousin.

After a while, Bean notices the time on the clock hanging on the wall behind the counter. "Oh, crap. It's getting late. We should probably head back. I've got a full afternoon of appointments booked, and I know G needs to get some studying in."

We all stand up, the air around us a little awkward again. After we say our goodbyes, Addison excuses himself to go to the bathroom. I wave as Gwenna and Bean head out and then sit back down at the table and wait. After about five minutes, Addison comes back and looks absolutely wrecked.

"Blooms, what's going on?" I usher him into a chair and push some water in his direction. I hesitate on where to sit before deciding on the chair next to him, but I scoot it over to give him space.

"Just... I don't date." He finally blurts out.

"Okay? I didn't think of today as a date." I'd have liked it to have been, but I don't say that. I don't want to send him further into a spiral.

"I'm sorry. I panicked. My head started swimming, and I couldn't really focus on anything."

"Yeah, you didn't seem to really be yourself at the end there."

"I'm sorry I ruined your reunion." He puts his head in his hands. I reach over and tentatively start rubbing gentle circles on his back. He melts at my touch.

"Whoa. No, Blooms, you didn't ruin anything. You're the reason I had the confidence to go through with it in the first place. Without you, today never would have happened," I counter.

"But I got awkward, and they left."

"Oh, Blooms, that's not because of you. You heard Bean—they had to go and get back to work. We spent almost an hour here with them. It's okay that it wasn't a full 60 minutes. We'll have more time to catch up in the future. I just need to know you're going to be okay."

"God, Colin, you're too good," he says with an air of frustration.

"What does that mean?" I'm starting to feel a little defensive, but I push aside the reflex that could quickly lead to anger.

"I'm not used to this. The whole getting taken care of. Usually, I'm the one taking care of people."

That breaks my heart. Addison's heart is so big, and he's so generous. To know that he doesn't get the courtesy of having people return the kindness and love he pours out at every opportunity makes me want to fight the world.

"We're friends, Addison. We take care of each other."

He leans into me.

CHAPTER NINETEEN
Addison (they/he)

Before we know it, August's Makers Market is here. Colin and I are set up together again. I got confirmation about our placement from Seth and Lilly with enough time that Colin and I were able to combine our booth layouts for a larger setup. Okay, maybe I badgered them a little about keeping us as neighbors so we could have a mega booth. As grumpy as he was about getting up earlier than usual, the double booth looks great and has been extra profitable for both of us.

The tension from our first meetup with Gwenna and Bean has dissipated, and we're back to our comfortable camaraderie. I don't know why I bristled when they implied that Colin and I were a couple. We're friends and close ones at that. If I had been with anyone else, it probably wouldn't have bothered me as much, but Colin is different. There's something about him that makes me hope, and hope is dangerous. I had hope with Liam and with Steve. Hope leads to heartbreak.

Despite my low-humming anxiety about my platonic relationship with Colin, I let myself enjoy the morning. It's so hot today, and the breeze feels nice. Colin and I have been huddled around our sketchbooks at every opportunity, working on finalizing our designs for the five sculpture pieces we're hoping get accepted to NAUA. Right around 2 o'clock, the breeze picks up to the point where it's windy. I'm glad we have everything weighted down.

Just as I'm thinking that, I feel the gust. Colin and I are nose-deep in our sketchbooks, but our heads pop up, and we instinctively grab the sides of our tents to give them a little extra anchoring. Not everyone is as quick to react as we are. We watch in abject horror as, almost in slow motion, Lane's tent, though weighed down, is lifted by the strong wind gust. We're powerless to do anything as it crashes into Cal's booth, taking out a corner of his table display. A collective freeze takes over everyone in the vicinity as hours of hard work falls to the pavement, and Cal's intricately handcrafted, one-of-a-kind sculptures break into pieces on the ground.

Before I can think, the paralysis lifts, and I'm acting. I rush over to the booth where Cal is staring at his work with an almost pained expression, completely silent. Lane is panicking at the destruction caused by their tent. Eyes turn to me, and before I can take command, Lilly and Seth appear. Lilly starts directing people not to touch anything before they can get pictures of the damage. While most vendors carry their own insurance, not everyone can afford it, so Seth and Lilly have a bigger policy that covers the whole show.

Lilly starts taking pictures with her phone, and Seth wraps Lane up in his arms, comforting them and whispering reassurances. I step towards Cal, but before I can get to him, his best friend, Samwise, is there.

I'm not used to not being the go-to, and I'm already feeling a little pushed aside and unneeded when a snide voice behind me sneers just quiet enough for just me to hear.

"Aww, poor mayor. Not sure where to stick his nose now that it's obvious nobody needs him. I don't know why you even try when no one really likes you anyways. I haven't seen a disaster this bad since you fucked up your last floral order at Stems & Such. Liam is right; you're just as useless now as you were then."

My blood chills. My breath stops, and I sway on my feet. Before I totally shut down, I feel Colin step up next to me, vibrating with anger. He starts to turn, but before he can really move, I reach out, grabbing onto him. And then my knees give out, and my vision narrows until the world goes dark.

CHAPTER TWENTY
Colin

I'm seeing red. I'm about to turn around and give Bethany a piece of my mind when I feel Addison start to slump next to me. I hold them up and practically have to carry them back to our booth. I set them down on one of the chairs temporarily and then move the other one behind the flower wall we've used as a safe haven away from prying eyes in the past. I'm so pissed off that I almost knock the wall over when the chair doesn't fit easily the first time.

As soon as I get the chair in place, I maneuver Addison over to it and set him down. They're practically catatonic. I'm so fucking pissed. How dare she? I won't hit a woman, but god damn, I need to punch something right now. Before I can register what I'm doing, there's a b-grade mug in my hand, and I'm so close to smashing it on the ground or in my hand, but I'm stopped as two people step into our booth. *Fuck!* I don't want to have to deal with customers right now. I need to do something. I need to... I don't know. I slam the mug back on the table.

"Whoa, what the fuck, Colin?" The voice of Addison's best friend cuts through the rage pounding in my head.

My head snaps over to look at Gri and Jodie. I must look murderous because they both recoil slightly.

"What the fuck is going on? Where's Addison?" she asks again.

I turn and look over behind the display wall at the pale and still blank face of the person who means the world to me. Gri's eyes follow mine and she starts walking over there. As soon as she sees the state they're in, she turns to me. Her fiery expression matches my dark rage.

"Did you do this to them?" she asks coldly.

I shake my head, unable to speak. My body is vibrating and tense. Tears burn at the corners of my eyes. I finally force myself to choke out one word: "Bethany."

Her face pales and she turns her attention back to her best friend, kneeling down in front of them. The place I know I should be. She begins talking to them in hushed tones and I see them nod before she reaches out and touches them. She's caring for them. I should be the one doing that. I step over and hover behind her, but the rage emanating off of me causes Addison to tense up which causes another wave of anger to pump through my veins.

"Colin, go take a walk," Gri instructs me with a stern voice. "Now."

I take a look at the anguished face of my Blooms and realize that I'm just making things worse by being here, so I do just that. I turn and leave the booth. Jodie gives me a sympathetic look as I pass her, and for some reason, that just feels like a knife in my gut. I don't want sympathy. I want Bethany to be held accountable for her words.

I storm past the destruction of Lane's booth and Cal's display, a bustle of cleanup still happening, and head down the aisle. I'm almost to the end when I see her. Bethany. She's back at her booth talking to a couple guys.

"What the fuck was that about?" I practically shout at her from outside her booth. I know better than to get too close. The Strickler family legacy of anger is boiling in me like it did in my brother and father before me. I may have changed my full name when Gram officially adopted me, but I can't scrub their blood from my veins.

Bethany turns towards me, the laughter on her lips morphing into a snarl as she sees my rage. If it would make a difference, I would burn this place down for Addison, but the market means too much to them, and she's not worth an arrest record.

"I didn't say anything that wasn't true."

"You're a fucking liar." I'm shaking so hard, the ground around me feels like it's vibrating.

"So eloquent." She rolls her eyes at the two guys standing with her. They both look judgmental and haughty. The one with dark hair has an especially punchable face, but they're not the ones I have issues with right now. I turn my ire back towards Bethany.

"Bethany, you want eloquence, here you go. You've been a nasty shrew since the day I met you. Clearly, you have some unresolved jealousy around how adored Addison is here. Just because your friends look like you smell like a rotting armadillo doesn't mean you have to try making the rest of us miserable. I hope you choke on a cow pie."

"Oh, fuck you, dick."

"No, thanks. I'm gay."

"What you are is a freak. An abomination. A disgrace."

Her voice morphs into the one that still haunts my nightmares. My father's final words to me ring through my head, though this time they're coming from Bethany. Before I can think about the repercussions, I snap. I'm springing back to lunge across the table at her and take her down, but two strong arms wrap around my middle and catch me. Instinctively, I swing my elbow back and just miss connecting with the side of Cal's head.

Seeing what I almost did causes the reality of the situation to bleed through. I'm no longer laser focused on Bethany and her two cronies. The adrenaline leaves my body, and I slump a bit against Cal. His arms are still around me, and for a brief moment, they hold me up. I regain the strength in my legs and shake Cal off, turning my attention to him.

"Thanks, man," I hoarsely whisper.

He stares into my eyes with a serious, no-nonsense expression, much like one I've seen from my team captains over the years. Yeah, he definitely played sports at some point in his life. When he's satisfied that my anger has dissipated and I won't attack anyone, he nods and gestures at me to go with him away from Bethany's booth.

The small crowd of onlookers who stopped to watch my verbal and almost physical spar with Bethany part as we walk past them. Cal doesn't say anything to me as we walk. He leads me around the long way to give me more time to cool down, and by the time my tent is in sight, the anger and tension I was feeling have been replaced by worry and concern for Addison.

How could I let my anger take over like that? They needed me and I couldn't help them. I *left* them. Granted, Gri told me to go, but I should have been able to tamp down the anger enough to take care of them. My priority shifts from vengeance to care. As soon as I see Addison, I'll make sure they're going to be okay, and I'll do what I can to make up for my blunder.

I rush back into the space Addison and I carefully put together just this morning, and I immediately know something is wrong. Addison is gone. I look around and don't see him or Gri anywhere.

"Jodie, where are they?" I ask Gri's girlfriend, who is seated behind our checkout area.

"Gri took them home. They weren't in any state to be here, Colin."

"Fuck." I try to hold back my tears and turn away from Jodie, bumping into a person whose arms immediately come up around me. I almost push away, but the sense of something familiar stops me.

"Whoa, Colin, what's going on, dude?" My best friend's voice cuts through the pain and regret that I'm feeling.

"I fucked up, T."

The fact that he doesn't make a snarky remark about messing up a testosterone shot speaks volumes about my relationship with Trevor. He wraps me up in a bear hug and lets me sob there into his broad chest. The last time I lost it like this was when Gram died.

As my sobs die down, I find my body facing a second adrenaline crash, and I feel so weak. I need Addison. I need my Blooms. I don't deserve them, but I need them. They ground me, and I fucked it all up because I couldn't keep my stupid anger under control. If I had any energy left, I think I would get angry again, but my body refuses to let me expend the remaining dregs that way. I pull away and wipe my eyes.

I see Travis standing outside like a bodyguard, keeping people away. Cal is over with Samwise, huddled over a table with pieces of sculptures organized out in front of them. Lane is biting their nails, glancing over at the two friends but not encroaching on their repair attempts. The mangled remains of their tent are nowhere to be seen. Many of the mirrors in their booth have been covered to keep the glare of the sun from blinding people walking by. Seth and Lilly are on their way over, and before Travis can try to keep them out, I go out to meet them.

"Thanks, Trav," I say as I pass by, patting his shoulder as I do.

"Anytime, C. We have your back, bro." I take comfort in his words. My true family is here, and they've got me.

I head Seth and Lilly off and invite them into my booth. Trevor is talking to Jodie a bit about what went down.

"Colin, what happened? Cal told us that he had to

stop you from a near fistfight with Bethany?" Lilly asks directly.

"She hurt Addison."

"What the fuck!? Today's a shitshow." Seth puts his hand on his forehead and swipes it down his face.

"How did she hurt them? Did she attack them physically?"

"No, she... Fuck it. She said some really shitty things about them and called them useless. It set them off into a really bad anxiety spiral. I don't know everything they've been through, but I do know PTSD symptoms when I see them, and that was pretty textbook." I pause before adding the next part. "When I went to go confront her, yes, I was pissed off, but I kept my distance. It was only after she said some transphobic shit about me that I lost my shit." *Deep breaths, Colin, you can do this.* "She specifically called me a freak, an abomination, and a disgrace." I say this last sentence as clinically and detached as I can. Trevor's head snaps up from where he's talking to Jodie, and he looks terrified. He's heard me utter those words once before when I told our support group about my story.

Lilly looks pissed. She turns to her partner with a set jaw.

"She's done. I want her gone, Seth. I don't care if we have to refund her the final month's booth fee. We've prided ourselves on making this a safe space for our vendors, and she is undermining that. We've had complaints about her attitude before, but nothing this serious. We couldn't kick her out for bad vibes, but we certainly can for breaking our vendor code of conduct."

Seth nods and turns to head toward Bethany's booth. Lilly looks back at me.

"Thanks, Colin. I'm sorry you had to experience that today. What you said lines up with what Cal told us. She won't be back, but I hope you will be."

With that, she clasps her hand to my shoulder and then follows off behind her partner.

I look over to where Jodie and Trevor are watching us. I don't give Trevor time to talk.

"I've gotta go make this right. I can't believe I left them here like that. Please, T." My voice cracks.

"Go. We've got this."

"Thanks. I'll text you."

I don't wait for a response before I'm sprinting through the almost fully diminished crowd to my truck and, if I'm not too late, to Addison.

CHAPTER TWENTY-ONE
Addison (they/he)

Bethany's words cut me to the point where I was numb and couldn't react. I remember reaching for Colin, and then the next thing I knew, Gri was crouched in front of me, talking in affirmations and rubbing the backs of my hands. I cried as soon as I saw her. I cried from the relief of not being alone, I cried from the hurt that Bethany inflicted, but I also cried because Colin wasn't there. I don't know how I came to rely on him so much in such a short time, but when it mattered most, he wasn't there. He abandoned me just like everyone else. The pain of his loss makes me shiver again, and Gri just wraps the blanket around me tighter.

She didn't wait too long before ushering me out of the booth and to my car. She drove me home and has been mothering me ever since. I was able to recount bits and pieces of what Bethany said to me, but mostly, I've just been in a numb state going along with the direction Gri's been giving me.

I finish my tea when I see movement outside.

"Blooms!" the concerned voice of Colin calls out. *He came.*

"Colin," I choke out in a near-whisper.

Gri looks up from where she's been sitting at the table, and her face gets a stony expression.

"I'll go get rid of him." She moves to get up.

"No, please. Gri. I don't want him to go. Not yet, at least."

Colin is timidly knocking on the back door as she gets up to open it. She slides the glass door so it's wide enough for her to block his way in. Standing there with her arms crossed, my best friend stares down this guy who has wormed his way into my heart despite every effort I've made to keep him out.

"Gri, please. I need to see them," Colin pleads. His voice is raw and full of emotion.

"Why?"

"I need to make sure they're okay. I need to apologize for my reaction. I need to explain."

"And if they don't want to see you?"

"If Addison wants me gone, then I'm gone, but please, Gri. I've gotta try. I can't let them go without trying."

Something in his voice must convince her because she looks over to me for approval. I give it with a nod. She slides the door open all the way and steps aside. Colin rushes in and kneels in front of me so we're eye to eye as I'm sitting on the window seat. I wrap my blanket around myself a little tighter as if it's the armor I need to protect my heart.

"Blooms, hey. How are you feeling?" Colin asks gently.

He's careful not to touch me, but there's an energy pulsating between us like he wants to reach out and hold me to make sure I'm real. I kinda want him to. He makes me feel centered and grounded. The loss of that at the market today during my panic attack is part of what's making my recovery take so long.

I meet his eyes. The darker grey is accentuated by flecks of an almost silver color, like the light peeking out from behind the clouds after a rough storm. His face is so full of emotion- relief, sadness, regret- I can read it all.

"I've been better," I finally respond with a little uptick to the side of my mouth.

Colin lets out a choked sob at my attempt to joke.

He looks pained not to be touching me, so I bridge that gap, reaching out to grab his hands and take them into my lap. As soon as they settle, his breathing becomes more even, and some of the tension he's carrying ebbs away.

"Why are you here, Colin?" I ask.

"I needed to make sure you were okay. I'm so sorry I couldn't protect you the way you deserve."

"What?" I'm confused. "How would you have protected me from her words?"

"I don't know, but I feel like I failed you in so many ways today. I'm so sorry, Blooms." He pauses, taking a moment for a couple deep breaths and to find the right words before continuing with a slightly steadier voice. "You're right that I couldn't have kept her from saying what she said, but I should have focused on what you needed rather than letting my anger take control. Gri was right to send me away to cool down, but I'm scared that made it worse."

I look out to where Gri is sitting on the back porch, typing on her phone. She must have slipped outside when Colin came in.

"She sent you away? I thought you left."

"No, but Blooms, you tensed up when I got near you. It's like you expected me to hit you or something. She saw it and told me to go walk it off, and she was right. I couldn't be what you needed in that moment."

I squeeze his hands in mine and try to think back to any sort of fear or reaction I had in the moment, but the whole episode is foggy. What he's saying makes sense, though. After what Liam put me through, it's no surprise I would have flinched or tensed when around anger palpable enough to penetrate my subconscious. I should tell him.

"I've worked so hard not to be an angry guy like my father and my brother. It's my biggest fear. Being like them. I can change my name, I can move away, but I can't change that predisposition," Colin admits. "I've gone to therapy for it, and I don't know the last time I had an episode like this, but Blooms, she hurt you, and I was powerless to do anything. I was so angry at myself and at her, but please know from the bottom of my heart, my anger was never directed to you. You are the brightest part of my life; you're a field of thistles and dandelions and all things beautiful, and she tried to set it all on fire and turn it to ash. I couldn't let her get away with it, but the rage just overtook me. I shouldn't have reacted that way. I should have pushed it aside so I could focus on what you needed, but I made it about me and my messed up sense of loyalty and protection. The anger terrifies me. So yes, I left because Gri told me to, but I also left because I felt it was the best way to protect you from the monster I was becoming."

I pull him up from the ground onto the loveseat next to me. I need more connection when I say these next words.

"Colin Jameson, you are not a monster. You are not your father. You are not your brothers. You are a protector- they are the monsters. They use their anger to harm; yours stemmed from a desire to protect and save. It doesn't make it right, but it doesn't make you a monster. You. Are. Not. Them."

He throws his strong arms around me, and I melt a little at the safety I feel with him there.

"I don't expect you to forgive me. I hope I can earn forgiveness for leaving."

"Where did you go?" My mind catches on something he said earlier. "You said you made it worse? How?"

"I walked away, and the next thing I knew, I was at Bethany's booth confronting her. She said some pretty shitty stuff to me, and if it wasn't for Cal, I would have tried to hit her."

I shudder, and I'm almost too scared to ask what she said, but I need to know so I can judge his reaction.

"What did she say?"

"She said the same things my dad did the night he kicked me out. Almost verbatim. Blooms, I've tried really hard to not be a violent person, but in that moment, I snapped. I wasn't big enough to defend myself back then, but I am now. She might have been the one to say it, but it was my father's voice I heard. I was taken back to that night again."

"I'm glad Cal stopped you."

"Me too," Colin admits. "Honestly, I didn't want to hit her, and I'm glad I didn't. Up until that point, I had kept my distance and only sparred with her verbally. I may be prone to anger, but I don't like to fight. I don't like to get physical. I don't want to be anything like my father."

We sit there for a few minutes in silence; Colin is stroking my hair, and I'm rubbing circles on his forearm, tracing his tattoos. I'm processing everything he's said so far. He got defensive and protective of me. We're just friends, but he felt this intense reaction because someone hurt me. Part of me is proud to have a defender like that, but my history is flashing alarm bells whenever the threat of anger is present. I don't know where we go from here, but I know how to take a step towards figuring it out. I have to tell him my story so he understands. I give a quick double tap on his forearm and move to gesture at him to get up. He does and follows me out the door.

"Hey," we're greeted by Gri. "Everything okay?"

"It will be," I reassure them both.

"Okay. I'm gonna head back to the Market then and help Jodie pack everything up. We'll bring it by after."

"Do you want to use my truck?" Colin offers.

"I think between Ad's station wagon and my truck, we can get it all loaded in. But thanks," she responds, no sign of any coldness or resentment.

Colin nods. "My bro—best friends are there watching my stuff. They can help you with the load out. Don't let them give you any trouble. They can be a bit clumsy if they get too distracted by each other."

It's Gri's turn to nod.

"Boss around the boys; I can do that." She comes up to give me a hug. "Love you Ads. I'll see you in a bit."

She walks away, and when I hear my car pull out of the driveway, I start walking. We head down to the garden, and I am more at ease the moment I see the late summer blooms. We walk side-by-side to the moss patch under the old oak, and Colin doesn't say anything to me as we sit. I sit with my back leaned up against his side, looking out at the rainbow of peace that I've cultivated over the years.

Colin doesn't pressure me to say anything or to start my explanation as to why I brought him out here, but after a few moments, I know it's time.

"So you know how I'm on the ace spectrum, right?"

I can feel Colin nod, but he seems hesitant to respond verbally.

"I'm not easily attracted to people, but when I do end up feeling that attraction, I fall fast, and I fall hard. Before..."

No, I can't say that. I'm not ready to admit that I'm starting to have feelings for him.

"The first time I fell was in college, for this guy named Liam," I say instead. "That's who Bethany was referencing today. We met freshman year in our Intro to Soil Science class and quickly became the core couple of our friend group."

I let myself remember those early days. Liam had the most magnetic personality. He was charismatic, and everyone flocked to him. That's how most of our friend group was formed—because people were drawn to him, not me.

"Part of why I fell so quickly and so fast with him is because I didn't know I could. I'd never experienced attraction like that before, so being the hopeless romantic that I am, I thought that it was fate; that we were meant to be. When he turned that attention on me, I knew that he was my soulmate. He quickly became the center of my universe, and for the first little while, he treated me like I was the center of his."

I was convinced that I finally had someone who loved and cherished me. It was exciting. I was sexually attracted to someone for the first time in my life, and I bought into the soulmate idea hard.

"We were together, and he was a lot of my firsts— first kiss, first boyfriend, first sexual partner. I always thought I was lucky. I figured it takes people years to find their person, but I did it all in one shot. I found my forever on the first try. I dreamed about our future- my goals and plans centered around him. For the first year or so, I truly believed that he loved me too, but then we started to change. It was college; people grow a lot in college. I kept growing in my dependency on him, but he outgrew me."

I take a deep breath and steady myself for the emotional pain that comes with telling the next part of my story. Colin shifts closer and the warmth radiating off his body helps mine relax slightly.

"I did everything I could to keep him happy, but over time, my sexual attraction faded. I don't know if it was because of anything he'd done or if it was because of external pressures and the general stress of life, but I just didn't feel it anymore. I know that libido and attraction aren't the same thing, so for a while, I coasted on the fact that my libido was still going strong, so I did whatever it took for me to make him happy and keep him satisfied. It wasn't healthy. I started to dread being physical with him. My anxiety would get the best of me, and the voices in my head would scream that I wasn't worthy of his love because I couldn't love him the way he deserved."

My eyes close for a moment as I press on. The gentle breeze wafts the scents from the garden towards me. My hands find the moss I often use to keep me grounded and connected to the world around me.

"Our senior year, we talked about opening up our flower farm together. We had all the plans figured out and I had been pouring a lot of time and energy into making sure we were set. It was a five year plan. We were both going to work in the floral industry to try and make some connections, and slowly, over those five years, we'd start up our farm and begin getting things ready to go.

"During that time was when my libido slowed significantly. That and my almost non-existent sexual attraction made it really hard for me to be physical with Liam. He was getting increasingly irritated and ended up cheating on me."

Colin's hand finds one of mine in the moss. He gently rests it on top, and feeling that added connection gives me the bravery to move on.

"He said it was a one-time, one-night thing. We hadn't done penetrative sex in a while because I just didn't like it, and he didn't bottom. I cried a lot that week, but I also was clinging both to the past belief that he was my soulmate and to all the future plans we had made together. I didn't want to throw that away because he made a mistake. I truly believed that it was my fault because I had all but stopped being physically affectionate. I felt so guilty. I figured if I could just get past my mental block, I'd be fixed, and he'd be happy with me again.

"So I tried. I researched things, I took herbal supplements, I ate foods said to be aphrodisiacs even though I hated them. I took medication, anything I could do to try and be what he needed. I went against my own comfort and desires and let him top me whenever he wanted. He didn't care that I never finished. I did everything I could to appease him and sacrificed myself and my happiness at the same time.

"After graduation, we moved in together, and it got worse instead of better. We no longer had the stress of school, but we had the stress of all the other adult things-loans, bills, jobs, family. My libido still hadn't recovered, and the fact that I never got fully hard, even with medication and aids, was a point of contention. He accused me of cheating on him, of not loving him, of pretty much everything, so I tried harder. I offered to bring another person into our bed so he could be sure to have what he needed, and that's when we brought in Nick. He was my coworker and I saw them check each other out and get a little flirty whenever Liam would come to visit me at work.

"It was only supposed to be a one-time thing for our five-year anniversary, but then it moved into a regular occurrence. I couldn't get hard and figured that as long as Liam loved me and still wanted me as his life partner, having a third in our sexual relationship was a great fix. Spoiler alert: it was not."

I choke out a laugh. It's not funny, but my body needs some sort of release so I can get through the story without breaking down more than I already have today.

"Liam kept being short with me, but one day, for whatever godforsaken reason, my libido woke up. I was excited, and I wanted to take advantage of the rare situation by having sex with him. The biggest issue was that I was out of town at a conference and wouldn't be back until that weekend. So we sexted, and we had a video session, but by the time I got back for the weekend, my libido had retreated again. In hindsight, it's probably because I dreaded being home with him at that point but hadn't realized it yet.

"I was frustrated and tired, and he was annoyed. He accused me of leading him on and teasing him. Called me a bunch of names and said that if I couldn't get it up for him, we might as well not even try anymore. That set my anxiety into a tailspin. We had been together for almost 6 years at that point, and I had been working hard on my end of our 5-year plan. So I tried everything. It didn't work, but I was so afraid of losing him that I just gave in and let him do whatever he wanted, even though I wasn't into it. I spaced out and let him use my body while my mind was elsewhere."

Colin's hand gripped mine tightly. I could feel the tears starting to pool at the edges of my eyes remembering that moment. I was numb, I felt so unworthy, I felt broken. I was miserable, but I didn't know what to do.

"That cycle of me spacing out and him just doing what he wanted when he wanted without checking in with me kept happening. I felt so numb. This man who I loved and planned my life around possessed my body like it was his property. All sense of self that I previously had was gone. He stopped prepping me well before he fucked me, and he never used enough lube or any sort of protection because he didn't like the feel of it. I developed a tear that got infected, and my mental health was tanked. I was sleeping like shit, having nightmares almost every night. Any time he tried to touch me, I flinched. He would yell at me and berate me whenever I reacted like that. I had isolated my family because I didn't want them to see me like I was. I was ashamed to have gotten it all so wrong.

"The last day was the worst day. After a few months of being a shell of my former self, I messed up an order at the flower shop where I worked and got fired. So I went home, and he was there with Nick- whose shift I had picked up because he begged me to switch so he could run a bunch of errands that he hadn't had time to do. Little did I know that one of those things on his to do list was a sex marathon with my boyfriend. They were just getting out of the shower when I got home early. When Nick asked me what happened, I told them. Liam lost his shit. He said that that was the final straw. I had changed, so he didn't love me anymore, and having sex with me was like trying to have sex with a corpse. He also told me that Nick was moving in, so I should pack my shit and get out since I couldn't help with the rent anymore.

"So I did what any nearly twenty-five-year-old would do in that situation. I came home. Mum couldn't treat me because she's my parent, but she got me help from a therapist she trusted. I recovered here. I expanded this garden. I leaned into my love for plants as a way of reclaiming my spark. All the plans that I had with Liam died when that relationship ended. The savings I had were thankfully not in any sort of joint bank account, but I ended up going through it quickly, just trying to survive between jobs. Since I was at-fault for my termination, I couldn't get back into the industry. I eventually landed where I am now, but it was difficult since I didn't have a reference, and it's not like I could list 'my abusive relationship caused me to mess up at work and get fired' as my reason for leaving my only post-college employment.

"Through gardening and being in a supportive and secure place with people I trust implicitly, I was able to learn a bit more about myself. That's how I discovered that I was grey ace. Most of the time, I don't usually experience any sexual attraction, but every once in a while, I'll connect with someone, and this weird ping sets off. After Liam, though, I was so scared and traumatized that I didn't think about dating for a while after that.

"A couple years of therapy later, though, I thought I was ready to try again. I went on a few dates, but most of those turned into friendships because I didn't feel that spark that I needed. But then I met Steve. He was an enigma. I was drawn to him in a different way than with Liam. He was a tractor beam, but Steve was a puzzle. I wanted to solve him. He was elusive- kinda like an itch you can't scratch, just out of reach but close enough to keep you trying.

"By that point, I had a better understanding of my identity and sexuality at that point, so I knew that I was on the asexual spectrum somewhere. I thought I was maybe demisexual, and Steve said he was cool with that. He had some ace friends, and I thought he really got it. I was excited to explore where my attraction was leading, but while my romantic attraction took off, my sexual attraction and libido never synched up. I told myself that after what had happened with Liam, I'd never try to force it again. It wouldn't be fair to me or to my partner if I'm not fully there, so when we had been exclusive for a few months, and I still wasn't able to perform to his standards, he told me that I was a tease with a broken dick, and if I wouldn't do anything to fix it, I should just lose his number because he 'didn't have time to fix another asshole who wouldn't put the work into themself'. He didn't let me explain and just left without looking back."

I start picking at the moss next to me with my free hand.

"So the only two times I've tried dating have ended really poorly for me. I know that it's not the largest sample size, but when Steve and I broke up, it sent me into another spiral. Thankfully I was still in therapy, so I was able to work through it a lot quicker, but being called broken brought back a lot of my self-doubt and insecurities that were deeply embedded from my time with Liam."

My voice cracks at the end, and we just sit. Eventually, I start to relax a bit as the adrenaline that comes from retelling the story leaves my body. Colin doesn't say anything yet. He just holds my hand, our fingers now entwined. We stay like that for a while, the late summer breeze surrounding us. It's not an uncomfortable quiet.

"Blooms, I'm sorry," Colin starts, his voice raw with emotion. "I hate that you had to experience that. No one should ever experience that kind of abuse and heartbreak, especially not from a person they love and trust. You were not to blame for either of those situations. No one is entitled to someone else's body, even if they're in a relationship. Consent isn't a one-and-done thing. Fuck, Blooms, I'm so sorry that you had to go through that nightmare and that you've had to carry it for so long."

I squeeze his hand back, not quite ready to talk again. After a few more moments of silence, Colin starts to fidget beside me.

"Can I make you some tea? That always would make Gram feel a little better, so it's kinda my go-to response when someone's going through it."

I already had a mug of tea when Gri brought me home originally, but another cuppa sounds nice. I nod and start to get up. When we start to walk up to the house, I reach out and hold Colin's hand.

We make it into the kitchen, and Colin grabs supplies for tea. He's really only been here once, but he seems to instinctively know where everything is. I only have to show him where we keep the actual tea.

Once the electric kettle is going, Colin guides me over to the window seat that overlooks the backyard and garden. He gently maneuvers me onto the cozy cushion and puts the light throw blanket I was wearing earlier back over my lap. I smile over at him and watch as he goes back to finish fixing my tea.

After it's steeped, he brings it over and carefully hands me the mug. Taking my first sip, I let the warmth of the tea consume and rejuvenate me. It spreads through my body like a hug. Colin pulls a chair away from the small table and sits facing toward me.

"Thank you," I say. My voice is raw. "This is perfect."

"I put some of the honey from your sister's hive in it. And it's an herbal- chamomile and yarrow, I think, so I let it steep at a lower temperature and longer than the usual 5 minutes I do for black tea."

"You sound like mum. Every tea has specific brewing instructions."

"She's not wrong. It makes a difference." He looks beyond me and into the garden. "Blooms, I... I just want to thank you for trusting me with what you told me today. I know it's hard to relive trauma, especially with what happened at the market. For the record, I don't think you're broken. I think you are an amazing person with a beautiful soul. I meant what I said earlier when I told you that you make the world light up just by being in it. You are worthy of being loved in whatever way it manifests for you. You are quickly becoming one of my favorite people, and I want you to know that I will do everything I can to be worthy of being in your life."

There's something unsaid that hangs in the air, but my brain is not in a space where it can process the hidden subtext.

Colin stays with me for a little while longer, but when it starts to get dark, he needs to go home, so I walk him out to his truck. Gri and Jodie have already come and gone with all of my items from our mega booth. I'm still wrapped in the blanket from the window seat, and when he wraps his arms around me, I finally feel reassured that everything will be alright. He lightly kisses my temple before pulling away. The all-consuming warmth I felt with that first sip of tea spreads throughout my body again.

"Get some rest, Blooms. Be extra kind to yourself tonight. Remember, some of the most beautiful flowers thrive in the worst conditions."

"Thistles and dandelions." I smile softly at him. I head back to the house as he drives away.

CLUARAN

A Cup of Chamomile and Yarrow

- …Just A Pause by Autumn Orange

- Safe & Sound [feat. The Civil Wars] by Taylor Swift

- Light Up Ahead [Acoustic] by Further Seems Forever

- Shelter by Joy Oladokun

- S.I.S. by Judah & The Lion

- Sensitive Badass by The Doubleclicks

- Keep Your Head Up by Andy Grammer

- Always Love by Nada Surf

- Breathe by Ryan Star

- Strip Me by Natasha Bedingfield

- I Feel Better by Gotye

- Embers by Ethan Hibbs

- Beautiful Soul by Jesse McCartney

SPOTIFY

APPLE MUSIC

https://bit.ly/TDATT-playlists

CHAPTER TWENTY-TWO
Colin

The next couple weeks are some of the most challenging weeks of my adult life in regards to my personal growth. Addison and I have been working on strengthening our friendship and rebuilding the trust we had before the Bethany incident. That night, when I got home, I went into the studio and channeled my emotions in a more productive manner. I ended up throwing a record number of vessels. The next day, I reached out to Gwenna, and she was able to connect me with a therapist. Starting therapy again has left me a little raw at times, but Blooms is always there after to help when I need them. Sometimes, I'll come back and work through my processing on the wheel, but other times, I connect with Blooms and help them with their garden.

I've considered asking them to help me create a small oasis in my backyard. We'll have to work around my raku kiln and fire pit, but if there's anyone who can make it work, it's my Blooms.

I'm sitting at my computer after another post-therapy marathon throwing day, sifting through the usual promotional emails before seeing a message that grabs my attention:

FROM: La Galerie D'Art

**SUBJECT: Your "New and Upcoming Artist"
Application Status**

My breath catches, and my heartbeat speeds up. I don't
know if I have enough mental strength to process a rejection right now. I hover the cursor over the email. But what
if it's not a rejection? I want Addison to be here either way.
Maybe we should open it together.

I should connect with him and see if he'd be willing
to come over tomorrow to check it with me. I close out of
the browser window and put my computer to sleep before
sending him a text.

ME

What are you doing tomorrow after work? The
DART decision email is sitting in my inbox and I'm
too nervous to open it by myself. I want you to be
here so we can know together.

It doesn't take long before a string of emojis and gifs
come back, practically blowing up my phone. I laugh at
Addison's response.

BLOOMS

Coming to your house to check an email
apparently. I'm bringing pizza and booze.

ME

Sounds perfect. I'm gonna be in the studio all day,
so If I'm not quick to respond you know why. 😊

In the morning, I do my best to avoid the urge to check
my email by heading straight into the studio, connecting
my phone to the speakers and charging dock as I pass it.
Looking at the bats of mugs and vases I made last night,
I think about what I want to do with them. I grab my

sketchbook and start to doodle. Apparently, Addison is on my mind because a couple hours later, I have a handful of floral motif designs I'm itching to feature on each of the vases. I haven't really done detailed sgraffito in a while, so the first couple attempts are definitely destined for my back table of discounted B-Grade items, but once I'm in a groove, the quality of my carving improves significantly.

I must lose track of time because when the doorbell rings, I look over at my phone and notice that it's well into the evening. I also see that I have a number of missed texts, mostly from Addison.

Grabbing it off the docking station, I head to the front door and open it to find Addison standing with a pizza and a brown paper bag that looks like it probably holds the promised booze.

"Hi," I greet him.

"Hi." He looks at me with a soft smile.

"Come on in." I step aside so he can easily enter my house. I take the pizza box from his full hands. "Sorry for being a little dirty. I, uh, got lost in the studio. Time blindness..."

"I see that," Addison says.

We head into the kitchen to get what we need for dinner. Before we can dig into the pizza, I gently grasp Addison's forearm and turn him toward me.

"Can I hug you?" I ask, my voice a little lower and breathier than I expect it to be.

Addison nods and steps into my arms, melting into the embrace, his ever present floral and dirt scent mixing with the earthy smell that lingers on me after a full day working with clay in the studio.

"Rough therapy session last night?" he asks.

"Yeah, we talked about Gram."

When the tears come, he gently rubs circles on my back. One of the things I learned when I moved in with Gram was just how touch-starved I had been for the first 14 years of my life. I had been skittish at first, but Gram persisted by offering me hugs, rubbing my back when I was having a depressive episode, or grounding me through touch whenever I had a panic attack. I've never told Addison this, but he instinctively does the right thing every time I need comfort.

"Sorry I'm a mess," I apologize after a few minutes.

"Cluaran, you never need to apologize for feeling how you feel, especially after such a raw emotional day as yesterday. Big emotions like that take more than one day to recover. When I told you my story, I needed like a whole week to recover. You not being back to 100% today is completely understandable. Gram was a big part of your life. I'd probably be more worried if you weren't still tender from yesterday. Come on, let's move over to the couch."

All thoughts of food and emails is forgotten as we slowly walk towards the couch. Carefully so as not to break our embrace, I sit down and pull Addison into my lap. Despite our six-inch difference in height, Addison fits like he's always been meant to be there.

I hold him and feel my emotions regulating a bit better. Between therapy last night and the pending email, I've been feeling jittery all day. After a few minutes of comfort, he gives me a final squeeze and kisses my cheek before climbing off my lap. My breath hitches, and I want to pull him back and kiss him properly, but I know that he's still a bit vulnerable after everything that went down last month, and I don't want to do anything that will hurt either of us. I can wait until he's ready, if he's ever ready, to take our relationship past the 'just friends' stage.

Standing up, Addison holds his hand out to me.

"Come on, let's go eat some lukewarm pizza and open this email. Then we can either celebrate or drown our sorrows with the gin I brought."

"Gin? Really?" I tease. Taking his offered hand and standing up, I follow him into the kitchen.

"I also brought tonic and limes. I wasn't sure if you had that or not."

"I do not."

"Then it's a good thing I came prepared."

"I've noticed that about you," I say as I pull out some plates for our dinner.

"Noticed what?"

"You're always prepared for pretty much any situation. You have your Mary Poppins toolbox at shows, and you had tissues at the cafe for me when we met with Gwenna and Bean; now you bring alcohol and my favorite pizza when we're about to open an email that could change our lives. You really are a demi-Boy Scout."

Addison blushes, and I didn't realize just how much I had missed seeing the redness on his cheeks until this moment.

"It's really no big deal. I like to make sure I can help people. I like feeling useful."

"It might not seem like a big deal to you, but Blooms, you make a difference in every life you touch. The Market community is better off because you're there for everyone. I'm so grateful that you've let me get to know you better over the past couple months. I know that without you, I wouldn't have my cousin back in my life. You make life better just by being in it. I hate that you've had people take your shine away from you, but please know that you bring color into the world around you."

Addison's blush deepens, but he stands a little taller, the confidence easy to read in his posture.

"After a pep talk like that, I don't see how we can put off checking this email any longer." Addison smiles widely at me and picks up his plate, heading towards the office. I grab my own pizza and follow after him.

It doesn't take long to wake up the computer and pull up my email. I hover over the message with my mouse and look over at the person who has brought so much joy into my life after only a couple months of knowing him.

"Should we do this together?" I ask.

"Sure." He puts his hand on mine.

"On the count of three. One... Two... Three."

We click. The email opens, and I shut my eyes, not ready to look just yet.

"What does it say?"

"Are you paying too much for your car insurance? You can save up to 10% by switching to—" Addison reads.

"Shut up. No it does not," I cut him off, confused, and open my eyes to read the screen in front of me. My eyes dart over the spam marketing email and see that it's very obviously not the email from the DART. I back out of the page to see that this email was above the email with our application status update.

"Apparently, the simultaneous clicking didn't work," I observe. I maneuver the mouse over the correct one and click before I can lose my nerve.

"Thank you for applying to La Galarie D'Art's New and Upcoming Artists (NAUA) exhibit. We had a record number of applicants this year, and while we can't accept all of them in the show, we appreciate your enthusiasm and desire to be a part of our biggest NAUA exhibit yet."

I let out my held breath and continue to read the rest of the email out loud.

"We read through every application that came through and were impressed by your vision, so we would officially like to offer you a space in this exhibit."

I stop reading because my head is ringing. I grab Addison's forearm and whip my head around to face him.

"Oh, my God. We got in."

"Oh, my God." He looks shocked.

"OH MY GOD!" We both jump up and start doing ridiculously cheesy dancing. It reminds me of the night I met Addison's family, and they had an impromptu dance party in the kitchen. We're laughing, hugging, jumping, and I keep looking back at the email to make sure I didn't misread it.

"We have to celebrate. Let me take you out for dinner or something." Addison tenses in my arms. "Not a date, just a friendly collaboration partner celebration before the hard work begins." I clarify and he relaxes.

"Okay. Yeah. Let's do that." He grins down at me. Our eyes meet, and I see a spark of something in his clear blue eyes.

"Ice cream?" I ask.

"Ice cream sounds good to me."

"Do you want to finish our pizza or skip it tonight and hit up the Stand and Grill?"

"Stand and Grill for sure. The pizza is pretty much cold by now."

I take Addison by the hand and lead him back into the kitchen where I make quick work of putting the remaining pizza away in my fridge. I grab my keys off their designated hook and head towards the front door. I stop before opening it and pat myself down doing my obligatory check to make sure I have everything I need before leaving the house.

"What are you doing?" Addison asks, with a chuckle as he sees me touch my pockets and crotch.

"Making sure I have everything. You know, keys, wallet, phone, packer, sunglasses."

"Smart," Addison concludes, and we head out to my truck.

Twenty minutes later, we're pulling up to the popular ice cream and burger spot. It's themed like a kitschy 50s diner and is a popular spot for late night hang outs, especially with teenagers during the summer. I usually avoid it, but they have the most extensive soft serve selection and some really delicious burgers. They're also open later than most other non-fast food restaurants, so at 9pm, we don't have many other options for our celebration meal.

We order our food and head back to the truck to wait. I pull a blanket out from behind the bench seat in the cab and put it down in the padded truck bed.

"We should probably finish planning out the other sculptures and arrangements," Addison starts as he gets settled against one side of the truck bed.

"Good call." I climb in and sit next to him.

By the time our number is called, we've planned out a timeline for the project and I've given Addison a list of words and phrases to include in the other arrangements.

"You know, I never would have pegged you for a cotton candy shake guy," Addison teases me when we get back from picking up our food.

We're sitting across from each other in the truck bed, our feet staggered together.

"Don't knock it til you try it." I take a big sip and hold the shake out towards him.

"Cotton candy or pegging?"

My eyes go wide, and I snort milkshake out through my nose. That was the last thing I expected him to say. Addison is laughing at my newly disheveled state while also wiping away some of the milkshake from my shirt with the extra napkins he must have grabbed.

"Sorry, that one was too easy."

"You are full of dimensions, Addison Baird." I catch his eye before continuing, "And for the record, I'm a fan." I wink and lean back, taking over the cleanup. That familiar blush starts to creep up his neck but doesn't reach his face this time. As disappointed as I am not to see his face get flush, I'm also excited that our relationship dynamic has shifted into one where he feels comfortable joking about sex with me. I don't think we would have been there before our heart-to-hearts in the garden, his or mine.

"Oh! I meant to ask you, what was with including that Jesse McCartney song in your last playlist? Kinda out of left field compared to all the other ones."

I let out a laugh so loud, some of the kids walking by turn to look at us.

"When we were talking in the kitchen, I said something about you having a beautiful soul, and the song got stuck in my head for the rest of the day, so it felt fitting to include it in the playlist."

"You're such a dork," he says, tossing a fry at me. I try to catch it in my mouth and miss horribly. Addison's laugh is one of my favorite sounds, carefree and unreserved. I can't imagine doing anything to take that away from the world.

"I am, but you wouldn't have me any other way." I smirk playfully at him.

"True." He smiles softly back at me, and I have to fight the urge to kiss every one of the freckles on his face.

We fall into a comfortable silence, our feet back to being entwined as we sit across from each other again. I have never felt this quickly comfortable with someone before. Maybe with Benji, but most of my friendships were brought together by trauma bonding over being queer or trans. I guess you could say that Addison and I have grown closer after we both shared our pasts, but our trauma isn't shared like mine and Gwenna's or even related like mine and Trevor's.

"What's your favorite flower?" I ask him finally. I want to learn everything there is about this person.

"Dandelions, obviously," he says without hesitation. I smile, thinking about the response he had to my resiliency comment the other day.

"What do they represent?"

"Well, they're another one with a double meaning. Most people see them in relation to magic, but they also can mean 'tell me I am wanted,' and that one really resonates with me. Most people don't want dandelions and are quick to get rid of them. They see them as a weed rather than a flower with a number of useful properties. You can eat the leaves, and the flower heads can be used in winemaking or as a vegan alternative for honey. Dandelions are great. And they're resilient. There are so many times I've been walking in an urban area, and there's a dandelion growing in the middle of the sidewalk. I love my crocuses and tulips, but there's no way you'd see them survive in those conditions. Dandelions are my all-time favorite, but I really like any of the overlooked flowers. You know? The ones that people either don't see or view as eyesores... dandelions, clovers, thistles..."

He looks over at me as he says that last one, and I see that spark from earlier come alive in his eyes again.

"I like that," I respond finally. My voice hasn't felt this weird since I was in my first year on testosterone. I clear my throat to try and get my voice back to its normal tone instead of the raw, huskier version it just was. "Well, Blooms, I have a song just for you. Two questions, though: do you like ska, and what's your level of religious trauma?"

Addison looks at me skeptically. "Umm, I haven't listened to ska in years- decades, possibly. Except for what you've sent me. And as far as religious trauma goes, pretty much none. You've met my family. Can you imagine Dr. Siobhan in a church?"

We both laugh, and I move over to sit next to him, pulling out my phone as I go and scrolling through my various playlists until I reach the song I'm looking for. A medley of horns fills the air around us. The rhythmic guitar and vocals come in, and we listen as the story of a young boy picking dandelions for his mother unfolds, with her treasuring the small bouquet that he picks for her.

"When does the religious trauma kick in? Oh, never mind." Addison chuckles a little awkwardly when the message of the song starts getting religious. I turn the music down a bit so we can keep talking.

"Yeah, their new stuff is less preachy, but they've always been one of the more progressive Christian bands from my youth. They're one of the only ones I still listen to, but I don't even know if I'd classify them as a Christian band anymore."

"I'm glad you still have that." He leans into me, and I instinctively put my arm around his shoulders. "What's the name of the band?"

"Five Iron Frenzy. I've put them on at least one of the playlists I sent you. I'm sure of it."

"The unicorn song?"

I laugh, "Yeah, that's them."

We sit there finishing our food and talking about random things until most of the other cars parked around us are gone.

"We should probably get back. I still have some work to do in preparation for this show I have on Sunday." I resign.

"Hmm?" Addison looks up at me from where his head has been resting on my shoulder. "Oh yeah, good call. I didn't realize just how tired I was until now. I needed a night like this."

I smile down at him, and while he kissed my cheek earlier, I hold back from kissing his forehead now. Instead, I lift my hand and softly brush back one of the curls that have fallen into his face.

"Me, too."

We move to untangle ourselves, and Addison goes to throw away our trash while I fix the truck bed back to its usual state and stash the blanket in the cab. Before he comes back, I take a moment to adjust my packer, which has been putting pressure on my T-boner. It's not a date, I have to remind myself.

On our drive home, Addison sits a little closer to me. I try not to be obvious about how happy that little show of comfort makes me, but I can't help the little smile that sits on my face the whole way back.

"We should do this again," Addison remarks as he gets into his station wagon.

"Yeah, we really should. I like going out with you. We'll have to have more 'not dates' soon."

"I'd like that." He bites his lip. Before I act on my desire to kiss him goodnight, I close the car door and watch from my front porch as he heads off down the street, knowing the smile on my face will be there long after I fall asleep tonight.

CHAPTER TWENTY-THREE
Addison (he/they)

Today is the final Makers Market of the season, and it's a bittersweet day. Colin isn't here as a vendor, as he wanted to get some work done on the sculptures for our exhibit piece, but on the plus side, Gri is back, and after last month, I'm glad to have a familiar anchor by my side. She's got her booth set up in what I'm coming to think of as Colin's spot, though it was hers for years before him. At least it's not that weird when I catch myself looking over that way a few times throughout the morning.

Colin and I have been on three more not dates since our celebration dinner. We went back to the cafe where we met Gwenna and Bean and then walked around the park a bit, where I showed him some of the inspiration flowers that I want to include in the bouquets I'm making. Another time, we went to the DART to scope out the space and spent the afternoon admiring the art. My favorite part was the outdoor sculpture garden they have in the courtyard. And then two days ago, we went to pick up some clay and glazes that Colin needed for restocking. We also happened to stop into the record store next to the ceramic supply store, and Colin showed me more of his favorite music.

Aside from our not dates, we've been talking every day. Sure, we talked before, but something changed the night we found out about getting into the show. As soon as I got there and saw Colin again, I felt my gut tugging me towards him. I'd been fighting anything resembling attraction, but the more time we've been spending together and the more we've been working on our communication, the pull has started to get stronger. Every time I see a text from him or get to witness his magnetic smile in person, my stomach gets all swoopy, like I'm riding a rollercoaster and we've just gone down a tall drop. But instead of feeling like I'm in a free-fall, like I have in the past, there's always a purposeful and grounding feeling of safety with Colin. It's confusing, but I don't hate it.

"Hey, Gri?" I call over to my best friend when there's a lull in customers.

"What's up, Ads?" She walks over and leans on my counter.

"Can I talk through something with you?"

"Always, babe. What's up?"

"I think I'm having guy trouble?" I say, my voice pitching up at the end like a question.

"Guy trouble?" Gri reaches over and puts the back of her hand against my forehead. I squirm away.

"What are you- stop. Geez, Gri, what are you trying to do?"

"I'm checking your temperature- making sure you're feeling okay."

"I'm fine." I snap. "I just want someone to listen and maybe give advice, not judge me for maybe actually having feelings."

"I'm sorry, Addison."

I sigh. "It's okay, Gri." *Damn my people-pleasing tendencies.* "Jokes like that just bring me back to that place with Liam and Steve and add to that feeling of brokenness I've worked so hard to get away from."

Gri's expression is somber and apologetic. "Thanks for explaining that," she says and then hastily adds, "not that you should have to. Especially after last month, I should have realized... I'll work on being better about that."

"Come here." I pull her into a hug and feel the tension release after a minute. She pulls away with a soft smile on her face.

"Thanks," I sit back down and gesture for her to do the same. She pulls her chair over to the edge of her booth so we can keep an eye on both of our spaces while talking.

"Okay, potential guy trouble. What's going on?"

"Well, I'm sure it's no surprise that I've been hanging out with Colin a lot recently. We're working on a collaboration for the DART's NAUA exhibit, and we've been going on these not dates, but part of me wants them to be?"

"Are you asking or telling?"

"Telling. I think I want them to be more than just friend hangouts and collaboration check-ins. We've gone to the museum, the cafe, the art store, the record store, and the public garden. All of our activities could be seen as relevant to the project, but something feels more with him. Like the night we found out we got into the show, something changed. I flirted, I made sex jokes, I opened up in a way I haven't in a while. He makes me feel safe, and that's terrifying."

"Safety is terrifying?"

"Yeah, because I've been wrong about it before. I thought Liam was safe. I don't know if I ever got there with Steve, but regardless of if he did or not, I don't want to go through that again."

"Addison, I get it. After Jordyn cheated, I wasn't sure if I could trust again. There were a few times in the beginning of our relationship when Jodie should have probably broken up with me because I was so paranoid."

"What helped?"

"Talking to her, explaining to her what was going on in my head, and being open to the possibility of heartbreak.

You can't predict the future, but you can take steps now to impact what's to come. If you close yourself off and don't take chances, you'll never find that fairytale love I know you dream about." Gri fixes me with a knowing look. We've talked so many times about my hopeless romantic nature. "Have you talked to him about your past at all yet? I'm not saying you have to tell him everything, but you might at least want to tell him that you've been hurt in relationships before."

"I have. I told him everything."

"Everything?" Gri is shocked. I don't talk about my past with everyone, and it took me a few years to be comfortable enough sharing it with Gri.

"Yeah. After the Bethany incident, when you left and we went into the garden. He listened and didn't judge. Then, when he got home that night, he sent me a playlist that night with a whole bunch of encouraging songs." I pull out my phone and pass it over to her so she can see the playlist.

"Jesse McCartney?" She side-eyes me.

"Inside joke." I smile, recalling Colin's response when I asked him the same thing.

"Well, I know last month was a bit of a shitstorm, but I'm getting a good vibe about him overall. I know safety feels like you're being lulled into a trick, but I don't think Colin is like Liam or Steve. He's heard your story and didn't bow out. He could have just as easily told you that you didn't get into the exhibit and left it at that, but it seems like you're finding more time to be together and do things. Sure, they've all related to the project so far, but that could just be a rouse to give you a comfortable setting so you can get to know each other outside of the context of dating. You might not be a horse, but you can still spook easily at times."

"Gee, thanks."

"It's not a surprise based on everything you've been through. It sounds like he's trying to be accommodating to what you need."

"Yeah..."

"Is there more?" She narrows her eyes in my direction.

"More?"

"Okay, now you just sound ridiculous with your one-word repetitive responses."

"Wemayhavecuddledabit," I rush.

"I'm sorry, repeat that please? And slowly this time. Remember to e-nun-ci-ate."

"We may have...cuddled a bit."

"And you think he doesn't like you?"

"I mean, if you were sad and needed a hug, I'd probably do the same thing."

"Addison, my dear darling demiboy, no. We don't cuddle. Sure, you're an affectionate friend, but any time we've hung out, we don't cuddle. We hug, and we platonically touch, but when we sit down to watch a movie, we tend to stick to ourselves. Do you cuddle with any of your other friends?"

"No, but he was sad. It wasn't like we were just hanging out. He was in a bit of an emotional hangover state from a tough therapy session, and we sat on the couch, and he held me in his lap—"

"You sat in his lap!?" Gri interrupts loudly. A couple of the shoppers passing by stall and look at us. We both smile and wait until they continue on their way to resume our conversation.

"Yes," I hiss. "I sat on his lap, and we cuddled. And I kissed his cheek after. Okay, I see it now. I think I have a crush on Colin."

I grin over at Gri's dumbfounded face. I wasn't sure if I wanted to share that piece of information, but seeing her shock was worth it. After a minute's stupor, she recovers.

"You don't say." She fixes me with a look so dripping in sarcasm, it could be used as the new universal visual definition. "How did he react when you kissed his cheek?"

"He blushed, and I'm pretty sure I heard his breath stutter. I don't know if he noticed the blush, but I did."

"And how did that make you feel?"

I roll my eyes at her. "Okay, Mom. Let's cool it with the Dr. Siobhan impression here. You're my best friend, not my therapist."

"Same difference." She waves her hand around flippantly. "What happened after that?"

"That's when I started getting flirty, and we went out to the Stand and Grill for burgers and milkshakes."

"Awww, did you share straws and drink your malts together while making heart eyes at each other?"

"Shut up," I nudge her foot with mine. She sticks her tongue out at me.

"Knock, knock," a voice interrupts us, and I look up to see the lavender-haired subject of our conversation.

"Colin!" I exclaim as I almost topple out of my chair from surprise. He's over to me in two strides and steadies me.

"Careful there, Blooms." He winks at me.

Gri is watching our interaction carefully. She catches my eye and mouths, 'Blooms?' with raised eyebrows. I give her a small smile before turning my attention back to Colin.

"What are you doing here? I thought you were working on the vases today." I find myself standing so I can be closer to him. My gut has started its free fall again.

"I am. I just wanted to take a break and come say hi and bye to everyone since I didn't get a chance to do that last month. I also figured you could use a pick-me-up since you were up late last night." He hands out an iced lavender latte from Micah's coffee cart. Looking over to Gri, he holds out a beverage for her. "I knew you were going to be here too, Gri, so I asked Micah to make you whatever your usual is."

"Thanks," she says sincerely and takes the iced chai from him.

"You're welcome. I'm glad you're here today. It's a relief to know that Addison has a reliable booth buddy in case he needs it today." He pauses and turns his focus back to me. "Actually, that was part of why I wanted to come by. I wanted to see if you needed a break or anything to do a walk around since it's the last show of the season. I also figured I could stand in line for food, so you would have time to eat without having to be away from the booth for too long."

Gri fakes swooning. I pointedly ignore her dramatics.

"You really don't mind?" I ask.

"Not at all." He smiles at me and then reaches out to squeeze my upper arm. "Besides, I'm sure Gri here wants to grill me about my intentions or give me a shovel talk because of all the time we've been spending together."

Gri shrugs. "He's not wrong."

I give Colin an apologetic smile. "Sorry for whatever she tells you. Chances are it's a lie."

Colin laughs as I stick my tongue out at my best friend, and she returns one. After all these years, Gri and I act more like siblings than I do with my own sisters.

I grab my phone and head out to go visit with some of the other vendors.

It doesn't take me too long to do my rounds, but I also don't want to deprive either of my best friends the opportunity to talk about what they need to cover. I stop down the row at Lane's booth to check in with them. They've got a new tent reinforced with extra weights, but their summer has been particularly disastrous this year, and I want to make sure there haven't been any avoidable ones today.

So far, so good, but I don't know how long that will last as a dad and his kid come into the booth right as I'm leaving. The kid is eating a PB&J, so I make a mental note to bring Lane some cleaning supplies later because PB&J + kids + shiny reflective surfaces generally equal a mess.

I'm about to make it back to my booth when I hear Colin's animated voice and decide to slip into Gri's booth to see what she thinks since he's distracted. I watch as Colin gestures around the booth, explaining things to potential customers.

"Oh, okay, so these are really cool, right? Addison, the artist, makes all the flowers by hand, which is awesome in its own right, but then, he puts together bouquets that have secret messages in them. I say bouquets, but technically, they're called tussie-mussies."

I try not to snort as I listen to him ramble on.

"Careful Ads, your heart eyes are showing." Gri sidles up next to me and gently nudges me with her elbow. "I'm impressed, though. He does your spiel better than I ever did. He sold three message arrangements. Must be nice to have someone who will let you go on about floriography."

I lean into her and sigh. "Yeah, he's great... Fuck, I'm scared."

"Be scared, but keep moving forward. Think about how many times you had an unsuccessful seedling transfer. Did that stop you from building your garden? No. You kept going and tried again, learning from the mistakes you made previously and applying that knowledge to become better. I'm not saying that you shouldn't be cautious and throw all your gut instincts to the wind, but you should follow your heart. And I think that heart is leading you to that man over there. He's head over heels for you, by the way."

"Did he say that?" I look at her, disbelieving.

"No, but the way he talks about you and the care and

enthusiasm he gives when talking to customers about your stuff shows it."

I smile softly and bite my bottom lip. Am I willing to give a relationship with Colin a shot despite my track record?

"I need a little more time to think about things."

"Understandable. But don't wait too long. I don't want you to feel like you missed out on life because you were too cautious."

Gri gives me a side hug and goes over to talk to a couple that just walked into her booth.

"Hey, you're back." Colin greets me with a wide grin. "I sold a couple bouquets for you." He hands over the key to the cash box.

"I heard. You do my spiel better than I do. I might have to figure out a way to put you on my payroll if you keep it up." I lean into his side and let myself hold my body there a beat longer than is normal for two guys who are 'just friends.'

"Did Gri scare you off?" I ask after we break apart.

"Nah, she was cool," Colin answers. "Though I didn't know you went through a kilt phase." He smiles at me, and the way it reaches his gorgeous grey eyes and lights them up like the sun breaking through clouds.

"I'm Scottish," I exclaim. "Of course I went through a kilt phase. It's part of my heritage."

"When you were 29?" Gri calls over as her customers head out.

I give her a stink eye. We really are like siblings.

"She knows too much."

"It's okay. I bet you rocked the kilt."

"No, I really didn't." I smile at him.

"Did you want me to go grab you both some food?"

"Sure. Can you bring something over to Lane for me on your way back?"

"Yeah, no problem."

"Great." I go into my storage area and pull out some all-purpose cleaner and paper towels. "There was a kid with a PB&J getting there when I was leaving, and with Lane's track record..."

Colin takes the cleaning supplies from me. "Got it. I'll stop there first. Gri, do you want lunch?"

"Yes, please. I'll have a chicken Caesar salad wrap and fries, please and thank you."

"You got it." He turns back to me. "Did you want your usual shawarma wrap today or something else?"

"The usual is perfect. Thanks."

Gri waits until Colin leaves before practically accosting me.

"Okay, yeah. If you decide to go ahead with this, I wholeheartedly approve and give my blessing. Addison, the man knows your lunch and coffee orders, and let's not forget how well he did with your customers earlier. And for some reason, I trusted him to take care of you last month despite his earlier angry reaction."

"Thanks, Gri. I'll take that under advisement."

More customers come through the booths and we spend time alternating between making sales and talking about life until Colin gets back with our lunch.

"Lane says thank you for the cleaning supplies." He sets down the lunch containers on my checkout counter, nudging Gri's over towards her booth. "The kid did a real number on the lower ones. That poor dad, though. Apparently, his daughter was practicing her skirt twirling after being told to stop touching things and bumped into one of the lower mirrors, knocking it over. Thankfully, Lane had put down those mats you recommended, so nothing broke, but it bounced, and the frame got scratched up. The dad was apologizing profusely when I got there. At least he bought the scuffed-up mirror."

"Yikes. Well, that's one way to make a sale." I shrug, taking my food. "Oh, this is so good."

Colin moans in agreement, and I feel my dick start to stir in a way it hasn't in years. My eyes go wide, and I cross my legs as casually as I can. *What the fuck is happening right now!?* I have to think of something other than finding a way to be the cause of those pleasured moans. He has some sauce on the side of his mouth, and I act before thinking, reaching out and wiping the sauce away, and then I lick it off my finger. *What. The. Fuck!? Who am I?* Maybe Gri was right, and I do have a fever or something.

Colin looks at me with heat and longing in his eyes. I break away from his gaze and look over to see Gri with her mouth agape. She's never seen me act this way. I don't blame her obvious expression, though. I've never seen me act this way either. There's something about Colin that brings my guard down and lets me just be in the moment.

I need to think of something to break the sexual tension in the air between us. Oh, yes. My birthday.

"Hey, uh, I meant to talk to both of you about something." I stammer.

"What's up?" Colin asks, his husky voice going straight through me.

My dick, apparently. Shut up, brain.

"Uhh, my birthday is coming up in a couple weeks, and I wanted to invite you both and Jodie to dinner with my family."

"Finally," Gri exclaims. "I've been waiting for this year's details."

"Uh, it'll be on my birthday, so the 17th. No need to bring anything, just yourselves."

"I'll be there." Colin smiles over at me. The electricity between us has lessened to a manageable amount, but there's still an air of longing coming from him.

"Great. It'll be at the house. I'll send you both details

when I confirm them with Mama, but I wanted to make sure you had the date reserved."

"Perfect."

Yeah, I think it just might be.

CHAPTER TWENTY-FOUR
Colin

Addison's been acting different lately. We've been meeting up with more regularity over the past few weeks. Sometimes we go out and have more "not dates", but most of the time, we've just been hanging out at one of our houses and tandem working on our respective parts of the collaboration.

None of that would seem out of the ordinary, except that Addison has been a little more withdrawn and reserved in his platonic affection. It's hard to describe; it doesn't feel like he's pulling away, but more like he's holding himself back.

I'm not gonna lie, it's been a little frustrating. I'm not frustrated at Addison, though; I'm mad at the assholes who hurt him and made him scared to love. Not that we're in love or anything, but yeah... maybe one day. There have been too many nights when I've gone to bed wishing he was next to me so I could hold him and protect him from any future hurt the world might try to inflict on him. It's not a realistic promise. Even if he decided to give me a chance, I can't promise that I'll never make mistakes that hurt him again, but I'm doing my damndest to avoid that. Addison deserves all the best things in this world, and I want to be the one who gives it to him. So I'm waiting and continuing to work on myself in the meantime.

Tonight is Addison's birthday dinner. I thought about having flowers delivered to their work since it's also their actual birthday, but I didn't want to overstep or cause him any panic. I also know his ex and his new partner are florists, and I can imagine that having a flower delivery might be triggering. A panic attack or even any steps towards one is the last thing I want to give them for a birthday gift. So the actual gift will have to wait for tonight.

I go into my studio and check on the vase that I thankfully finished just in time. I'm going to hate to see it leave the studio, but I'm happy that it will go to Blooms. This vase has been one of the most time-intensive and technically fulfilling projects that I've completed thus far. It really pushed my limits in the best ways, and I got to have a lot of fun with fire while doing it.

Not every ceramic artist plays around with raku kilns, and those that do usually don't do so in their backyard. But when your best friend is a firefighter, sometimes there are perks you can take advantage of. Mine just happens to be ridiculously hot fires in controlled areas with professional supervision—thanks, Trevor.

Raku firing has always been my thrill-seeking adventure of choice, and this project took it to a whole new level. I think having an emotional connection to the piece I was working on added to the increased adrenaline I felt through the whole process.

After I made all those vases the night Addison told me about his past, I decorated all but one of them with my normal process, but my gut told me that I needed to save one of them specifically for Addison. And then, when he confided in me that his favorite flowers were the overlooked ones, especially dandelions, I knew that I had to incorporate them, but I wasn't sure how. I've seen so many carved and glaze-painted dandelions that doing that didn't feel special enough. I thought about pressing them into the vase to create a relief, but that didn't seem right either. Then I remembered a technique that would combine my love of raku with the use of actual dandelions in a way that would bring my vision to life. After speaking with some of the experts down at the ceramic supply center, I got to work.

After hours of collecting flowers, burnishing, creating a batch of terra sig—a process which takes three days to complete—and polishing, I was finally ready for my very first ever saggar firing. The whole process took me about a week from start to finish, which may not seem like much, but let me tell you, every stage was intense. Half the time, I was holding my breath, knowing that one little misstep could derail the entire project. In the end, the work was worth it. I have the most gorgeous piece I've ever made, ready to go for the person I care for the most.

The copper and cobalt had a gorgeous effect in outlining the dandelions and thistles that encircle the vase, leaving gorgeous imprints of negative space among the pinks, blues, purples, and smokey greys.

I definitely will be trying this method again, but probably not until after we've finished the pieces for NAUA.

I pick up the smooth vase and bring it inside, where I have a bag waiting so I can wrap it. It seems cheap to use a paper bag to hold this vessel, even if it does have handles. I tried to find something more suitable, but honestly, outside of a custom crate that I wouldn't have time to commission, the only thing that came to mind was a silk bag, and the closest thing I could find was a pillowcase, which is most decidedly not the same thing.

Sighing, I carefully wrap the vase in tissue paper and place it in the brown kraft paper bag I use for the rest of my ceramics before heading to my truck and driving over to Addison's house.

When I get there, I can tell that it's going to be a fun night. There's music playing around back and balloons tied to the front porch. A sign on the door is pulled from Bilbo's party in *The Fellowship of the Ring*, but since I am here on party business, it doesn't apply to me, and I make my way inside. Addison texted me earlier to just come in when I got here, and since it's their birthday, I follow their instructions.

When I get to the kitchen, I'm greeted with a round of hugs by Addison's moms. His sister Aisling is talking to who I can only assume is his other sister and her husband based on the woman's curly red hair and nose which look just like Addison's.

Addison, Gri, and Jodie come in from the back patio, and I see that Jodie has traded her rollator for a cane today. I smile when I see the birthday boy.

"Hi," I say, the smile growing bigger when Addison sees me.

"Hi." They return my smile, and the blush that I've loved on them since the first time I saw it takes its usual place on their face.

We stand there, oblivious to what everyone else in the room is doing, caught in each other's gazes. I take a tentative step towards them and hold out the bag. Why am I so awkward? *Say something, Colin.*

"Happy birthday, Blooms." We close the gap.

"Thanks, Cluaran." They reach out and take the bag. Our fingers touch during the exchange, and goosebumps shoot up my arms like wildfire at the contact. I've got it bad.

"Now kiss!" A voice says off to my left. The illusion breaks as I whirl around to see everyone watching us. I can practically feel the heat radiating off Addison's skin as I'm sure their blush deepens. Gri is being too obvious to be innocent, so I fix her with the practiced glare I've given

Trevor way too many times to count.

I turn back to Addison to see them sending a similar look towards their best friend. Jodie swats at her arm.

"Ingrid Tennant, behave," she chastises.

"Sorry, Ads," she apologizes before turning to her girlfriend and kissing her.

"What's in the bag?" Aisling pipes up as she joins us in the middle of the kitchen.

"Yeah, what'd you get, Addi?" Their other sister asks as she approaches. "Hi, I'm Gillian, the other sister, and this is my husband, Clay."

"Nice to meet you both, I'm Colin." I shake their hands and then turn my attention back to Addison as they're opening my gift.

I watch as Addison's expression changes from jovial to awestruck as they remove the final pieces of tissue paper.

"Colin, I... This is... How?" They carefully trace their hands over the shadowed imprints left by the dandelions and thistles, turning the vase slowly in their hands, admiring every unique reaction the chemicals created during the firing.

"Lots of burnishing and patience," I say.

"But you hate burnishing."

"You're worth the risk of carpal tunnel," I admit, and I can practically see my own heart eyes as I watch them admire my work. They carefully pass it off to one of the others, and the next thing I know, they've stepped into my space and are throwing their arms around me.

"Thank you for making me feel so cherished and seen," they whisper in my ear.

My arms close around them, and we are once again caught up in our own world. In this moment, Addison is all that matters.

"Thank you for inspiring me," I reply, placing my hands on either side of their face and gently pulling him down towards me so I can kiss their forehead. "And happy birthday, Blooms."

Their blue eyes meet mine, and I can hear the same siren song I heard the first time we met, enticing me to stay trapped in their gaze forever. And I would. I'd sacrifice nearly anything to have Addison keep looking at me like this, with such affection and an ember of longing pulsing and growing brighter.

CHAPTER TWENTY-FIVE
Addison (they/he)

It's time. Gri was right. I'm 33 now, and I can either wait in fear and keep denying myself any chance at being happy with someone else or I can take a risk, and everything he's showed me so far gives me hope that Colin will be worth the risk.

Longing radiates throughout my body, originating from the spot on my forehead where Colin placed his gentle kiss. I drop my hand to his, entwining our fingers, and quietly lead him outside to a spot that is quickly becoming less mine and more ours.

Neither of us speaks until we are nestled in the moss patch under the old oak tree. I avoid the instinct to look up at the house because I'm pretty sure at least one person will be watching out the kitchen window. I keep my focus on the man in front of me. The one who has somehow slipped past every wall I've built around my heart and brought it back to life. The previously cracked and cooled heart is roaring like the raku kiln Colin uses to fire my favorite of his art.

He sits across from me now, nervously playing with his lip ring and running his fingers through the moss below us.

"Colin," I start. "I can't do this anymore. It's not fair to you."

His face falls. "I understand. I'm sorry, Blo—Addison. I can just go."

He starts to get up, but I place my hand on his to stop his movement.

"No, that's not what I meant." He settles back down, and I rub my hands across my face. "I can't keep denying this connection between us. I've tried, but you've shown me time and time again that you aren't anything like anyone I've ever met before. I don't want to hold back anymore."

His expression brightens with every word I say, so I continue.

"I really like you, Colin. I tried not to, but you make me feel safe in a way I've never experienced with someone outside my family and Gri. You have become my best friend over these past few months and more than that over the last month. I wake up every day, and you're the first person on my mind. I can't stop thinking about you and wanting to be with you all the time. Fuck, Colin, I've even had *feelings* for you." I gesture down at my crotch. His eyes go wide, and he bites back a smile.

"Whenever we are together, my body feels like it's a piece of metal, and you're a magnet pulling me towards you. I want to be touching you all the time. The little arm squeezes and hugs, and gods, that kiss to my forehead. Mo chridhe, I could just melt. I put up so many walls, and you bypassed all of them, not through force but with the key to unlock the doors that I put there as failsafes. You've let me lead at every step, making sure I'm comfortable and safe and confident in whatever we've done. I don't want to keep putting up these fences. Colin, I..."

Here goes nothing.

"Colin, I'd really like to kiss you."

I look up and meet his eyes.

"Please," he whispers in that husky voice that wakes up my dick every time.

I don't hesitate any longer. My lips are on his, and I'm pouring every pent-up emotion and longing hunger I've been feeling into this kiss. One moment, I feel like I'm falling, and Colin's pillowy lips catch me before I get hurt. The next, he nips my bottom lip, and I'm sent flying. He tastes like butterscotch, and I'm grounded by his campfire and earth scents. Together, they blend and fill my senses. I reach up to hold the back of his head so I can deepen the kiss. We've shifted, and I'm practically sitting on his lap now, straddling his legs. His hands encourage my closeness as they rub my back in a motion that both calms any pending anxiety and urges me to get closer to chase this connection. I run my fingers through his thistle-colored hair and melt into his embrace.

His mouth leaves mine, but he doesn't pull away. Instead, he moves his way down to my shoulder, holding me close and kissing my jaw, my neck, and my collarbone on the way. If we weren't physically connected, I'm pretty sure I'd float away from the ecstasy.

His lips return to mine, and unlike the hungry kisses from before his wandering interlude, this is a soft one. He's in the lead this time, pouring in every ounce of the care and affection that I've grown to expect from him lately.

We finally pull apart and he looks wrecked. His hair is sticking up like an anime character or any boy band member from the early 2000s. His eyes are dazed and he blinks a few times to pull everything back into focus.

"Wow."

"Yeah," I laugh and blush, burying my face in his neck.

"Blooms, that was hands down the best kiss I've had in my life." He chuckles, and I feel his chest move with the laughter. I haven't moved out of his lap, and his arms stay wrapped around me, holding me and showing me that he wants me to be right where I am.

I feel him turn his head, and he plants a gentle kiss to

the crown of my head, right above my bun. I sigh and nuzzle closer. His hands resume their soothing pattern. I don't want to leave this bubble, but I know that we can't stay here forever.

Right as I have that thought, I hear Aisling's voice call from the patio.

"Hey lovebirds, if you've stopped sucking face, Mum says dinner is ready."

I groan.

"Can't we just stay here and not go back?"

"It's your birthday, Blooms. We can do whatever you want."

I give him a squeeze before slightly pulling back so I can see his face again. He has a little dirt streaked across his cheek, and I chuckle as I wipe it away.

"So uh, before we go back. I just want to see where your head is at." I start, nervously.

"I'm all in if you'll have me," Colin responds without hesitation.

"Absolutely." I smile, and he shifts to give me a brief kiss before gently moving me off of his lap and standing up.

He holds out his hand to help me up.

"Come on, Blooms. Time to go meet the family."

"You've already met my family," I say, a little confused.

"True, but not as your boyfriend." He winks and pulls me into his arms.

Boyfriend. I have a boyfriend. Colin is my boyfriend. For the first time in nearly 15 years, that thought fills me with giddiness and warmth instead of sending a shockwave of terror through me. I lace our fingers together, and we head back to the house.

More than Buds, We're Blossoming

- Stargazing by Myles Smith

- So High School by Taylor Swift

- I Really Like You by Carly Rae Jepsen

- Sweet Symphony (feat. Chris Stapleton) by Joy Oladokun

- Blush (Only You) by Plumb

- Butterflies by Kacey Musgraves

- Big Love Ahead by Mon Rovîa

SPOTIFY

APPLE MUSIC

https://bit.ly/TDATT-playlists

CHAPTER TWENTY-SIX
Colin

It's been three days since Addison and I made things official, and tonight, we're going on our first date. I went back and forth on things that I wanted to experience with him. The list is long, but we have time to explore it. I just hope I made the right choice for our first date.

I leave my house at 5:30 and make the drive over to the Stamp-Baird residence. The bouquet of wildflowers sits in a mason jar secured in the cup holder. I checked every stem's meaning before adding it to the bouquet. I didn't want any ominous messaging to put a shadow on our new relationship.

I'm nervous as I pull into the now-familiar driveway of my boyfriend's house. The thought makes me smile. *I have a boyfriend.* I asked if he wanted me to use a different term for him, but he confided that he love the idea of being someone's boyfriend, so that's what we're using. I love it, too. I haven't had the best experience when it's come to dating in the past. Most of my dates haven't progressed past one or two dates, and the few relationships I've had were short-lived. My history doesn't worry me, though. I recognized a while ago that I wasn't in a place where I could sustain a relationship and be the man that my partner needed.

I've gone on a few dates and had a couple hookups in

the past couple years, but nothing serious until I met Addison. I've mostly taken the past few years to work on myself and really learn who I am as an individual.

Taking a deep breath, I grab the flowers and head up to the front door. As soon as I knock, Addison's moms are there, opening the door, and his sister, Aisling, is hovering behind them.

"Hey Colin, come on in. Addison is just finishing getting ready," Lolli welcomes me in and hugs me when I cross the threshold. I'm careful not to drop the flowers.

"Oooh, flowers! Are those for me?" Dr. Siobhan teases before wrapping me up in a hug as well.

"Sorry, Dr. B," I say as we pull away, and a big dopey grin finds its way on my face. "These are for my boyfriend."

"Awwwwww," the three women playfully tease my besotted tone.

"Are you badgering my boyfriend?" Addison's voice calls from down the hall. In four long strides, he's in front of me and I didn't realize my smile could grow bigger, but it does. It feels like it's gonna take over my whole face.

"Hi, Blooms," I say softly. "I brought you some flowers."

I hand the mason jar out to him, careful not to let go until I feel it secure in his hands. His gaze takes in each stem of the carefully hand-picked and curated arrangement, and his smile rivals my own by the time he passes it off to his sister. Addison takes my hand in his.

"It's perfect. I love it. Thank you." He kisses me on the cheek, and now I'm the one blushing. Three things I never imagined ever happening are all taking place at the same time. I'm a boy being shown affection by his boyfriend in front of loving parents and siblings who affirm and support us. It's almost enough to bring tears to my eyes, but I refocus on being in the moment instead of mourning what I'll never have with my own living flesh and blood.

"I'm so glad. Are you ready to go?" I ask as he entwines

his fingers with mine.

"Yeah, let's blow this popsicle stand."

I laugh.

"Have him home by curfew, young man. And no funny business," Dr. Baird sternly instructs with a mocking tone.

"Hand to heart, I would never." I put my free hand to my heart as Addison protests.

"Mum, I'm 33. I don't have a curfew."

"Oh, that's right, we forgot to give you one." She turns to her wife. "Lolli, what do you think? Is 10:30 too late for a 33 year old?"

"Have fun, you two," Lolli laughs, dismissing her wife's question.

We head out to my truck, and I do the chivalrous thing of opening Addison's door for him and making sure he's settled before closing it.

When I round the front of the truck, I notice Aisling in the doorway of the house, and she signals that she's watching me before turning around and retreating further into the house. I laugh and climb in to the truck cab.

"Could they be more embarrassing?" Addison asks as I get in. Clearly, he saw his sister's vaguely threatening gesture, too.

"Probably," I answer honestly.

"Yeah, you're probably right." He looks over at me and slides over on the bench seat until he's right up against my side. Score one for the old-school truck.

"Hi." I turn my head to look at him. My grin has simmered down to a smirk, but it's still very evident that I'm happy to be there with them.

"Can I kiss you?"

"Any time you'd like, Blooms. Unless I say otherwise, you have blanket consent. Enthusiastic blanket consent."

I turn my torso towards him and meet his kiss with my own. It's hungry but reserved. As much as I want to have another make-out session with him, doing it in front of a potential audience of his moms and sister isn't exactly my thing. We can save the heavy stuff for later, as long as he wants it.

My fingers play with some of the stray curls at the base of his neck. He has his hair up in its usual bun, but some of the shorter strands aren't long enough to be tied up.

Addison smells like his garden and tastes sweet, like honey and lavender.

"You taste delicious," I pull away to remark before going back in for more.

"Mmmm." Addison's pleasurable moans send a spark of lust all the way down to my dick. He briefly deepens the kiss before pulling back. "We should probably head out before giving them another show."

"Good call."

He scoots away, and I adjust the packer in my pants, trying to give my T-boner a bit of relief before starting the truck and backing out of the driveway.

"Where are we headed?" Addison asks when we finally get on the road.

"I figured we'd do dinner first, and then I have an activity planned."

"An activity?" He waggles his eyebrows at me.

"Calm down, Casanova. It's low-key, but I want to keep it a surprise. Though, we could absolutely skip it if you wanted to do other things. No pressure though." I add that last bit to let him know that I don't want to rush into anything he isn't ready for, and I know that we're gonna need a long conversation about boundaries and consent before we get more intimate than make out sessions.

"Thanks, mo chridhe." He leans into my side from where he's buckled in the middle of the bench seat. I'm tempted to put my arm around him, but I need to keep two hands on the wheel so I'm not more distracted than I already am.

I pull into the parking lot for the local pizza place we both love and give Addison a kiss on the forehead.

"I'll be right back. This isn't our final stop."

It doesn't take me long to pick up the pre-ordered pizzas and get back on the road towards our true destination. We drive for about 20 minutes until we're outside the city. I pull off the road down a fairly hidden path.

"If I didn't know you better, I'd be worried right now," Addison jokes.

"Nothing to worry about. Welcome to my sanctuary," I say as I maneuver the truck to a clearing that overlooks a valley. I back it up to the overlook and turn it off. "Come on, we're having a truck bed picnic."

I get out of the pickup and head to the back where I have a duffel bag full of pillows and blankets ready to be set up similarly to the night we went to the Stand and Grill. This set up is a bit more cozy since I had time to actually plan it.

Once we're settled in with our pizzas, I look out at the beautiful sight before us.

"This is one of my favorite places to go when I need inspiration," I admit. "When I was having a hard time, especially after Gram died, I would come out here and just be. Some of the most beautiful sunsets I've seen were witnessed from this spot."

Addison cuddles closer to me. "That's beautiful. Thank you for bringing me to your sanctuary."

"I figured it was only fair since you've shared yours with me." I lean on him a bit more. The September air is just starting to chill and gives us a reason to stay close.

"It's fitting that you call this your sanctuary."

"Why's that?"

"There's a patch of Queen Anne's Lace over there." Addison points to a patch of the off-white flowers with the purple hearts in the center. "Queen Anne's Lace represents 'sanctuary.' The shape of the top resembles a shield protecting everything below it."

I smile softly and put my arm around my boyfriend, nuzzling close to his side. We sit like that for a while, eating in silence and watching birds fly across the sky. It's not long before the sun starts to set, and beautiful reds, purples, and blues paint the sky before us.

"I get a lot of my raku glaze inspirations from watching the sunsets out here- all the different color combinations that I haven't thought of or patterns when clouds change the texture. It's gorgeous."

"It is," Addison agrees.

When the sun has set, we start to pack up the blankets and pillows.

"I'm not ready to go home yet," Addison admits.

"Well, it's a good thing I had more planned for us."

"Really?"

"Yeah. If you're up for it, I have another activity planned." I grin at him.

Addison grins back and hops into the cab, scooting over to take the middle seat next to me. I secure the duffel bag in the back and climb in beside him, starting the truck and driving us back to my house.

CHAPTER TWENTY-SEVEN
Addison (he/they)

I'm a little confused when we pull up to Colin's house, but tonight has been pretty magical so far, so I'm trusting that he's got something fun in store for us.

I follow Colin as he gets out of the truck and leads me into the house, pulling me into a kiss when we get inside. Before either of us escalate the kiss into make-out territory, he pulls away and takes my hand.

"Come on. I have something fun planned in the studio."

"Lead the way, Cluaran." I smile and follow him out to the garage studio.

He turns on the lights and my breath catches as I see a number of electric votives on and setting a romantic mood.

"So I love the idea of those 'paint your own pottery' places, but there isn't really one around here, and I have a perfectly good ceramic studio at my disposal, so I thought it would be fun to get a little messy and play around with the wheel a bit."

"Like *Ghost?*" I ask skeptically.

Colin rolls his eyes. "Ugh, that scene is so unrealistic. I like you, Blooms, but if I'm trying to throw something on the wheel and you're just trying to wipe raw clay all over my arms, we're gonna need to have a conversation. Besides, who wants drying slip all over them when they're trying to have sexy fun times? It would be so gross and uncomfortable as it dries."

I try to stifle my laughter at his rant, but it bursts out of me anyways. "Got it," I chuckle.

"There are ways to do it where it's intimate, but that scene is most definitively not it."

"Prove it." I goad him.

"Which part?"

"That tandem wheel throwing can be intimate."

"Okay," he says as he claps his hands together. "Let's do this."

Colin goes over to the coat rack and grabs an apron off of it. He hands it to me and as I'm putting it on, I notice that it's longer than your normal kitchen apron and has split panels to cover each leg. I watch as he prepares the rest of the wheel throwing area with the tools and materials we're going to need. When he's got everything set up, he motions me over.

"Your seat, my Blooms." He's called me that before, but the possessive signifier ahead of his nickname for me causes my stomach to swoop, and I give him a kiss before sitting down on the stool he has set out for me.

"Scooch up to the edge so I can get behind you," he instructs. I do as he says and feel him nestle in behind me. We connect at the hips, and I can feel his packer press into my ass. I have to bite back a moan, but that makes me smile to myself. *Welcome back, libido.*

"Before we start, is there anything in particular that you want to make?" Colin's question breaks me away from the fantasy.

I think for a moment. "What's easier for a beginner—a mug or a vase?"

"A wide-mouth vase would probably be the easiest. It's similar to a mug, but without having to worry about a handle."

"Okay, let's do that."

"Great."

I try to pay attention as he takes me through the steps in getting the clay ready for forming through something called coning. When he folds himself over me in order to get my body into the proper position for centering the clay, I have to stop listening for a moment so I can remind myself to breathe. It's been so long since I've willingly been this close to another person. Every point of contact is sending heat coursing through my body. I'm glad this apron is made from a heavy canvas because I'm finding it extremely distracting to follow Colin's instructions with a growing boner, and I'm sure if he saw the effect he has on me, he'd be distracted, too.

Somehow, we make it into the forming stage and Colin manipulates my hands into the shape needed to thin out the walls and draw them up higher, guiding me through the right amount of pressure to apply.

When I'm satisfied with the shape of my piece, we slow the wheel down to stop it but don't make any movements to get up. Colin wraps his less dirty arms around me and kisses the side of my neck. My head tilts back to rest on his shoulder. I'm lost in his affection. I go to put my hand in his hair when he swerves away. I snap out of the blissful state I was falling into as a cold wave of rejection washes over me.

He must feel me stiffen because he goes back in for another kiss to my neck before speaking.

"Blooms, you've got clay all over your hands, and it's a pain in the ass to get out of hair. Especially with the way you tease mine." He winks and kisses me again. "Let's get you cleaned up and go inside. I want to make sure we talk through some stuff before going further. I want to know your boundaries and limits and make sure you're aware of mine."

The chill is gone, and I'm swept up in the warmth of the care that Colin has exuded every day I've known him.

He leads me over to the sink and leaves me to clean up before returning to my creation and getting it off the wheel and onto the drying rack he showed me when I toured the studio the first time.

"I see what you mean about drying clay being unsexy. My skin feels so dry."

"Yeah, it'll do that. I have some lotion inside that I'll let you use."

When we're both cleaned up to a satisfactory point, Colin comes over and pulls me into a hug, tilting my head down so he can kiss my forehead. I am quickly becoming addicted to that particular sign of his affection. My eyes flutter closed, and I sigh contentedly.

"Come on, let's go inside."

I follow as Colin leads me back to the living room and pulls me into his lap just like he did the day of his emotional hangover, though this time, there's a playful, lighthearted air around us.

CHAPTER TWENTY-EIGHT
Colin

Addison feels really great in my arms and on my lap. I could easily spend all night teasing little sounds of pleasure from him and seeing just how deep I can make his blush go, but we need to talk before we get too far into things tonight.

I hate this conversation, but I know we can't avoid it. It would be so much easier if I was cis. I have no doubts that Addison will be understanding, but the fact that I have to have this conversation at all can amp up my anxiety and trigger my dysphoria.

"Hey, Blooms?" I pull back from our kiss and see my boyfriend's lust-filled eyes. "Can we talk about boundaries and limits and stuff before we get too swept away tonight?"

"Yeah." He shakes his head like he's trying to clear the haze. "That's a good idea."

Addison slides off my lap, and we turn to face each other. He doesn't move away, though, and I feel like keeping a physical connection is going to be important in keeping us both grounded while we talk through things. His knee touches mine, and I hold out my hand as an offering to hold his if he needs it. He does.

"Do you want me to go first?" I ask tentatively.

"Sure." Addison bites his lip.

"Okay, well, first things first. In case you were unaware, I'm trans," I say as a way to try and lighten the tension building in the room. It works. Addison rolls his eyes and nudges my knee with his.

"You're such a dork, Colin."

"I know." I wink before continuing, "So my hope for this talk right now is to make sure that we're both comfortable with each other and with communicating about sex. I also want to make sure that we're clear when it comes to expectations and boundaries. I don't want to do anything that you're not into, and I hope that you'll respect my limits, too-"

"I will," Addison interjects.

"I have no doubts you will." I lift his hand to mine and kiss it. "I want you to always feel safe, protected, and heard when you're with me. I know that I do when I'm with you.

"So right off the bat, I want to reassure you that no matter what we decide to do, I won't get pregnant. I got a hysto right after college. With that said, though, I don't like front hole penetration, so one of my limits is that we don't do that."

Addison nods in understanding. I take a deep breath and continue.

"I am on PrEP, and I've had my HPV vaccine. I always use condoms with one-off partners or until after an exclusive partner and I get tested. I was tested after my last partner, and my results were negative, but if we eventually decide to do more than making out—which I'm fine with, by the way. I've been loving it. But if you want to do more, I'd really like for us to get tested before we do any sort of penetrative sex. I'm exclusively committed to you and have no desire to have multiple partners. That's where my head is at."

"Mine too." Addison's voice is a little tight. "I agree with everything you're saying. I'm not sure if I'm going to be ready for penetrative sex, but I agree that getting tested before ditching condoms is a smart idea."

"Okay, great." I pause to think before getting into this next part. I had a feeling that penetration was going to be a concern, and I'm hoping I can ease Addison's mind.

"So I use prosthetics. I have no desire to get more surgery at this point in my life. I'm happy packing every day and using a prosthetic with a partner. I've been on Testosterone since I was in high school, so I do have a T-dick. Most of the time, I use the prosthetics to help with stimulation, but I am also okay with oral without it as long as you avoid my front hole."

"Got it," Addison assures me. I wait to see if he wants to continue or if he wants me to go on. The hard part for me is over.

He takes a deep breath and starts. "I don't want to bottom."

"Okay," I squeeze his hand.

"Liam hurt me, and I don't know if I'll ever be in a mental place to do that. I trust you, but that's a hard limit for me. Maybe we can revisit it later–"

"We don't need to," I cut him off. "Blooms, I want you to tell me what you need to feel good so I can give that to you. In my mind, you will always come first. I have toys I can use if I really feel the need to fuck something. Bottoming is a hard limit for you, and that's great for me to know. I don't need to put my dick in you to show you how much I care and how much you turn me on."

I waggle my eyebrows at him to keep him present in the moment. He laughs and rolls his eyes playfully.

"Thanks, Cluaran." I wait, giving him the space he needs to continue however he wants. "So I've never tried it before, but I might be okay with topping if that's something you'd be into."

"If you want to try it, I'm more than willing to be your

experiment buddy, but there's no pressure if you decide against it."

"I've really loved making out with you, so that one can definitely continue. I'm also cool with hand jobs and blow jobs as long as you don't fuck my face or force me to deep throat. Putting your hands in my hair during oral also gets a green light as long as the touch is caressing rather than forceful. And please, no degradation. It brings up too much."

"I understand, and I can agree with all that," I assure him. He smiles and continues with a little more confidence.

"Basically, everything up to penetration is great. Hand jobs, blow jobs, rimming—God, I've missed rimming. I'll need to go slow with it, though, because it's been a while, and it honestly might be a little triggering."

"Understood. I'm also good with all of that." I'm practically salivating at the thought of being able to get my tongue on his hole, but I've been patient this far. I can keep waiting.

"I'm going to need to take things slow, and please know that my body reacts differently. I'm not always going to be in the mood, but I don't want you to think that means I don't care about you. And sometimes, I'm going to be in the mood mentally, but my body won't work with me, but in those instances, we can always use toys if you're okay with that."

"I'm very okay with toys. I'm happy to follow your lead here. If there are moments when I need to get off and you're not up for playing around, are you okay knowing that I'll be masturbating, or would you rather not know?"

He thinks for a moment before responding, "You don't have to tell me every time. I mean, you don't need my permission to take care of yourself. That would be absurd and a level of controlling that doesn't make sense for me. Just don't lie to me about it."

"Easy enough." I lean over and kiss his forehead.

"Mmmm. More of that. All of that. The little affection. I love that."

"Happily." I pull him into my arms so we can cuddle and hopefully make out some more.

"I know it's a little late, but do you want to watch a movie or something?"

"But what about my 10:30 curfew?" Addison teases.

"Yeah, babe, we're already past that point." I smack my lips to the side of his neck, laying a loud kiss there.

"Oh no," he protests with mock sincerity. "I'm gonna be in so much trouble." He smiles at me. "Yeah, let's watch something."

I throw on an episode of **The Great Pottery Throwdown** that I've already seen in the hopes that we'll ignore it and go back to making out.

Ten minutes later, Addison and I are both sucked into the show. We've moved to a lying position on the couch, and I have my arms wrapped around his waist while I spoon him.

"This is so cool. Have you ever tried it?"

"Raku? Yeah, I have a kiln out back. I usually do it at least once a month whenever Trevor can join."

"Why Trevor?"

"He's a firefighter, and since I live in a residential area, I've found it eases my neighbors' minds to have a professional on-site in case there are any issues."

"That's cool. Do you think I could be here next time you do it?"

"You'd want to?" I ask excitedly. He shifts and turns to face me.

"Yeah. It looks like it could be really fun."

"Oh, it is. But it's also pretty dangerous."

"I mean, there's fire involved. Danger kinda feels pretty obvious."

"I was thinking of raku firing the pieces for the exhibit. I think the crackle effect of the glazing will work with the story we're telling. Would you want to come for that one?"

"I'd love to."

"We could even prep the vase you threw tonight so it'd be ready to go into the kiln. That way, you could try it out if you want."

He surges forward, and his lips find mine with force, all pretense of watching the show long past. Kissing him is bliss; even the best television show could never compare. I let Addison lead, but any reservation or queasiness I was feeling earlier has dissipated since we've talked about how much we're willing to do.

We nip and pant against each other, kissing anywhere we can find in our current positions. Addison plays with my lip ring and runs his hands through my hair. I play with the hem of his shirt, paying close attention to any auditory or non-verbal cues that indicate he wants me to stop. When he just deepens the kiss, I let my fingertips brush the skin on his lower back, and when he melts at the touch rather than tensing up, I let my hands explore a little more, my full palm gently urging him closer to me. I can feel his hardening cock bump up against my leg. Instinctively, I grind against it. Addison lets out a moan with the little bit of friction and starts to chase it for himself.

I break apart our kisses, my hands still under his shirt while his are in my hair.

"Addison, can I touch you?"

"You already are," he teases, nipping at my bottom lip. I smile.

"I meant, can I touch your dick? I'd really like to give you one of those hand jobs we talked about."

After a brief pause, Addison nods. "Yes."

"Remember, if you need to stop at any time, just tell me.

Say 'apple pie' or something."

He chuckles and starts to take off his pants. I lick my bottom lip, biting my piercing at the slow and sensual sight before me. When his cock is free from its restraint, I surge forward and kiss him. He relaxes into my kiss, and I let him guide my hand where he wants it.

"Blooms," I say, looking at his face once my hand is in place, gripping his dick softly. "You're in control here. If you don't like something, just tell me, and if words are too hard, feel free to readjust me or tap me twice if you want me to stop." I try to impart all the sincerity and seriousness I can into my words.

He nods and smiles at me before kissing the tip of my nose. I start to slowly stroke the shaft, and it occurs to me that we should probably get some lube, but I don't want to get up and go into my bedroom. As if he's read my mind, Addison grabs the unscented lotion we used earlier after cleaning up from the studio and squirts some onto his palm before transferring it over to mine. With the lubrication, I continue stroking Addison's dick from base to tip and back again, applying pressure and staying attuned to his reactions. I end with a little twist near the head, and he gasps. I give him a few more strokes before I try that move again.

He turns towards me and straddles my lap. This new position makes it a little more difficult to grip him, but our bodies add some extra friction. He grinds down into my hips, and I almost lose my mind at the pleasure. I didn't change into my prosthetic before we started, but the friction from my packer rubbing against my t-dick is everything I need in this moment.

His mouth captures mine and we grind together. I'm stroking him with more intensity, trying to chase his pleasure. He moans into my mouth. I break our kiss and start moving my mouth down his neck. The blush I love so much has crept over every part of his body that I can see.Knowing that I'm the one causing him to be so aroused is heady.

Before I know it, his breathing starts to quicken, and he grinds against me faster. My arousal is distracting, but I'm determined to give Addison the orgasm he deserves.

"Col, I'm...I'm gonna..."

I quickly use my free hand to lift up my shirt so it won't get cum all over it. I keep stroking and kissing Addison.

"I've got you, Blooms. You can come. I'll catch you."

With those words of reassurance and a loud cry of ecstasy, Addison comes on my stomach, and he collapses towards me in a sticky, sweaty mess. I hold him as he comes down from the high of his orgasm, rubbing circles on his back and whispering sweet praises in his ear.

When some time has passed and he starts to squirm, I know I need to clean up this cum before it dries. I kiss his forehead and gently guide him off my lap, grabbing a leftover napkin from somewhere and using it to wipe up what I can.

After we've cleaned up a bit, Addison curls up into my side and I put my arm around him.

"Thank you," he says.

"Anytime, Blooms. Any time." I squeeze him tighter to me and kiss the back of his head.

We go back to rewatch the rest of the episode we missed and then another before I feel Addison start to drift off.

"Come on, boyfriend. As much as I want to invite you to stay the night, I should probably get you home."

He smiles up at me with sleep in his eyes and nods.

After I drop him off back at home and wait until he's made it safely inside, I head back to my house. It feels lonelier without my Blooms brightening up the space, but I still fall asleep with a smile on my face. It's becoming a habit of mine, and I don't hate it.

OCTOBER

CHAPTER TWENTY-NINE
Addison (he/they)

It's really difficult to focus on your dead-end job when you keep replaying the incredible orgasms you've had with your boyfriend in the last month. There was that first time on his couch, the time in the kitchen after Travis and Trevor left from brunch, in the back of Colin's truck up at the overlook where we went on our first date, behind the garden shed, and at my house on the rare occasion my family was gone. I smile and squirm in my seat thinking about the beard burn I got during our last tryst. I never realized that sex could be so fun. Colin has been the most attentive and caring partner I've ever had. It's healing to be with him.

We've gotten into a bit of a routine over the past month. He comes to my place for dinner and time with my family once a week, and I'm over at his house for Sunday brunch with the guys or to just hang out. I'm there most evenings, actually. And I'm going back tonight. We're planning on doing a final check of the figures for our NAUA exhibit before they get fired in the raku kiln tomorrow.

I'm really excited that I'll get to experience this with Colin. Travis and Trevor are coming over, and we've also invited Jodie, Gri, and Aisling to witness the process. We'll have a campfire and cookout after. I know Colin is nervous because it's a risky process and anything can go wrong, but he texted this morning that all of the pieces came out of their first firing in one piece without any signs of flaws, so that's a bit of a relief and hopefully a good omen as to how tomorrow will go.

Along with the exhibit pieces, we're also going to be firing the vase I threw on our first date. I get to decorate it tonight to get it ready. I'm pretty excited to see this through to completion. I snort at the thought of the word completion, getting side-eye from one of my coworkers. I'm pretty sure being with Colin has reverted my brain into thinking like a twelve-year-old boy.

When it's finally time to leave for the day, I shut everything down as quick as I can and fight the traffic to get over to Colin's house. He opens the door and pulls me into a tight embrace, and I melt as he reaches up to kiss my forehead. Ever since I admitted that I really like them, he goes out of his way to kiss me like that at every opportunity.

When we pull apart, Colin has yet again lifted my leather satchel onto his shoulder and holds out his hand to lead me further inside. As we make our way towards the kitchen, I notice a mouthwatering aroma. Colin's been cooking, and it smells amazing.

"What are you making?" I ask.

"Mushroom and goat cheese galette, steaks, and jalapeño poppers."

"Mmmm." I kiss his temple and follow him into the kitchen, hand in hand. "Any particular occasion or just in the mood?"

"Well, I mean, you're here, and that's a pretty special occasion in my opinion. And it's raku weekend. I'm hoping that a good night of good food and good company will kick off the weekend with all the good vibes we'll need for the firing tomorrow.

"Good." I wink. "Fingers crossed for all the good." I hold up the tangled fingers on my free hand. "I feel like I should have made a bouquet. Maybe I could clip some heather from my garden to bring over."

"What's the significance of heather?"

"Well, it means good luck and protection, and it's got a bit of Scottish folklore associated with it. It's actually the bloom that got me into floriography. Mum would keep a bundle of dried heather above her and Mama's bed. When I asked about it, she told me the story of the Scottish warrior who was dying in battle and sent a bundle of heather to his fiancée, whose tears turned it from purple to white. Despite her sorrows, she wished for white heather to bring good fortune to all who find it. When I first started researching floriography, I realized that Queen Victoria was a large proponent of sharing that story, and that's how it became the official meaning."

Colin listened, enraptured. "That's pretty awesome. I love learning about this stuff. And I love seeing you light up when you talk about it."

I feel my face start to blush. He's really good at making me do that.

"Thank you," I say sweetly and kiss his temple. "I have some in bloom still in the garden. I'll have to check in the morning to see if I can bring enough for a clipping tomorrow if you think we could put it in the fireboxes."

"That would be awesome," Colin's enthusiasm grows at my suggestion. "We could absolutely do that. I love the idea of using something so significant as a combustible."

I don't know why I didn't think about doing this earlier, but I'm glad we have the opportunity to do it now.

After the delicious dinner, we head into the studio.

"Okay, Blooms. Are you ready for this?" Colin gestures to a table he has set up with a cloth over top some forms.

"Let's do this." I clap my hands together and cautiously move towards the table.

Colin carefully peels back the covering, revealing the

five forms and my vase, which pales in comparison to the literal works of art next to it.

"So I've already started getting things ready to go for the sculptures, but I wanted to check with you before adding any of the wax resist or glazes."

Colin takes me through each of the sculptures with care to point out just where he plans to put the surface decoration.

"Most of the beauty will come from the glaze crackle that occurs in raku, but I wanted to make sure that certain things, like my top surgery scars, were going to be very evident. I thought about adding color, but I'm not sure. What do you think?"

I look over the forms again and think before responding. "I'm not sure if color would benefit. We're already showing the growth through the bouquets we chose. Adding color might detract from the statement you're trying to make with the crackle glaze."

Colin ponders my words for a few minutes before nodding and pressing a kiss to my forehead. "See, I knew I lo—liked you for a reason." He winks, and I try not to focus on the words he didn't say. Surely, it's too soon for that. I smile, but I can tell it doesn't fully reach my eyes.

"We can use all the color you wanted to use on those forms on mine." I wink, trying my best to force the playfulness back into my expression. It must work because Colin's eyes light up like he's a kid, and I've just handed him the keys to a candy store.

The next few hours go by fast as we set out to decorate our vases. Despite having more work to do, Colin is done well ahead of me—probably because he already has a vision, and I'm just following my intuition when it comes to what colors to use.

The pieces earmarked for the gallery are drying on one rack, and we've put my creation on a different one, so there's no potential for them to intermingle. The last thing we need at this stage is for my color-bombed vase to rub off on the white glaze covering Colin's forms.

We clean up and go back into the main part of the house.

"So Travis and Trevor will be here around 8. I figured we could do breakfast first and then get started by like 9? That way, if we batch fire, we should be able to get everything through the kiln by lunch, and then we can clean after we eat. Does that sound good?" Colin says as we sit cuddled on the couch.

"Yeah, that's doable." I yawn. "I should probably head home, though, if I need to be back so early." I cuddle a little more into him, obviously making no effort to actually get up and go back to my house.

He plays with his lip ring for a minute, and then he looks down at me. "Or you could stay?" he asks tentatively.

"You wouldn't mind?"

"Fuck, Blooms. Having you in my bed so I can hold you and cuddle you all night? Getting to wake up to you in the morning? That sounds like heaven. I've wanted to ask you to stay over for weeks now, but I didn't want to overstep or make you feel pressured."

"I'm your boyfriend. I'm 33. It's not overstepping. And I want to stay. No pressure. I like being with you as often as I can. You make me feel like life is the way it always was meant to be. When I'm with you, my past doesn't feel so haunting."

He surges forward and kisses me. The tiredness I felt earlier is gone, and my body is waking up under his touch.

"Bedroom?" he asks. I nod and go to stand up so I can follow him down the hall.

We make our way into Colin's bedroom, kissing and groping at each other. My mind goes to the blissed-out place it finds whenever Colin's hands are on me. Everything about Colin is intoxicating. He still smells like clay and fire, and I'm a little worried that I'm going to have a boner all day tomorrow when I see him in his element.

We get to his bedroom, and without thinking, I'm tugging at his shirt and trying to take mine off at the same time. My body needs to be pressed up next to his. I need to feel my skin on his. I don't know why, but something about his invitation for me to stay over flipped a switch, and I have this overwhelming longing to be naked with him. A little voice in the back of my head reminds me that this will be the first time I've been naked with someone since Liam. I shudder briefly and push it away. Hopefully, I was able to hide the shudder with my effort to pull my shirt off. It gets stuck on my head, and I hear Colin chuckle as he tugs it back down and unbuttons it.

"Blooms, baby, it'll be a lot easier to get off this way." He kisses the tip of my nose. The heat from our passionate rush earlier has boiled down to a simmer. My body shivers as Colin's fingertips graze my skin, and I feel the goosebumps radiate from where he's touching me. That's the thing about simmers; turn up the heat briefly, and they turn back into a rolling boil.

It doesn't take long for us to be almost naked after that. We're down to our underwear, and I bite my lip, drinking in the view of Colin wearing tight boxer briefs that emphasize his bulge. My own underwear is full with my erection. I'm craving friction, and I reach for Colin. I grind my hips against his and let out a moan. Pre-cum leaks from my tip, and a small wet patch appears on the front of my underwear. Colin's hand reaches down between us and presses into me.

"God, you're so hot," he says, already slightly breathless.

"You are too," I respond before nipping at his earlobe.

I found out during one of our earlier makeout sessions that it's a sensitive area for him. He moans, and his eyes roll back as he squeezes me tighter.

I capture his mouth with mine, biting his lower lip and playing with his piercing. His hands pull me closer so our chests are flush, our breaths heavy.

"Blooms, I need...I've gotta change," Colin pleads as soon as I release his lip.

Change? It takes me a moment, but then I realize what he's saying—he needs his prosthetic.

"Okay." I slide onto his bed, and he starts to get up. We stay connected until he's out of my reach.

I watch him grab something from the top drawer of his dresser and go into his en suite bathroom.

I take off my underwear and sit on the edge of the bed to wait. My breath starts picking up, and I realize the seriousness of what we're about to do. We both got tested a couple weeks ago, but we haven't done much more than make out sessions and hand jobs. I was serious when I told him that he makes me feel safe and that when I'm with him, I'm able to let go in ways I haven't done in over a decade. But he's not physically right in front of me right now, so the grounding I feel in his presence is just out of reach. I try to focus on my five senses exercise. I hear the shower turn off, and I realize that I didn't even know it had turned on. What is Colin expecting us to do tonight?

I think about leaving, but before I can make up my mind, the bathroom door opens, and there's my boyfriend. My breath returns to a somewhat regular pace, but Colin's got a worried expression on his face, and when I see the condoms and lube in his hand, it picks up again.

"Blooms? Baby, are you okay?"

"Yeah," I choke out. "Maybe? I don't...I don't know."

Colin is in front of me before I realize he moved.

"Can I touch you?" he asks. I realize that despite us being mostly naked, there's no heat in his question, just concern.

I nod, and he kneels. His hands find mine, and he touches my forehead with his, our noses centimeters away.

"Blooms, baby, can you tell me what's going on in your brain?"

I open my mouth, but the words won't come. I can't find my voice. Instead, I just shake my head.

"Okay, let's breathe together." Colin instructs me through the same breathing technique I used with him that day he had a panic attack at the Market. Steadily, my breathing evens out. Colin kisses my forehead and then moves to sit next to me on the edge of the bed, always keeping at least one point of contact between us.

"Blooms, baby, is this too much?" He asks.

"It might be?" I say, unsure of my answer. "I realized that you're the first person to see me like this since... since Liam and Nick. And I started to freak out about that."

"It's okay. This is a big step. We don't have to do anything. Tonight or ever. Let's get under the covers and just cuddle. We can put our clothes on if it would make you more comfortable."

"No, I want to be close to you like this, but I just don't think I'm ready for that tonight." I gesture to the condom and lube he threw haphazardly on the bed when I was having my panic attack.

"Addison, please look at me. I want to make sure you know that I'm serious when I say this next thing." I look up at him, and he continues, "You are so important to me, and I am so happy to be in your life. I will always respect your boundaries. When I told you to tell me if you were uncomfortable with something, I meant it. I'm with you for who you are, not for anything you can do for me. My priority is you, not myself."

I nod, choked up again. Colin moves to the head of the bed and folds the sheets back. He guides me in and tucks the blankets around me before walking over to the other side and climbing in. My body finds his, and we cuddle for a while before speaking. His hands sweep in a soothing gesture along my arms and my body melts into his as it starts to relax.

"Thank you," I whisper, my voice a bit crackly.

"For what?"

"For never pressuring me into more. For not calling me broken tonight when I changed my mind."

"Broken? Oh, Blooms, I would never. You are the furthest thing from broken." He gently kisses my forehead before continuing, "You have so much strength. You told me what you wanted- what you needed despite having past experiences where that didn't go well. That took a lot of bravery and courage. I'm impressed by you. I don't know what I did to earn your trust, but I do know that I'll do whatever I can to keep it."

I'm crying now. Those were exactly the words I needed to hear from him. For the second time tonight, I can't find my own voice in the moment, so I just squeeze him and hope the physical touch says everything I can't.

We lie there wrapped in each others' arms, all thoughts of finishing what we started abandoned like the condom and lube that are somewhere tangled in the sheets. I let myself just be. I finally understand that there's no pressure to do more than I'm ready for. Colin's hands continue to stroke my back, and every once in a while, he gently kisses my forehead or the tip of my nose, but there's never an expectation to go further than that. Eventually, my eyes get heavy, and I feel myself drifting off to sleep.

CHAPTER THIRTY
Colin

My alarm goes off way too early for a Saturday. I try to turn so I can reach my phone to shut off the alarm, but there's a weight on my left arm keeping me from rolling over. I open my eyes and smile at the sight before me. Addison's auburn hair has fallen down around his face, and his freckles are highlighted by the sunbeam shining across his nose. I shift as softly as I can without disturbing him to grab my phone and turn the alarm off.

I check my phone for any notifications and see one from Addison's sister, Aisling. I texted her after he fell asleep last night to let her know he was staying over and asked her to bring him some clothes and the heather clippings when she came for the activities today.

She agreed but also promised to do her fair share of teasing us when she saw us. Fair enough. It's been far too long since I've had a sibling tease me. Actually, I don't think I've ever had that. The closest has been Gwenna. I should invite her and Bean to come today if they're available.

ME

Hey Geeje- doing a pottery thing at my house today if you and Bean are free. Gonna have a few people over for a cookout in the afternoon and a campfire this evening. No pressure and I totally

> get if you have plans, but you're welcome to come if you want. Most people are getting here starting at 10, but we'll be going all day.

I put my phone back down and gently try to pull my arm out from under where Addison has it trapped. He stirs and tries to roll into me.

"Blooms, baby. I've gotta get up, but you can stay and rest some more."

I kiss his forehead and listen to his soft, contented sigh as I get up and throw on some clothes. The faintest smile creeps across his face, and I watch from the doorway as he grabs a pillow and snuggles up against it. Yeah, I could definitely get used to this.

I grab my phone and shoot off another text, this time to the group chat I have with Travis and Trevor, asking them to bring coffee and giving them Addison's order.

After checking the drying progress of the pieces we glazed last night, I head outside to get the boxes ready. I pull three metal trash cans and one of my containers full of sawdust out of the shed and get them set around my raku kiln. Travis and Trevor should be bringing over the propane we'll need, but I have everything else here. I go through the motions of filling the trash cans, setting up a table, and putting out the tongs and safety gear- including the new set I picked up for Addison last week. When I'm satisfied, I head back inside, and the sight I see nearly stops my heart.

Addison is cutting up fruit at the kitchen island, head-phones in, and dancing—badly—to whatever he's listening to. That sight alone is enough to melt the coldest part of me, but what really gets me is what they're wearing. Addison has on the shirt I was wearing when we first started talking. It's a little baggy and short on him and fits more like a crop top than a regular t-shirt, but it suits him. He's also wearing a pair of my gym shorts, rolled at the waist to keep them from falling down. His hair is also back up in its trademark messy bun.

My feet are rooted to the ground, and I can't believe that this man is in my life. I hope I get the chance to show him every day just how cherished and loved he is.

There's that word again—love. Outside of Gram, Trav, and Trevor, I don't know if I've experienced it. I definitely haven't ever fallen in love with someone before. These past five months have been some of the happiest I can remember, and I have my Blooms to thank for that.

I'm broken out of my reverie by a knock at the door, followed by the sound of it opening.

"Everybody better have clothes on, or we're joining in," Trevor's voice calls from the entryway.

I move to get into Addison's peripheral vision, so I don't startle him and then signal towards where I know Trevor and Travis are coming from.

"We're in the kitchen," I call out. "Enter at your own risk." I wink at Addison, who blushes. I wait for him to put the knife down before stepping up behind him and wrapping my arms around his waist, placing a kiss on the back of his neck as I do.

"Awww, so cute," I hear Travis say at the same time Trevor protests.

"Ewww, too mushy. I expected hot, filthy action."

I roll my eyes at my best friend and go to grab the coffee order from Trevor's hands and pass the lavender latte to Addison.

"Thank you," he says, giving me a small smile. I get lost in that smile for a beat before Trevor puts the rest of the grocery bags down on the table with unnecessary force.

"Dude!" I turn towards him and fix him with an expression that reads 'are you serious?'

"Sorry, just didn't want you to forget that we were here and start making out or something."

"I thought you wanted 'hot filthy action,'" Addison pipes up, and Travis snorts into his coffee. I beam and hold out my hand for a high five, which Addison supplies without hesitation.

My best friend is only silent for a moment longer before he narrows his eyes at us. He opens his mouth to say something but is cut off by his boyfriend.

"Hey, so breakfast? We brought HeftyFeline challah bread again for French toast."

"I'll get the mix started," I reply and walk over to the fridge to grab the ingredients we need.

"Do you guys want parfaits?" Addison asks. "I brought over some of my sister's honey last week, and it tastes really good with the granola topping."

"Aisling has bees?" Trevor asks. "Yeah, that tracks."

Travis and Trevor have gotten to know Addison's sister over the past couple months since she joined our monthly D&D game. Addison still doesn't play, but he usually hangs out and watches. I'm still hoping he'll get into it at some point, but I'm happy for him to be our audience for now.

"Yeah, she's been raising them almost as long as I've had my garden." He turns to me. "I texted her this morning and asked her to bring some heather clippings, but apparently, you already beat me to that."

"Yup," I grin and kiss his cheek. "Didn't want to get on the moms' bad side by not letting someone know that you were staying over last night. We kinda got distracted before you could tell them."

Despite all his earlier protests, Trevor is sitting on a stool at the island with his chin in his hands, watching our conversation with rapt attention.

"Don't mind me. Feel free to go on," he encourages.

"Trevor, honey, behave," Travis warns. Trevor cocks his eyebrow at his boyfriend and smirks. He knows when to play up the bratty side.

"You're gonna get along scary well with my best friend," Addison says and then turns to me again. "Actually, maybe I should uninvite Gri and Jodie. Those two in the same room are going to be terrifying with all the dirt they collectively have on us."

I laugh and hug my Blooms around the waist again, this time kissing his shoulder blade and inhaling his familiar floral scent that is laced with the briefest hint of clay.

Travis takes over the French toast preparations, and he and Addison finish cooking breakfast while Trevor and I haul the propane tanks out to the backyard and get the kiln set up.

"He's good for you, C," Trevor says when we've got the first tank hooked up. "Love is a good look on you. Both of you."

"Love? We've been together for a month. Isn't it too early for that?"

"Maybe you've only been official for a month, but I saw it back in July when we stopped by to see you at the market. You don't trust people easily, but I've watched you let your walls down for Addison. You might not be *in love* just yet, but you're definitely headed that way, and I'm proud of you for it."

"Thanks," I respond, and then he says the one thing that could bring me to tears.

"Colleen would have loved him. She loved you, and she was vocal about her opinions of anyone you brought home, but Colin, she would have loved Addison like he was her own."

He claps me on the back and heads back inside, where our boyfriends have presumably finished making breakfast. I hang back for a moment and let Trevor's words sink in. Looking over at the rocking swing Gram insisted we bring up from Texas when we moved despite it being old and almost unmanageable to move, I see a cardinal land

and stare at me for a moment before moving on. After learning about floriography from Addison, I went on a bit of a research spiral, looking up other symbolism folklore, and cardinals are said to represent a loved one coming back to visit after they've passed on. I take it as confirmation of Trevor's words and wipe my damp eyes before following my best friend into the house. As I pass the swing, I see the cardinal dropped a couple feathers. Instead of going straight inside, I pick them up and turn around to bring them back to the fireboxes. Placing one in each of the bins I intend to use for my exhibit pieces, I look back at the swing and say a silent thanks to Gram.

After breakfast, we carefully bring the pieces outside in crates and place them on the table. It's almost time for everyone else to get here by the time we're truly ready to get the first batch of three loaded into the kiln and start it up.

Travis and Trevor have helped me with every firing I've done at this house, but Addison hasn't ever been around it before. Over the past week, I've given him the rundown, but Trevor insists on doing a fire safety talk for all of us as he does every time. It's a bit strange seeing him slip into his responsible first responder role. When he's done, Travis and I give him our customary round of applause.

"Thanks, Smokey," Travis says admiringly.

"Yeah, thanks, Fire Daddy," I tease.

"Now who's being a brat?" Trevor asks.

I grin at him and waggle both of my eyebrows. Addison laughs as he puts on his safety gear.

I check my phone once more before we really get into it and see that I have a couple texts—one from Aisling letting us know she's on her way with the heather and one from Gwenna.

GEEJE ☺
> Sounds like fun. Send me your address and we'll try to stop by.

I respond to her quickly and then put my phone on the table, away from the heat.

"Everyone knows to come around back, and Aisling said she's on her way with the flowers, so she should be here before we pull the first batch out," I inform my friends.

"Let's burn some shit!" Travis says. He gets really enthusiastic about raku days for some reason. Probably because seeing Trevor in his element really gets him going.

Trevor starts the kiln and lets it get up to temperature before I load it with the first three vessels and shut the door.

"And now, we wait," I say, mostly addressing Addison.

Aisling arrives about 15 minutes later. She grabbed a ride with Jodie and Gri. Aisling eyes her brother's wardrobe selections and hands us a clipping of white heather.

"Thanks, Ash," Addison says, taking the flowers from her and putting them on the table next to the bag of dandelion and thistle blooms we've been collecting for today.

"Nice outfit. Seems real safe." Aisling side-eyes her brother.

"Yeah, well, I didn't exactly plan to spend the night."

"Good thing you have a nice boyfriend who asks me to bring you appropriate attire."

As much as I'm going to miss seeing Addison wearing my clothes, I know it's smarter for them to change into something a bit heavier. I go up to him, wrap my arms around his waist again, and whisper, "I've got a hoodie that should fit you in my closet if you want to wear one. I like seeing you in my clothes."

He melts back into me and turns to place a kiss on my temple. "Thanks, Cluaran. I like wearing your clothes." I help him finish taking off the safety gear and watch as he heads inside.

Addison comes back a few minutes later, wearing jeans and one of my hoodies. He stop at the swing and talk to Jodie and Gri for a bit. Both women are nursing coffees and are cuddled up under a blanket that I laid out this morning. Aisling is talking with Travis and Trevor over by the kiln, probably about something nerdy, and I just take it all in.

This is my life now. It feels so full. Everyone here is part of my chosen family. I never would have expected this in all my childhood daydreams. I'm at peace. I see the cardinal again, this time perched in one of my neighbor's trees, just watching over the laughter and love radiating from everyone gathered.

"Knock, knock." I'm broken out of my thoughts by the appearance of my cousin and her partner.

"Gwenna, Bean!" Addison exclaims. "I didn't know you were coming."

"Yeah, it was kind of a last-minute thing. Sorry for the late invite," I apologize. "I realized all my people would be here today, but it wouldn't be the same without you. Because you're my people, too."

Gwenna smiles at me and squeezes Bean's hand.

"We brought donuts," Bean supplies as they hold out a box of one of the local favorites.

"Oooh, you're my new best friend," Gri says as she hops off the swing.

"Hey!" Addison exclaims. "I take offense to that."

"Sorry, Ads. Bring me donuts and we can talk."

"I buy you food all the time," Addison argues with a pout.

They both reach for the same donut, and Addison grabs it a fraction of a second before Gri can. He holds it up above his head, and the two friends tussle together before Jodie calmly walks over and snatches the donut with a well-timed grab. She starts eating it, and Gri follows, knowing that she has a better chance of getting it if she sticks with her girlfriend.

"Thanks for coming. And for the donuts," I say to Gwenna and Bean, giving them both hugs in turn. "This is my house. We're firing some pieces for the DART's New and Upcoming Artist exhibit at the end of the month."

"Wow, that sounds huge, Colin. I'm so happy for..." Gwenna's words cut off, and I follow her gaze to the swing Gri and Jodie are cozied back up on. "Is that..."

I nod. "Gram insisted we bring it up when we moved here. It was the one piece of furniture she didn't want to part with."

"Oh my God, Colin."

We walk over and Gwenna walks around to the back left support and crouches down. Her eyes well up with tears when she sees the engraving that she made in our childhood. We got in trouble for borrowing my older brother's knife and carving our names into the leg. Gram thought it was great, but my dad flipped his shit. 'You girls need to behave. Pocket knives are not appropriate for young women'. Pocket knives, no; kitchen knives, yes. I internally roll my eyes at the memory.

Gwenna points it out to Bean and recounts the story for them. I don't necessarily want to hear it and excuse myself to go check on the kiln.

CHAPTER THIRTY-ONE
Addison (he/they)

"We're at about 850 C," Trevor informs Colin as I walk up to them. I slip my hand into his, giving it a little squeeze, hoping to silently convey my support and a little comfort after overhearing Gwenna tell her story.

"Okay, so here's how we're gonna do this first batch. Trav, you get the door. Trevor, you get ready to cut the gas. Addison, you get ready with the combustibles, and I'll move the vases." Colin instructs.

"We should probably add in the flowers now," I suggest.

"Good call."

The two of us move over to the bucket of sawdust, and he divides it into three smaller buckets while I split up the flowers and mix them in with the sawdust.

Before stepping away, I snatch back one of the heather stems and tuck it in Colin's apron.

"For luck," I say and give him a kiss. We hear catcalling from Gri and Trevor and each flip off our best friends in a synchronized move that looks well-rehearsed, all without breaking the kiss.

I grab the bucket, and we head back over to the kiln, where the temperature seems to have risen to the right point.

Travis tilts back the kiln door so Colin can take a look.

"What's the temperature?" he asks Trevor, who has

been monitoring the thermometer.

"992."

He must like what he sees because he nods to Travis and picks up the tongs. As soon as Travis takes away the door, Colin is moving. The first two vases transfer easily and quickly to the waiting container. There's a bit of a scare with the third transfer when the vase Colin is moving slips and drops a few inches into the sawdust bed below. There's a collective gasp from everyone behind us who has gathered around to watch. From what I can tell, though, it's okay.

Colin signals to me, and it's go time. I grab the box we prepared and dump the top combustibles over the top of the vases, making sure to distribute it evenly so all three pieces are covered.

When the lid is on, I let out a breath.

"Well, that could have been a much bigger disaster. Now, all we can do is wait on these to make sure they're good to go." Colin informs the waiting group. "We've gotta let the kiln cool down a bit before we can load in the second batch."

The group of us, minus Travis and Trevor, who are turning off the kiln, head back up to the porch. We all relax for a bit. I tag along as Colin gives Gwenna and Bean a tour of the house. Gwenna giggles when she sees the pictures of their Gram leading the Pride Parade. I listen as Colin recounts the story fondly, and Gwenna gives him a big hug when his eyes start tearing up.

They're broken apart when Travis finds us and informs Colin that the kiln is ready to be loaded for round two. We head back outside, and I survey the remaining three pieces.

"Do you want to take yours out yourself?" Colin asks me.

"Kinda? I'm nervous about dropping it or damaging the

other vases while I try to get it out."

"Why don't I put it in the back so it's the last piece to get removed, and you can see how you feel when the time comes. I've got a separate firebox for it, so we can put it as close as is safe so you won't have to go far with it."

"Okay," I agree tentatively. I'm really nervous about messing up and destroying all of Colin's hard work with the other vases, but if Colin has a separate container for me to use, it might be okay.

I watch as he puts his gloves back on and loads the warm kiln with my vase centered in the back, as promised.

When the door is shut and the heat is rising, he kisses me on the forehead and then runs into the studio.

He comes back out moments later with three vases about the same size as the one I have in the kiln now.

"Here. You're going to practice," he says to me, putting the pieces down on the table. He grabs the tongs and moves the trashcan next to the table.

"This is about the same distance and placement you'll be dealing with when you pull your piece out."

He stands behind me and guides me through the proper technique for grabbing the vase. It reminds me of the night at the wheel when we created the vase. I can tell Colin is thinking the same thing by the way he reacts when I grind my hips back into his.

"Careful," he whispers in my ear and gives it a little nibble.

"I'm finding it very difficult to concentrate right now," I admit.

"Same, Blooms. Very much same, but we'll have more time for that fun tonight."

The smile on my face grows wider. He kisses my neck, and then we return my focus to the task at hand. We concentrate and practice until I'm comfortable handling the vase on my own. With every successful transfer, my confidence grows. I practice for a while until everything feels burned in my muscle memory.

When the second batch of pots are ready to come out of the kiln, Colin faces me and puts his hands on my upper arms.

"Blooms, I have the utmost confidence in you. You've got this." He rubs my arms and kisses my forehead before nodding at Travis to remove the kiln door.

He makes quick work of the two remaining exhibit vases, and then he turns to me, handing over the tongs.

"You've got this, Blooms," he encourages. "Just like we practiced. Get a secure hold on it and then pull, rotate, lower, and release. I'll be right there with the combustibles to put on top." He transfers the white heather stem to my apron and kisses my forehead before going to grab the bucket of sawdust and flowers.

I take a deep, steadying breath and then go for it. It takes me a few tries to get a good hold of the vase, but once I do, the rest of the transfer goes fairly smoothly. Colin sprinkles the remaining combustibles on top of my vase and then closes the lid. His strong arms come around me and lift me off the ground in celebration. He kisses me as we ignore the cheers and catcalls from everyone around us. Their joking barely registers because I'm caught up in just how impressive my boyfriend is, and I can't stop beaming with pride at what we've accomplished together so far.

"I'm proud of you," he tells me.

"I feel so jittery," I respond.

"It's the adrenaline. It'll calm down in a bit. Come on, the hard part is over. Let's go grab some food." We link arms and head into the house.

CHAPTER THIRTY-TWO
Colin

We all enjoy a nice spread for lunch, and Trevor lights up my fire pit so we can roast hot dogs and marshmallows later for s'mores.

Addison keeps looking at me and finding ways to touch me more than usual. After we've finished lunch and have started scrubbing the ash off the vases, I cock my eyebrow at him after the fifth time he's nudged me.

"Blooms, baby, not that I'm not loving the extra touchy-feelyness you've got going on right now, but what's up?"

"I'm still feeling the adrenaline high from earlier, and I have a bunch of extra energy that I need to expel," he confesses before looking down.

I gaze down and notice a bulge in his pants.

I look around at our friends and family all doing their own thing and abandon cleaning my vase before grabbing Addison's wrist and urging him to follow me into the house.

We pass Travis on the way, and he gives us a knowing look before nodding at me in an unspoken agreement I'm hoping means he'll cover for us.

We rush into my bedroom and start stripping before the door is even fully closed. I lock it for good measure. It's on the side of the house, so I'm hoping no one has any reason to come over to that side of the yard. The bathroom is in the other direction off the kitchen, so no one should have any reason to come down towards my room, but I still don't think we have more than 15 minutes before someone notices and comes looking.

"What do you need, baby?" I ask as we get down to our underwear.

"Your mouth," he responds without hesitation and with the same confidence that was radiating off of him earlier.

I whine. This isn't a side of Addison I've seen before, and it's making me weak in all the best ways.

"Colin, I want you to blow me. I'd ask you to rim me, too, but we don't have enough time for me to clean up first."

"Tonight then," I suggest, dropping down to my knees and rubbing my face against his tented underwear. "I'll do anything you want, Blooms," I promise.

I suck on his dick through the fabric of his boxer briefs. I would love to spend time teasing him and bringing him to the edge before finally getting him to release, but we don't have time for that right now. Maybe tonight.

I pull down his underwear and put my face back in his crotch, breathing in the scent of flowers and sawdust and fire and something distinctly Addison. I nibble at the base of his cock, and his knees buckle.

"Oh fuck, Cluaran, yes." He reaches one hand onto my back and one hand onto the dresser behind him. When he's secure so I know he won't fall over, I pull back and reach my tongue out to lap at the precum leaking from the tip of his cock. I moan loudly at the taste, and he moves his hand from my back into my hair. He loves playing with my hair, and this is a new feeling as he grips it and tugs me back.

"Shhh. We've gotta be quiet, Cluaran." Oh, my Blooms is bossy when he's confident.

I bite my lower lip and then lick it before moving forward to take him as deep as I can. Addison's dick isn't the biggest I've seen, but when you have a prosthetic dick, you can see them in some pretty big sizes. Addison's delicious cock is about six inches and not super girthy, but it tastes like heaven, and I'm pretty sure it was made custom to fit in my mouth.

I'm able to take Addison's cock all the way to the base, and I inhale again, breathing in the scent of him. My eyes close in bliss, and I swallow before I pull back and play with the head. It's Addison's turn to moan this time. He's leaning against the dresser with both hands in my hair now, gripping tightly. I look up at him and see just how wrecked he looks already. It's a heady feeling knowing that I'm the one to make him look so free and uninhibited.

I'm so distracted looking at him that I almost don't realize it when he starts thrusting his hips, fucking my face. I moan in delight and pull the backs of his hips towards me in a sign of encouragement. I take him deep a few more times this way, and when Addison's legs tense and his vocalizations get louder, I can tell he's close to coming. I swallow down and hum before pulling back until my mouth is just covering the head of his dick, sucking harder and licking the vein underneath on the way. That does it. I feel the tension in his body release as he comes in my mouth. I swallow his cum with pleasure and pride. As I'm milking the last bit out of him, I feel his legs sag. His hands release the tight grip of my hair, and he leans back onto the dresser.

I pull off and stand up, wiping the drool and cum from my chin.

"Can I kiss you?" he asks.

"Always," I respond. I wasn't sure if he'd be into kissing after I just had a mouthful of his cum, and I'm proud of him for asking for what he wants.

We fall onto the bed and lazily make out for a few

minutes before Addison realizes that I haven't gotten off yet. He reaches down and grinds the palm of his hand into my packer.

"I want…I need…" He looks at me with pleading eyes.

"I know, baby, but we probably don't have time right now. We've already been gone for a while, and we should probably get back."

"But it's not fair," he protests.

"Blooms, your pleasure is my priority. I am so turned on by you, but I know that you'll take care of me later when you have more time to make me come apart at your hands."

He groans. "Please don't be so self-sacrificing. I want to take care of you, too. Please, Cluaran. I need this. I need you to want me."

That shocks me. I didn't realize that denying my orgasm after I got him off would make him feel like he wasn't wanted.

"Oh, Blooms." I cup his face and kiss his nose. "I very much want you."

My lips slam into his with force, and our hands roam all over each others' bodies. I grind against his leg, and the pleasure I feel at the friction compels me to want more.

"Blooms, I- I need you," I pant against his mouth.

He bites my ear, sending a jolt of goosebumps cascading down my body. His hand moves to my boxers, and I help him push them down. I don't have my prosthetic on, and I feel a little vulnerable as I'm splayed out on my bed, but I trust Addison.

He kisses and nips his way down to my dick and positions himself in between my legs. I bite my lip piercing as his tongue flits out and flicks my dick. The sight of his head between my legs is one that will sear into my brain and live with me for the rest of my life. His tongue feels magical. He sucks and teases my dick, and I have to grip the headboard on the bed so I don't interrupt the world-changing blow job he's giving me. He pulls off my dick and sticks two of his fingers in his mouth. The reprieve gives me a moment to catch my breath. I'm all sweaty, and I never want to leave this bed. I'm daydreaming about ways we can live in this room forever when Addison returns to taking my dick in his mouth. He shifts and throws my leg over his shoulder and then places his arm on my stomach. My other leg slides up so my knee is in the air. Addison's wet fingers find their way to my anus, and I see why he positioned himself that way because I buck up.

"Blooms-" I cry out. The sensation of his fingers circling and tapping my hole and the pressure from his mouth on my dick are almost overstimulating in the best way. It doesn't take long before I can feel my entire body tense up.

"I'm gonna- Oh fuck." The release is unlike anything I've ever experienced before. Addison stays where he is as my body deals with the aftershocks of my orgasm. When everything stops pulsing, and my breathing calms down, he kisses just below my belly button and joins me at the head of the bed, where I pull him into my arms and kiss him deeply.

"Thank you," he says when our lips pull away.

"Thank me? Why are you thanking me? I'm the one who should be thanking you for that world-bending, mind-shattering orgasm. Fuck, Blooms. That was..." I let out a breath because I don't have words for how amazing it was.

He snuggles against me, and I hold him there.

"Thank you for not debating me when I told you I needed to do that for you. Some of my trauma manifests in a major way whenever I feel rejected. And you don't make me feel rejected, but in the moment, when I know you wanted to get off, but you were denying yourself, and it felt like you didn't want me to be the one to give you the same pleasure you give me."

"I'm sorry, Blooms. I never intended to make you feel unwanted. Thank you for telling me." I make a silent vow to never give him any reason to question how much I want him.

After a few more minutes of cuddling, we get up and change into new clothes. I put on a hat to hide my very obvious sex hair, and Addison is back to wearing the clothes of mine he wore this morning, but he keeps the hoodie from earlier since it's almost sunset and the temperature is getting colder.

We walk back outside well past the fifteen minutes we originally gave ourselves, and our best friends are standing there with grins on their faces. They start slow clapping for us as soon as we step out the door.

"Well done," Trevor says, clapping me on the shoulder like a proud dad.

"I'm so proud," Gri adds, wiping a fake tear from her eye.

Addison turns to me and buries his face in my shoulder. My arm comes over him in an automatic and protective maneuver.

"Cute," I deadpan, giving them both a side-eye.

"Are they done yet?" Aisling calls from the opposite side of the house. She turns the corner with a stack of pizzas.

"Oh my god," Addison mumbles into my shoulder. The campfire has nothing on the blush radiating from his cheeks right now.

"Let's eat," I nudge him from his hiding spot and then kiss his forehead sweetly.

"Sounded like you already did," Travis jokes.

"Not you, too," I scoff.

"Hey man, I tried covering for you. You were the ones who couldn't keep it quiet. At least I kept them from going inside. Those two wanted to stand outside and throw confetti or some shit when you opened the door."

"Oh my god, Gri, no!" Addison shoots a dirty look at

his best friend.

"Please stop talking about my brother having sex, or I swear I will take this pizza and leave," Aisling threatens.

We all agree and turn the topic of conversation to other things. A few slices in, and I remember that we still have to finish cleaning the last couple pieces. While I know it should be done now, I have my boyfriend in my arms and my chosen family around me. The pottery can wait.

When everyone leaves for the evening shortly after a second round of s'mores, Addison helps me bring the important things inside and pick up the yard to acceptable conditions for one night. Any additional cleaning can be left for tomorrow. Right now, my main goal is to shower and curl up in bed with my favorite person, my Blooms.

FROM ADDISON'S SKETCHBOOK

Dandelion, Thistle, & White Heather

- Dandelions: Tell Me I Am Wanted

- Thistles: Worthy of Effort

- White Heather: Good Luck; Protection

CHAPTER THIRTY-THREE
Addison (they/he)

I shake out the nerves as I triple-check the arrangements. Tonight is the opening reception for the New and Upcoming Artists exhibit at the DART. Colin packed the vases up in secure boxes, and each of my bouquets has been fit tested, and reference pictures have been taken, so it should be fairly easy for us to get it set up. I thought about binding them so we could easily just plop them in but decided against it in case we had any last-minute changes. It's hard to stop revising.

I look up when I hear a noise behind me. My jaw drops as I see my handsome boyfriend in the outfit he selected for tonight. Every detail has been thought through like the artist that he is. His chinos match my hair, and the navy open-knit polo has a floral pattern similar to my shirt, but he's wearing it open over a 'Protect Trans Kids' shirt. It's short-sleeved and shows off the tattoos and muscles in his arms. I bite my bottom lip, thinking about all the glorious things those arms and strong hands have done to my body. I look away before I get distracted and drag us both to the bedroom. My eyes rove back up his body and get caught on a flash of green. He's wearing the Oscar Wilde carnation I made and gave to him in June. I abandon the flowers I was fiddling with and walk over to kiss him.

"You are the most handsome man I have ever seen," I

say as I pull away. Those arms I love so much wrap around my waist, and he pulls me towards him for another kiss before twirling me so he can see my outfit.

"You obviously haven't looked in a mirror recently because I would like to Uno Reverse that compliment back at you. Addison Baird, you take my breath away. You are stunning."

That familiar heat in my cheeks starts as I feel my blush creep on my face. I don't think I look too out of the ordinary. I basically just piece-mealed different parts of my wardrobe until I had something coherent. The only special item I got for tonight was the bow tie that I bought because it matches Colin's lavender hair. The rest is pretty standard Addison flair: a floral button-up, a tweed vest, and brown linen pants. I've worn this same outfit to some of the more upscale markets before. I wasn't sure if it would be okay for tonight, but Gri assured me that it would. The way Colin is looking at me now reinforces her opinion, and I'm feeling a bit less nervous now.

"Are you ready for your speech?" I ask Colin. He agreed to do the quick presentation for our piece. We both could have spoken, but this project was originally his idea, and I want to make sure that he gets the recognition he deserves.

"Yeah, I think I have it all done. You're sure you're okay with me doing the whole thing? I know how much you love talking about floriography. I wouldn't want to deny you the opportunity to talk about it to a captive audience." He winks at me.

I roll my eyes at him and head back over to the table. We close up all the crates and load up Colin's pickup, taking extra care to secure everything in the truck bed.

It doesn't take us too long to get to the DART downtown, and we sit for a minute in the truck and let the weight of the moment wash over us.

"I'm proud of you," I tell my boyfriend. "It takes tremendous courage to be yourself, and you're putting yourself and your story out for the world to see tonight. That is the bravest thing I can think of. You should be proud of tonight. From what everyone has told me about her, I know your Gram would be too."

Colin nods and puts his head on my shoulder. Both of his hands are still gripping the steering wheel. I turn my head and give him one of the forehead kisses that I love so much.

"Thanks, Blooms." He takes my hand and laces our fingers together. "It means the world to me that you're here and that you helped. I don't think I'd be half as brave without you."

I squeeze his hand in a show of confidence and support.

"Come on, let's get things started." He moves, and we get out of the car. We each grab a crate and head towards the entrance.

We meet one of the exhibit organizers in the foyer and are directed to our area, close to the main door. It's pretty prime placement; we'll be one of the first exhibits everyone walks by as they come in. As we requested, there are five plinths set for us, and the artist statement that we co-wrote is already set up on the wall. We double-check to make sure that everything is in the right order, and then it's time to set up.

Once we're sure everything is in order, Colin gives me a kiss on the forehead and heads back out to the truck so I can start with the set-up. I pull out the first vase and start arranging flowers. I'm just finishing the first arrangement when Colin comes back with the next box.

"Blooms, that's stunning. I know we did the practice arrangement back at the house, but it's just so impressive in this setting. Your work is... perfection."

I back away from the plinth and let Colin wrap me in

his arms while he stands behind me so we can look at the completed first piece.

"It's only that good because of your work. Colin, your vases are breathtaking. The story and flow you've been able to impart into each piece is unparalleled. I'm continuously impressed by you."

"Okay, Blooms. You're gonna make me blush now." He nuzzles into my neck and kisses me before pulling away. "Two more boxes, and then I can help you however you direct me."

"Sounds good." I walk forward and pull out the next two pieces.

I'm lost in my work when Colin returns with the fourth box and don't actually see him place it down. I'm arranging the thistles in this bouquet and daydreaming about the fantastic rimming session Colin gave me last weekend after we closed down my garden for the winter when I hear the voice that sends chills down my spine.

"Thistles? Really? It's just like you to choose a weed as the highlight for a bouquet. And I see you're still using the fake stuff."

He's here.

Fuck.

My breathing starts to pick up, and I feel my hands go numb. The room around me starts to spin, and I bump into the vase I'm working on before steadying it and stepping away.

I turn and look into the cold eyes of my ex-boyfriend. Liam stands in front of me with the haughty, judgmental expression that haunts my nightmares even a decade later. I look towards the door, but it's not Colin who comes through- it's Nick. He sees me and freezes. A disappointed expression crosses his face, and I feel like I'm a kid about to get scolded by their parents.

Nick steps up next to his boyfriend, and I'm frozen.

"Honestly, Addison," Liam continues, "it's like your education was wasted on you. These fake flowers are so tacky. You have the training to use the real thing, but apparently, you still lack the talent to make them work. It's no wonder you couldn't make it in our industry."

My mind is blank. He steps forward with his hand reaching out. I take a step back out of reflex. My body hits something hard, and I feel it slide. And then I hear the crash.

I turn and pray to every deity I know that the crash wasn't what I think it was. I sink to my knees and see that my arrangement is scattered across the floor, and Colin's creation is chipped, broken into pieces, disfigured beyond recognition.

Oh my God. I did it again. Flashbacks of my failed final project with my only floral job flood into my head. Worthless, waste of space, incompetent, never going to make it in this industry, clumsy, foolish. All the insults I remember being called during that time in my mind are overtaking my thoughts. My vision tunnels, and my hands are shaking. I try to pick up the pieces. Colin is going to be devastated and so mad. The best relationship I've ever had is gonna be over because of my lack of spatial awareness.

I hear a scoff and two pairs of footsteps walking away. My airway feels like it's closing. I can't breathe, and I think I'm going to be sick.

CHAPTER THIRTY-FOUR
Colin

I walk back into the gallery after moving my truck from the loading area and bring in the final box, excited to see the magic that Blooms has created with his arrangements. There's something about the gallery lighting that makes everything just glow.

As I step into the main exhibition hall, I notice the air is tense. My eyes dart around and see that everyone is staring at our space, but when I look, I don't see Addison anywhere at first. And then I notice they're on their knees next to an empty plinth. Flowers are scattered around them, and my heart drops. *Fuck.*

I tighten my grip on the case I'm carrying and rush over to them. I hastily, yet carefully, place it on the ground and then slide onto my knees next to them. Among the carefully handcrafted stems are pieces of raku pottery, and my fears are confirmed. The vase broke. It's the big one, too, the one meant to represent the me of today. I turn to Addison to ask what happened and truly take them in. They're trembling, and they look pale. They're clearly going through some sort of panic attack, and it's probably the most intense one I've witnessed.

"Blooms, baby. Can I touch you?" I ask softly and move my hands slowly so as not to startle him.

They're unresponsive but shaking. I don't think you're

supposed to touch someone in this state, but at this point, Addison's panic attack is turning into something like shock, and I can't stop myself.

"Blooms...Addison. Look at me." I cautiously touch their leg, and they look up at me. Tears are streaming down their beautiful face. They wipe their cheek to clear it, and a streak of red is left behind. I grab their hand and turn it to see that they're bleeding from a cut in their palm.

"Baby, you're hurt. We've gotta get you cleaned up so it doesn't get worse." I look around and notice Addison's trusty toolkit. I open it to find a cloth and a mini first aid kit. Addison still isn't responding verbally, but they don't fight me or pull back as I carefully clean the wound and wrap it in a bandage.

When I know they aren't going to bleed out, I take stock of the mess around us. I'm rubbing comforting circles on their wrists, trying to bring them back to me so I can find out what happened. Sure, I'm pissed that one of my sculptures broke, but I don't think it warrants a reaction this intense.

We sit there, and Addison's breathing slowly starts to even out. When I think they'll be able to answer, I gently ask the question.

"Blooms, what happened?"

They open their mouth to answer, but the words just aren't coming out.

"It's okay, baby. Take your time." I try to mask my frustration at the situation while encouraging them to open up.

When they try again a few minutes later and still can't get the words out, I look around to see if I can figure it out. I look up to see that we've amassed a small crowd around us. One of the other exhibiting artists must see the panic in my eyes because she starts to explain.

"They were just minding their own business working

on setting up the piece when a couple guys came over and said something to them. One of them looks like he might have pushed them or something because the next thing I knew, they stumbled back into the plinth, and the force knocked the piece off. Are they going to be okay?" she asks with genuine concern.

I ignore her question because I honestly don't know. What I do know is that Addison's in no state to be around people, and I'm ready to abandon this whole thing and bring them home. I just need to make sure that I don't need to bring them to the hospital first. My head is swimming now as I process her words. Two guys? Why would someone push Addison? What the fuck!? So many thoughts are running through my head that I almost miss Addison's voice, soft and small.

"Liam."

The name sends my anger into a boil, and I immediately stand up.

"Where did they go?" I ask the artist.

"They went out that door." She points at a door in the back of the hall. I follow where her finger is pointing and take a half step before stopping.

I look back at Addison and know that I can't leave them. After my misstep at the market with the Bethany incident, I know my place is here. It's an easy decision to make, and as much as I would like to dish out a long overdue and well-deserved heaping serving of good ole' Southern ass-whoopin', I put aside my anger for the moment. I promised to care for them, and they need me now more than ever. I won't let them down this time.

My new therapist has also been working with me on controlling my anger, so I guess we'll see if her techniques work. I take a deep breath and close my eyes. I focus on the sensations in my body, mentally moving them towards my core. They gather and grow like raindrops until I'm left with one big ball of collective anger. I take another deep breath in and then visualize the anger leaving my body as I breathe out. I'm a little surprised when I feel calmer, but that jubilation is short-lived as I hear Addison dry-heaving. I've gotta get them out of here. I don't care that tonight is my biggest break and opportunity to take my career to new heights; the person I love is in pain, and I need to help them.

I crouch back down next to my Blooms, careful not to kneel on any ceramic shards.

"Baby, I'm here. I've got you." I gently start rubbing their back. When they stop dry-heaving long enough to catch their breath, I hand them a clean tissue so they can wipe up the snot and tears before having to face anyone in the crowd around us.

"Blooms, baby, let's go get you cleaned up properly. Can you walk with me?"

I start to get up when they nod. I help them up and start to lead them towards the bathroom. Thankfully, the DART recently renovated, so the single-use bathrooms are close by. I maneuver Addison to sit on the toilet and grab a wet paper towel. I wring out the excess water and fold it into a strip before placing it on the back of their neck. I hand them another damp paper towel so they can clean their face.

Their breathing is starting to come back to normal, and when they finally look up at me, I see trepidation and anxiety behind their puffy eyes.

"I'm sorry," they whisper and choke back another sob. I hand them a fresh towel for their eyes.

"Oh, Blooms, baby. There's nothing you need to apologize for." I rub their back and try to communicate my sincerity through my touch.

"But I broke the vase."

"That wasn't your fault. You were pushed."

"No, Liam raised his hand and stepped towards me, but I moved back before he could touch me. I'm the one who knocked it over."

I guess that makes sense. As manipulative as Addison has told me Liam is, I can't see him physically assaulting someone in the middle of a room full of security cameras and witnesses.

"I still don't blame you, Blooms." I kiss their forehead.

"You're not mad?" They ask.

"Oh, I am, baby, but not at you. Never at you. You had a trauma response. Your body told you that you were unsafe, so you moved on instinct. I'm pissed that that ass-hole even messed with you, but I'm not mad at you." I tilt their chin up so I can meet their gaze when I repeat my last words with extra emphasis. "I am not mad at you. And I will say it as many times as you need to believe it."

They stare at me, and tears start to well in the corners of their eyes again.

"Thank you." They reach out and squeeze my hand. "What do we do now?"

"Well, we have a few options. We can head back over to our exhibit area, clean up, and go home. Or we can see if we can fix the vase and stay. If for some reason they have an issue with both of us leaving, we can call Gri or your moms to come get you, and I will stay until they let me go, and then I'll come straight over to you for extra cuddles."

"I think we should both stay," they decide. Their voice is getting stronger as they continue speaking. "Let's try to fix the vase and stay. I won't let him scare me away. We've worked too hard to just leave now."

Itaketheirhandandhelpthemstandup.Assoonasthey're on their feet, I pull them into a hug. My heart is screaming at me to tell Addison that I love them, but I can't think of a less romantic place to confess that than in a bathroom. Instead, I pour all of my love into our embrace and hope that I'll get a better chance soon.

CHAPTER THIRTY-FIVE
Addison (they/he)

I'm still a little shaken, but here in Colin's arms, I feel safe. He stayed. I needed him and he stayed. I know he's still upset about the sculpture breaking, and I am too, but he still stayed. For whatever reason, I'm having a hard time getting past that. I'm always the one who is there for other people; people don't usually stay for me. Sure, I've had Gri and my moms—they stay when they can, but they always have other priorities. Colin makes me feel like I'm his priority. The reality of that almost brings another round of sobs, but I choke them back and try to get myself together. Colin has been here because I needed him, and now it's time for me to be there for him.

I give my boyfriend a final squeeze and pull out of his arms. I assess myself in the mirror and do my best to look presentable. My once-tidy outfit is wrinkled, and it looks like there might be a little tear in my pants from the sharp edge of the broken ceramic piece. I look down at my hand and see Colin has wrapped the cut well. I straighten my bow tie, fix my hair back up into its trademark bun, and put my game face on. Years spent being the Market's unofficial mayor have trained me for this moment. The mishaps with Lane, the disputes between vendors, dealing with Karens—all of it has prepared me for what we have to do tonight.

"Okay, let's do this," I say, clearly in my mayoral persona.

"Well, okay then, Mayor Blooms." Colin smirks at me playfully. "What's the plan?"

"Right. I should have some glue and sandpaper in my toolkit that will work for fixing the vase. Let's head back and see what we can piece together." I look at my watch. "We have about 90 minutes before the show officially opens, so if we can prioritize getting the vase functional for now, we can make it work."

I go to open the door, but Colin is already there. He opens it for us, and we walk out the door and into the lobby. I stop when I see two figures on the other side of the room. Liam and Nick. When a low growl sounds from next to me, I reach out and grab Colin's forearm in a gesture meant to ground me but also to keep him from doing something we'll both regret. There is no room full of witnesses this time. We're in a standoff. I take a deep breath, and just the reassurance from touching Colin gives me the strength I need to finally put Liam and Nick behind me once and for all.

Liam cocks his eyebrows and looks smugly at us. "I thought you left."

"You thought wrong."

"Hmm. I'm surprised that one hasn't kicked you to the curb yet after you wrecked his piece." He turns his attention to Colin. "You know, this one doesn't put out. He's a tease and a flirt, but he can't get it up when it counts."

Colin's jaw tightens, and his forearm tenses under my touch. I squeeze him and let go, stepping in front of him to put myself physically between them.

"Mo chridhe, he's trying to get a rise from us both. Don't let him win," I whisper back to my boyfriend. I feel his anger dissipate slightly. I turn back to the man who has haunted me for too long. "I don't know why, after 10 years, you are still obsessed with my life. I know you've been spying on me through your network. Why should it matter whether or not I'm having sex or who I'm with? You lost the privilege of knowing that when you discarded me like I was nothing more than a piece of shit under your shoe. I'm not that guy anymore. You can't step on me. I know who I am, and who that is isn't broken. I'm perfect just the way I am, and not that it's any of your business, but I've found someone who accepts me for me. Sex with him is fun and exciting and makes me want to be an active participant. You said sex with me was like having sex with a corpse, so go fuck an amorphophallus titanum and leave me alone. You're an abuser and an asshole, and I'm done letting you have any power in my life. Now if you'll excuse us, we have a show to do."

I reach out and take Colin's hand and lead him back toward the gallery. We pass by Liam and Nick's shocked expressions, and out of the corner of my eye, I can see Colin's smirk at their speechlessness. As soon as we're far enough away, Colin takes control and leads me through a door. Instead of going back to our exhibit, he leads me out to the sculpture garden. The door shuts behind us, and almost as soon as it does, he's got me pressed up against it.

"God, Blooms, that was so fucking hot." He kisses me deeply, and I'm returning his fervor with my own.

"It felt hot," I admit as Colin moves to kiss my jaw. I rake my hands through his hair.

"If I didn't know there were cameras all over this place, I'd blow you right now," Colin says between kisses.

That gets my dick perked up. Colin's mouth is addictive- kissing him, fucking it, the words he says. That man has a magic tongue, and I am fully under the spell. I groan and pull away.

"Later, mo chridhe. I promise." It takes me a lot of effort to stop what we're doing, but this night has been a roller coaster already. I don't exactly feel like adding a public indecency charge and getting banned from the museum to the docket. I kiss his nose. "We've gotta go fix that piece, Cluaran."

He whines.

"I know. I promise we can have all the fun we want after the reception," I assure him.

"Okay," he pouts.

"At least my outfit is wrinkled from an intense make-out session this time instead of a breakdown and panic attack," I laugh and go to fix my hair again. Colin pats his down as well and then kisses my forehead before opening the door to bring us back inside.

We actually head into the gallery this time and find our setup untouched. In my head, I was catastrophizing the moment; I saw thousands of tiny pieces, making our task impossible. In reality, the vase is in less than a dozen larger pieces. It seems that the felt flowers cushioned the fall and kept it from fully shattering.

Colin stoops down and starts to gather the pieces we can see while I rummage through my toolbox to find the glue and supplies we'll need to fix things up. As I hand them over to Colin, he pulls me in for a quick kiss. Even though it's brief, it still settles any lingering anxiety I have about this repair.

"We've got this, Blooms. I believe in us," he whispers.

Along with the pieces of the vase, Colin has picked up the fallen bouquet and placed the stems on the plinth. He starts working on the puzzle in front of him, and I busy myself with preparing the arrangement as best I can. I still have a few more bouquets to finish setting up, so after I've gotten this one as ready as it can be without the finished vase in place, I move on to the others.

Colin is done before I am. The glue I gave him techni-cally won't be fully cured for 24 hours, but it sets quickly enough that we should be okay for tonight. With the natural cracks in the raku glaze, you can barely see the actual breaks.

Metaphorically, it makes the piece stronger. Scars heal, but they don't always go away fully. Colin is still dealing with the scars his family left on him. I'm still dealing with the scars my past relationships left on me, but together, like the way the vase and flowers fell earlier, we can keep each other from shattering.

I place the final bouquet in the repaired piece, adjust a few stems, and step back.

"It's beautiful." I turn to Colin, and he's got tears in his eyes. He tries to speak more but is too choked up in the moment.

My arms instinctively go around him and offer him the comfort he so freely gives me. "I've got you, mo chridhe."

The throughline of the thistles is evident. The first vase features so many flowers choking out the one stem most people would pick out as a weed. The form is small and closed off. Colin's fear and trauma are clear in the torso's pose.

The second vase has those more popular stems clipped off and lying under and around the vase. The thistle is a little more vibrant and is joined by a couple other stems. The theme of growth continues through the bouquets in each vase, and the forms show a growth in confidence and comfort as each torso changes to reflect the physical transformation Colin has made over the years. It's breathtaking.

I give Colin another squeeze. "I'm so proud of you."

"Blooms, this wasn't a solo effort. It wouldn't be as nearly as powerful and complete of a piece without your help. You brought my vision to a whole new level." He kisses my shoulder.

A voice calls out through the hall as the exhibit's lead curator steps into the gallery space.

"Artists, thank you so much for your attendance tonight. We're looking forward to a phenomenal opening night to our New and Upcoming Artists exhibit. Here at La Galarie D'Art, we have a long tradition of lifting up unheard voices. We're excited to give you the opportunity to showcase your talents."

I smile at Colin as she goes on to give the logistics of how each artist talk is going to go and what to do if you want your piece to be listed for sale. I'm really glad that Colin decided to be the one to give the talk tonight. After our run-in with Liam and Nick, I'm feeling lighter, but I'm definitely not in the mental space I need to be in order to talk to a crowd.

We also decided not to sell the piece. It's too personal. Colin is going to keep it at his house after this since it's representing his journey.

Before we know it, the doors are opening, and people are filling in. I take a deep breath, hold onto Colin's hand, and prepare myself to face the hordes.

CHAPTER THIRTY-SIX
Colin

Tonight hasn't been anything like what I expected it to be. I never expected we would run into Addison's ex and his new boyfriend. I never expected that my piece would break. What I did expect, however, was being nervous before giving this speech. With everything that happened earlier, I haven't had much time to overthink it, which is good, but I also haven't had the chance to practice it a final time. Thankfully, it's pre-written, and I've been practicing it all week.

When the lead curator gives my introduction, I step up to the podium and look out at the crowd. In a sea of faces I don't recognize, there are bright spots in the family I've curated since my story began. Seth, Lilly, and Lane stand in the back with Samwise and Cal and a few of our other Market family. Lolli and Dr. Siobhan stand with Addison's sisters and brother-in-law at a high-top table, Jodie and Gri are seated on a bench in the middle of the room, and Gwenna and Bean are over with Trevor and Travis by our piece. But the brightest part in the room and the focus of my attention is on Addison, my Blooms, my boyfriend, the person I love most. With my eyes on them, I start my speech.

"I was kicked out of my house at age 14 for being trans. I was physically beaten and bruised by the people who were supposed to care for me and love me, their own flesh and blood. Instead of nurturing and growing with me, they discarded me. Thankfully, I had one person in my life who didn't abandon me. My grandmother took me in and raised me to be the man standing in front of you today. The piece I've worked on, in collaboration with the extremely talented Addison Baird-" I gesture in their direction- "is representative of my journey from that broken and bruised child to the healthy and thriving adult I am today.

"Healing hasn't been an easy journey, and there are some scars and cracks that will never truly disappear, but my wounds have mostly closed. I wouldn't have gotten to this place without the support and love of those around me. First, my grandmother, then my chosen family," I take a brief moment to look at each of them before continuing.

"There have been setbacks, new cracks and tears have emerged throughout my life- most notably when my grandmother passed away a few years ago- but I've continued on. While every stem in these arrangements have their own meaning, the central theme of growth is represented by a thistle. Many may see this as an annoying and stubborn weed, but to me, it represents resilience and being worthy of effort. It's taken me a while to find myself, but I know now that I am worthy of putting effort into myself and the relationships that feed me. I have found support and love once again, and I will continue to nurture those relationships as I move through this life."

Pride and love radiate from Addison as I step off the stage and return to their side by our piece. Gwenna and Bean stop me for a hug as I get to them.

"You were phenomenal," Addison whispers to me as the next artist takes the stage. I slip my arm around their waist and kiss their temple.

"Thank you, Blooms. I couldn't have done it without you. I mean that."

They hum next to me.

When the speeches wrap up, we're greeted by everyone who showed up to support us. They congratulate us both on our piece and me on my speech.

"I'm proud of you lads," Dr. Siobhan. "And Colin, I'm glad you're a part of our family. Lolli and I are proud to consider you a son."

My eyes can't hold the tears back. She hugs me, and I lose it. It's been years since I've felt a maternal hug. Gram was the closest thing I've had to a mother, but I was always her grandson. The Stamp-Bairds have welcomed me without reservation, wholly and just as I am.

As the tears calm down, I turn to find Addison, my ever-prepared boyfriend, is there with a tissue. I can't help but laugh when they hand it out to me.

"I love yo—your preparedness. How did you know I'd need this tonight?" I say, hoping that I covered my declaration of love. This isn't the place for it. I don't want to blurt out those words here in the middle of a crowd.

"Oh," they blush. I think they know. "I, uh, brought them for me. I figured your speech would be emotional, and I wanted to make sure I had them on hand in case my crying got ugly."

I wipe my eyes, stash the tissue in my pocket, and then turn to kiss my Blooms, first on the nose and then the forehead like they love so much.

As our small group of found family filters out, Lolli informs us that there's going to be a small afterparty at the Stamp-Baird house when we're done. The reception is only scheduled to go for another hour, so that should give them enough time to get everything prepared before we get there.

Addison and I spend the evening talking to other artists and collectors who have come out to see the exhibits. A few people inquired about purchasing individual pieces, but since we talked about not wanting to split up the set or even sell it at all, we handed them our contact cards and talked about commissions.

At one point, the director from the LGBTQ+ center where my support group meets comes up and asks me about doing a small talk to the youth at the center. We exchange cards, and they tell me that they will reach out when this exhibit is over. A few other small gallery owners stopped by to get our contact information.

I check over to see how Addison is doing and notice them engrossed in a conversation with an older lady in a grey pantsuit. They're pointing out different flowers, and just by checking the expression on their face, I can tell they're on a roll talking about floriography.

All in all, the night is a success. By the time the reception is over, I'm ready to take Addison home so we can make out and then pass out, but first, we have to go back to their house for the afterparty. Apparently, when their moms left, they mentioned that the cheesemonger, Dauphine, was setting up a 'delicious spread with all the good stuff'.

"Leave it to your moms to get a cheesemonger to cater an afterparty," I muse.

"Oh, that's just a typical Friday night for them," Blooms jokes.

With a look back at our exhibit, we leave the DART hand-in-hand.

CHAPTER THIRTY-SEVEN
Addison (they/he)

When we get to the house, we're greeted by everyone who had joined us at the gallery. Mum wasn't lying when she described Dauphine's charcuterie board. I laugh when I see the dandelion wine and cheeses cut to look like thistles.

Our night is spent talking with our friends and family, basking in the love and warmth that surrounds us. It's easy to lose myself in the comfort and security of this place, but I catch myself reflecting on the day, and my body shivers when I think of the confrontation with Nick and Liam. I'm a little surprised that thinking about it doesn't make my body tense or go into fight or flight mode. My anxiety doesn't take over and cause me to be a hopeless, unresponsive mess like it used to. Speaking out and telling them off was freeing. I'm sure that I'll go through a rollercoaster of emotions as I process everything, but right now, the confidence I felt immediately after is pumping adrenaline through my veins again.

I walk over to my boyfriend to politely pull him away from the conversation he's having with Samwise and Cal. I wait until they're done talking about some comic and gaming convention that Cal is going to in a couple weeks and then make my interruption.

"Excuse me, guys, I need to borrow this one for a little

bit." I tug on Colin's hand and start to lead him towards the door to the garden. We're able to slip out the door without getting pulled into other conversations.

We don't talk as we head to the familiar moss patch under the oak tree. So many of our relationship milestones have taken place in this spot. I know that this is where I need to tell Colin the words that have been dancing in my head all night.

When we get to our spot, I feel a lightness that I haven't felt since I was younger. There's a hopefulness in the air around us. The garden we sit in is dormant and will be for the rest of winter, but with that comes the growing excitement about the potential for the future, and that's what Colin and I have. A future. Together.

"Hi," I say as I straddle Colin's lap. His arms automatically wrap around me, lying on my lower back. I want to be face-to-face with him as I confess my feelings for him. I'm pretty sure he feels the same. I think he almost said it earlier when we were at the gallery.

"Hi, Blooms." He smiles at me and kisses my nose. I let out a little giggle as the cold October air tickles the spot where his lips were.

"We did good tonight." I'm stalling, and I think Colin knows because his smile turns into a knowing and playful smirk.

"Yeah, we did, baby. We make an excellent team."

"We do." I'm stalling. *Why am I stalling? Come on, Addison, you can do this. Be brave, lad.*

I take a deep breath and pull out a paper from the pocket of my vest.

"So I wrote something down in case I had to talk today or something."

Colin quirks his eyebrow at me and tightens his hold on me, bringing me a little closer.

I look down at the words I wrote and start to read.

"Art tells a story. Every artist here tonight has made that story personal by making the piece about themself. Some might say that makes us a room full of Narcissus, but unlike that particular subject of Greek mythology, we're not obsessing with our reflections. We're pouring out our hearts and souls for you all to see. Every artist in this room has presented themselves in a raw, unfiltered way. I had the distinct honor to work on a collaboration with Colin Jameson, whose story is represented in our piece. Colin's journey is one that too many young trans kids face. He was neglected by his family while still a child, and if it weren't for the goodness and love of his grandmother, he admits that he wouldn't be the man he is today.

"Colin is one of the strongest and most loving individuals I have ever met. He is passionate about his art and the people who are blessed to call him family. I'm grateful that I can count myself among that lucky few. Colin is a talented ceramicist and storyteller. Our piece features a number of flowers whose meanings correlate to different times in his life. Through floriography, we have been able to show Colin's mental growth from a fearful child to the man he is today. Through the handcrafted figure vases, Colin has been able to express his physical changes as he moved away from the abusive home in which he was raised and grew into the confident, independent artist he is. I am proud to call this man my friend, my boyfriend, mo chridhe." I look in his eyes for this next part. "I love you."

I put the paper down next to us, and before I can say anything else, his mouth is on mine. His hands slip down to my ass, and he scoots me forward. My hardening cock pushes into his stomach, and I grind down against his packer.

He moans and breaks the kiss.

"I love you, too, Blooms."

This time my mouth crashes down on his. We make out

for a while until the porch lights over the back deck flash and break us apart.

"I think we're being summoned."

I groan. I know we abandoned the party being held in our honor, but there's no place else I want to be right now than with Colin. I'm still hard and don't exactly want to walk back inside with the obvious sign of my arousal visible for all to see. I get off of Colin's lap and adjust my dick to make it a little less noticeable.

"It's moments like this that I'm glad I'm trans." He winks at me.

I stick out my tongue at him.

He kisses my forehead. "I love you, Blooms."

"I love you too, mo chridhe."

Colin takes my hand, and we head back inside.

"Hey, Blooms, what does 'mo chridhe' mean?"

"My heart."

And that's what he is. My Colin. My thistle, worthy of effort. My heart.

A Bouquet For Love

- Apple Blossom: Preference

- Cornflower: Hope in Love

- Sweet William & Eucalyptus: Protection of a loved one in the face of adversity

- Heather & Rose: Luck in a new relationship

- Honeysuckle: Devotion

Dandelion & Thistle

- Enchanted (Taylor's Version) by Taylor Swift

- The Best Thing by Relient K

- My Home by Myles Smith

- Heaven In This Bed by Nur-D

- Coffee by Beabadoobee

- Kiss Me by Sixpence None The Richer

- Electric Touch (Taylor's Version) by Taylor Swift & Fall Out Boy

- You'll Always Be My Best Friend by Relient K

- Just Let Go by mae

- Honey and the Bee by Owl City

- I'm in Love!! by SubRadio

SPOTIFY **APPLE MUSIC**

https://bit.ly/TDATT-playlists

8 MONTHS LATER

EPILOGUE
Colin

"Uh, that one goes to the studio. Down the hall, second door on the left." I direct Samwise as he carries a box of Addison's art supplies into the newly cleared room that used to be Gram's bedroom but is now going to be their studio.

Blooms is moving in today, and along with the usual suspects, a bunch of the Makers Market crew is helping us get their stuff relocated to our house. Travis and Trevor are in the backyard helping them position some of the planters they brought over so their garden could live on here. They helped me plant a few things this spring out front, but I want them to be able to turn the backyard into their oasis. The only caveat being that I needed to be able to keep Gram's rocking swing, my raku kiln, and the fire pit. Everything else is their domain.

Mum and Mama, as they insist I call them now, are in the kitchen with Aisling getting food prepared for everyone. Unsurprisingly, there are a couple cheese trays.

Satisfied that things are going smoothly inside, I head out back to check on the progress. I sidle up to my boyfriend and my best friend, lightly raking my nails over the itch on my chest.

"No scratching!" Addison grabs my hand and pulls it away from where I was scratching.

"But it itches," I complain.

"You would think that with the 20 other tattoos you have, you'd know not to scratch at a new one."

I huff before smiling and giving them a kiss on the forehead.

"How's it going out here?" I ask as I stand behind them and wrap my arms around their waist, my chin reaching up to rest on their shoulder.

"Good. We've almost got things sorted. Trevor gave me a good idea of the heat perimeter for the kiln, so we've been marking the boundaries so I'll be able to plan properly later."

"I'm amazed you want to tackle this so quickly."

"I'm gonna need it for my portfolio."

Addison has been talking more to the woman he met the night of the NAUA opening reception, Brianne. She's an investor and was enthralled by the concept of floriography. The two of them hit it off, and Brianne offered to invest in Addison's next venture as their benefactor. It's all very House of Medici.

They thought about opening a florist shop but ultimately decided against going into an industry where they'd have to be in direct competition and sometimes contact with Nick and Liam. While we haven't run into either of them since that night, we also have no desire to chance it. Addison has done a lot of growing and more healing, and I don't think bumping into them would have the same impact it once did, but we still have no desire to put ourselves in their path. Instead, they decided to start a landscaping business focused on storytelling gardens. Using their knowledge of floriography and their talent and training from school, they've been able to come up with a business plan. They've even taken on a few smaller clients like Gwenna and Bean. Between the funding they secured from Brianne and what they bring in from the markets, they were able to quit their receptionist job to focus on all their creative endeavors. I'm increasingly proud of them and how passionately they're pursuing their dreams.

After the success of the NAUA, we were able to secure a few commissions, and I got contacted by curators in a couple larger galleries about exhibiting there. Right now, I've got a series of saggar pieces I'm working on for a private collector, and I'm finishing a raku tea set for an exhibit featuring trans artists. Our collaboration piece holds a place of pride above the mantel in the living room. We've been contacted about including it in a few other shows, but aside from the one at the LGBTQ+ Youth Center, we've kept it displayed here. Neither of us feels comfortable shipping it anywhere despite having properly repaired the broken parts using Kintsugi.

I've also expanded my business a bit to include pottery lessons. I teach hand-building down at the youth center and have a couple students who come by the house for lessons on the wheel. We're actually having a group of the kids and their families over next weekend for a raku firing. It's gonna be awesome.

The rest of the day flies by. Addison didn't have too much to move- most of their clothes have already migrated here over the past couple months. When I asked them to move in officially, they'd practically been living here already, having had their own key since New Year's.

Finally, when everyone is gone for the night, we sit down on the swing in the back. I put my arm around my boyfriend, and they settle into my side, feet tucked up underneath them.

"Welcome home, Blooms."

"Thanks, mo chridhe."

"I got you something," I say. "A bit of a housewarming gift."

"Funny that," they retort. "I have something for you, too."

We each head into our respective studios before coming back outside and settling onto Gram's rocker swing for real this time.

I hand over the large, poorly wrapped piece with the contents of the package that arrived just in time yesterday. Addison hands me a linen bag, and I'm pretty sure I can decipher the contents.

I watch as they unwrap the planter I made and each of the seeds intended for them to plant within it: honeysuckle for the bonds of love, lilac primrose for confidence, marjoram as a reminder of the blush I love so much, sweet alyssum for worthiness, and something called milkvetch which is meant to symbolize that Addison's presence softens my pain. The last are some snowdrop bulbs. They symbolize hope, especially hope after a dark time, and I hope they serve as a reminder that we're both resilient and will survive anything that gets put in our way. We have so far.

They gesture for me to open my gift, and I unwrap a bouquet of some of the most beautiful flowers I've seen them create.

"I started a list when I first met you of every flower with a meaning that reminded me of you. These are all of them."

I'm choked up with gratitude. My hand grasps theirs, and I hold it to my heart, where the new tattoo depicting an entwined dandelion and thistle is healing on my chest.

"You are everything I have ever dreamt of, Addison Baird. I love you with all my heart. Thank you for finding me worthy of the effort."

FROM ADDISON'S SKETCHBOOK

Colin's Bouquet for Blooms

- Lilac Primrose: Confidence

- Marjoram: Blushing

- Sweet Alyssum: Worthiness

- Milkvetch: Your Presence Softens My Pain

- Honeysuckle: The Bonds of Love

- Snowdrops: Hope & Resiliency

Floriography Dictionary

- **Moss:** new beginnings; resilience; growth
- **Oak:** bravery
- **Dandelion:** tell me I am wanted; wishes; magic
- **Thistle [Colin's Version]:** worthy of effort
- **Clover:** think of me
- **Chamomile:** energy in adversity
- **Olive:** peace
- **Larkspur:** levity
- **Ivy:** fidelity & attachment
- **Narcissus & Clover:** hope for change
- **Sweet Pea & Zinnia:** token of appreciation
- **Zinnia:** everlasting friendship
- **Iris & Clematis:** admiration of ingenuity
- **Begonia:** warning or repay a favor
- **Laurel:** glory; victory; success
- **Forget-Me-Not:** remembrance
- **Protea:** change; transformation
- **Lavender:** distrust
- **Anemone:** forsaken love
- **Rue:** regret
- **Datura:** deceit
- **Wormwood:** bitterness
- **Heliopsis:** joy; warmth; happiness
- **Queen Anne's Lace:** sanctuary
- **Mistletoe:** surmounting all difficulties
- **Lily of the Valley:** return to happiness
- **Snowdrop:** hope after a dark time; resilient

- **Eucalyptus:** protection
- **Belladonna:** silence
- **Bramble:** jealousy; envy
- **Wolfsbane:** sadness
- **Dogbane:** deceit
- **Yellow Acacia:** fear
- **Red Columbine:** fear; foolishness
- **White Heather:** good luck; protection
- **Apple Blossom:** preference
- **Cornflower:** hope in love
- **Sweet William & Eucalyptus:** protection of a loved one in the face of adversity
- **Heather & Blush Rose:** luck in a new relationship
- **Honeysuckle:** devotion; bonds of love
- **Lilac Primrose:** confidence
- **Marjoram:** blush
- **Sweet Alyssum:** worthiness
- **Milkvetch:** your presence softens my pain

...

Want to learn more about floriography? Check out these books:

- *Floriography: An Illustrated Guide to the Victorian Flower Language* by Jessica Roux
- *Flowers and Their Meanings: The Secret Language and History of Over 600 Blooms* by Karen Azoulay
- *The Language of Flowers: A History* by Beverly Seaton

Acknowledgements

Thank you. Thank you. Thank you, dear reader. I'm so grateful that you took a chance on my debut novel. It means the world that you would read the story that means so much to me.

Thank you to my husband, Bacon - Your continual support has made my dreams possible. Without your encouragement, I'd never be where I am today. I love you.

To Matt - thank you for the invaluable advice and answers to all my many questions.

To my beta readers - Cait, Ona, Shannon, Micah, Daniel, and Katie. Your early feedback and hype really helped me press on.

To my awesome artists - Léa and Micah. Thank you for bringing Colin, Addison, and the Market family to life.

To my editor, Charlie - working with you has been so encouraging and educating in the best way. Thank you for pushing me to continue improving.

To my cousin and best friend, Sarah - you are the best hype buddy. Thanks for your unending support and encouragement.

To Casey and the amazing team at Golden Bee Bookshop - without you, I never would have gotten this far. Thanks for always talking books with me.

To the Peach Pit - butts and peen.

To Ninabeth and Shannon - Thanks for being my found family and listening to my many ideas over the years. I love you both.

To Rafa & Daniel - Thank you for talking me through my early gender journey. Y'all are the best.

To Amy - Surprise! Thank you for all your sweet words and encouragement. I'm so glad Colin & Addison mean as much to you as they do to me.

To Cait (again) - Thanks for letting me gush on and on about my stories and being one of the earliest champions of my writing.

To Nina and my D&D crew - Thanks for giving me a place to be myself and make magical stories with you.

To my craft show friends - we've been in the trenches together and you've inspired me so much.

To those who came before - thank you for paving the way.

To all the bands whose music has made it on to my playlists (especially Five Iron Frenzy and Kat & The Hurricane) - y'all are the real ones. Your music has kept me going even in the darkest of times. Keep rocking.

And finally, to Grandma - Thanks for getting me into reading and the Red Sox. You were the most badass person I knew and absolutely the inspiration for Colin's grandma. I will continue to miss you every day. Fuck Cancer.

About the Author

Pip Dolyn (they/them/he) is a queer and trans creative.

They believe trans and queer people have always existed and deserve to have our stories told- stories of happiness, love, challenge, heartache, jubilation, pride, sadness, and reality. We exist like anyone else, our individual stories are unique to our experiences- no community is a monolith and that includes ours.

He is inspired to tell these stories of imperfect people loving imperfectly but still finding their happy ending.

The Dandelion & The Thistle is their debut novel.

Pip lives in the Northeastern area of the US with their spouse and two cats, Queso and Taako (yes, from tv).

...

Also by Pip

The Dandelion & The Thistle
Makers Market Book 1
is Pip's debut novel and, unless something is seriously
wrong and their nightmares have come to pass, you're
holding it in your hands right now.

...

An Unconventional Journey
Makers Market Book 2
Coming as soon as it's written.

...

About the Font

The Dandelion & The Thistle is set in Kyle Letendre's
Dotties Chocolate, Light, 11 point.

Text messages are set in Dotties Vanilla, Regular, 11 point.

To learn more about the Dotties Chocolate and Vanilla
typefaces and Kyle's designs, visit their website:

kyleletendre.com

...